THROUGH THE EYES OF
A SPY

KENNETH A. WINTER

WildernessLessons

JOIN MY READERS' GROUP FOR UPDATES AND FUTURE RELEASES

Please join my Readers' Group so i can send you a free book, as well as updates and information about future releases, etc.

See the back of the book for details on how to sign up.

* * *

Through the Eyes of a Spy

Published by:

Kenneth A. Winter

WildernessLessons, LLC

Richmond, Virginia

United States of America

kenwinter.org

wildernesslessons.com

Edited by Sheryl Martin Hash

Cover design by Dennis Waterman

Cover photo by Lightstock

ISBN 978-1-7341930-1-5 (soft cover)

ISBN 978-1-7341930-0-8 (e-book)

ISBN 978-1-7341930-3-9 (large print)

Library of Congress Control Number: 2020900050

DEDICATION

* * *

To
Kordan Josiah and Kenton Isaac,

as you grow to become two of God's mighty men, just like Caleb,

in the hope and prayer that you will always

hold fast the confession of our hope without wavering,
for He who promised is faithful.
(Hebrews 10:23 ESV)

CONTENTS

FROM THE AUTHOR

A word of explanation for those of you who are new to my writing.

* * *

You will notice in the Preface and Epilogue that whenever i use the pronoun "I" referring to myself, i have chosen to use a lowercase "i." It is not a typographical error. i know this is contrary to proper English grammar and accepted editorial style guides. i drive editors (and "spell check") crazy by doing this. But years ago, the LORD convicted me – personally – that in all things i must decrease and He must increase.

And as a way of continuing personal reminder, from that day forward, i have chosen to use a lowercase "i" whenever referring to myself. Because of the same conviction, i use a capital letter for any pronoun referring to God. The style guide for the New Living Translation (NLT) does not share that conviction. However, you will see that throughout the book i have intentionally made that slight revision and capitalized any pronoun referring to God in my quotations of Scripture from the NLT, as well as any other Bible translation that does not do so. If i have violated any style guides as a result, please accept my apology, but i must honor this conviction.

Lastly, regarding this matter – this is a <u>personal</u> conviction – and i share it only so you will understand why i have chosen to deviate from normal editorial practice. i am in no way suggesting or endeavoring to have anyone else subscribe to my conviction. Thanks for your understanding.

* * *

PREFACE

In time, Joseph and all of his brothers died, ending that entire generation. But their descendants, the Israelites, had many children and grandchildren. In fact, they multiplied so greatly that they became extremely powerful and filled the land.[1]

✳ ✳ ✳

This work is a fictional novel set in the midst of true events. At its core, it is a story of faithfulness. A fictional storyline has been created to weave certain parts of the narrative together. The narrator and main character of the story, Caleb, is seen in Scripture from Exodus through Joshua. Caleb is one of only two men – the other being Joshua – who were firsthand witnesses of the Israelite's journey from their days of slavery as adults in Egypt through their possession of the Promised Land.

His life of one hundred years and his unique role in the events as they occurred give us a tremendous vantage point with which to see the exodus unfold. Though Scripture tells us a great deal about Caleb, there are many details about his life we do not know. This story fills in those blanks with a fictional storyline. That is also true with other historical characters in this book. i have included a character listing as an appendix at the back of the book where i describe the factual and fictional framework for each character.

As the story unfolds, you'll be introduced to several fictional characters who have been added to advance the storyline. You'll also encounter fictional twists and turns that are an attempt to fill in the blanks where Scripture is silent regarding day-to-day events. My prayer is that nothing in the story detracts from scriptural truth, but rather tells the biblical story in a way that creates an interesting and enjoyable reading experience.

Throughout the novel, you will find that whenever i am quoting Scripture it has been italicized. The Scripture references are included in the back of this book. Those remaining instances of dialogue and teaching that are not italicized are to help advance the storyline. i have endeavored to use Scripture as the basis in forming that dialogue as well, with the intent that i do not do anything that detracts from the overall message of God's Word.

As you already know, this story begins in ancient Egypt. In researching the pharaohs who ruled from the time of Joseph's elevation to prime minister through the Exodus account, i found disparities in the timelines between the Egyptian and the Hebrew accounts. In order to tell historical events from both sides of those timelines, i was compelled to alter the timelines in order to bring them into alignment. i have included the timeline i created as an appendix at the back of the book. i do not include it as historical fact; it is not. But i have provided it so you might have a clear chronological order for the events as they unfold in this novel.

Most of the characters in this novel come from the pages of Scripture or history books. i have used their Hebrew or Egyptian names – which, in most instances, are difficult for those of us who are native English speakers to pronounce. The ancient native Hebrew or Egyptian speakers would probably experience the same struggle with our contemporary English names. So please, do not get lost in the dilemma of pronunciation. As a matter of fact, feel free to make a game of it by shortening the names and allowing yourself to use simpler, abbreviated names as you read.

The story begins with the promise God gave to the patriarchs and continues through the fulfillment of the first part of that promise – His gift of a land where His people would dwell. The promise extends well beyond the pages of this story and continues today. But at its essence this story is one of faithfulness – the faithfulness of a spy – but even more importantly, the faithfulness of God.

i pray the novel stimulates conversation; so, like my other novel, i have established a Facebook discussion group for that purpose. If you are on Facebook, i invite you to join the *Through the Eyes of a Spy* group and i look forward to hearing from you there.

May the grace of the Lord Jesus Christ be with you.

* * *

1

Eventually, a new king came to power in Egypt who knew nothing about Joseph or what he had done.[1]

* * *

"'A braham! Abraham! Don't lay a hand on the boy!' the angel exclaimed. 'Do not hurt him in any way, for now I know that you truly fear God. You have not withheld from Me even your son, your only son.'"[2]

Though I had heard the story many times before, my heart still raced as my father spoke those words. The boy was Isaac, who my father told me was fifteen years of age when his father, Abraham, took him to the top of Mount Moriah in obedience to God's command. That meant he was only five years older than I was now.

God had told Abraham, *"Take your son, your only son — yes, Isaac, whom you love so much — and go to the land of Moriah. Go and sacrifice him as a burnt offering on one of the mountains, which I will show you."*[3]

. . .

I was astonished by the trust Abraham had in God. There was no question he loved his son – and yet, he knew he must obey God. But I also marveled at the courage Isaac had demonstrated. Abraham was one hundred fifteen years old. Isaac could have easily resisted his father. But he knew his father was being obedient to what God told him to do. So, when his father tied his son's hands and laid him on the altar, Isaac knew that he, too, must trust God.

Many years earlier, God had promised Abraham he would be the father of a great nation. At that time, Abraham and his wife, Sarah, did not have any children, and they were very old. How could Abraham be the father of a great nation if he didn't have any children?

"And yet, Abraham still believed God would fulfill His promise," my father said, "even as he raised the knife to kill his son as a sacrifice. Abraham knew God did not lie. He knew God would keep His promise, no matter what things might look like. Nothing would ever prevent God from honoring His promise and carrying out His word.

"Caleb, you must always remember that truth. No matter your circumstances. No matter what you might see around you to the contrary, God will bring about His promise. Trust Him!

"God provided a ram that day to be the sacrifice. He provided just what was needed – right when it was needed. Not just on that day, but He has done so ever since. Almost four hundred years have passed since then. You and I are a part of that great nation, Caleb. God was faithful to His promise to Abraham and Isaac, and He has been faithful to each of us since then. And He always will be!

"Caleb, my son," my father continued, "walk in the courage and faith of your patriarchs, Abraham and Isaac, no matter where your journey leads!" I never tired of hearing that story. And I never wearied of hearing my father's reminder.

. . .

It was hard to believe we could ever be a great nation, though. We were slaves! God had made a way for us to come to Egypt through our patriarch, Joseph, over one hundred eighty years ago. Egyptian Pharaoh Merneferre Ay the First had made Joseph his prime minister to oversee the storage and distribution of grain. Through his oversight, the Egyptians, as well as our people – the children of Israel – had survived the famine. And our people had continued to live here peacefully for the generations that followed.

We had entered the country as honored guests. The pharaohs had welcomed us with open arms and allowed us to prosper. Our patriarchs had known we were only to be sojourners in this land. God had promised a land to Abraham in Canaan that would be our land. But, over the years, we had settled and become complacent.

Throughout our time here we had multiplied and had now truly become a nation within a nation. We numbered approximately two million men, women, and children. All from one man, his wife, and a son who had once been laid on an altar to be sacrificed! But over the years, as our numbers increased, the Egyptians became frightened of us. They believed we would one day overrun and take possession of their country.

Then, slightly more than sixty years ago, Ahmose the First had become pharaoh. His immediate predecessors had allowed the different territories of Egypt to become fragmented. The nation's solidarity and power had weakened. A once prospering economy was languishing. Some blamed the deteriorating condition of Egypt on the presence of the Hebrew people.

Ahmose's first mandate had been to restore order in the country and reassert Egyptian power throughout the territories. He had used his armies to turn us into a nation of slaves serving the bidding of our Egyptian taskmasters. It was said he was a pharaoh "who knew not Joseph."

. . .

Ahmose scattered our people throughout the land. He reopened the quarries and mines that had become dormant and now operated them with Hebrew laborers. He dispatched large numbers of our men to build the store cities of Pithom and Raamses. Many worked laying brick and mortar in the newly established capital city of Thebes, located along the West Bank of the Nile River in upper Egypt. And great numbers were used to cultivate and work the fields in Goshen in lower Egypt.

Egypt began to prosper after years of decay. Ahmose re-established trade routes and massive new construction projects were undertaken. Pyramids were rising out of the earth anew. Ahmose's success endeared him to the Egyptian people. Their national pride and unity were returning. But it was all on the backs of the Israelites. And as life got better for the Egyptians, life became much harder for our people.

About ten years into his rule, Ahmose dreamt the Hebrews would one day overtake the Egyptians based on our numbers. So, he sent for the Hebrew midwives and commanded, *"When you serve as midwife to the Hebrew women and see them on the birthstool, if it is a son, you shall kill him, but if it is a daughter, she shall live."* [4]

But the midwives feared God and disobeyed the pharaoh, allowing the male babies to live. Ahmose then commanded the Egyptian people, *"Every son that is born to the Hebrews you shall cast into the Nile, but you shall let every daughter live."* [5] Death and fear spread throughout the land. So, a great cry from our people went out to our God to save us.

Ahmose reigned for twenty-six years before his death. His son, Amenhotep the First, assumed his father's throne. Thankfully, God heard the cries of His people and the killing of the male Hebrew babies ceased. Amenhotep's decision to stop the practice was not prompted by any moral conscience or compassion; rather, he was motivated by his desire to raise up an even larger enslaved labor force.

. . .

He did not fear that our people would revolt against the Egyptians. He believed the strength of his military was more than sufficient to keep any revolt in check. Our numbers grew throughout his reign, as did the number and magnitude of pharaoh's building efforts and his increasing demands on our people.

Soon after the male Hebrew babies were no longer being murdered, my father, Jephunneh, was born. My father was a firstborn son and was raised to be a hunter, as was his father before him, and his father before him.

My father was taught a good hunter needed to study and understand the animals he intended to hunt. He needed to learn their ways, their habitats, their preferred foods, and their migration patterns. He needed to be a student of his surroundings and be respectful of his prey – killing, in a humane way, only what he was going to use. These were skills he would later instill in my brother and me as we grew up.

As a slave, my father, like his father before him, was commanded to serve the royal household under the direction of the palace manager. He was tasked with keeping pharaoh's personal food larders well stocked with fresh meat and his clothiers supplied with animal furs and skins.

On occasion, the royal princes joined my grandfather on a hunt. Pharaoh wanted his sons to be well educated in all aspects of life and leadership, including the skills required to be a successful huntsman. My father was twelve years of age when, for the first time, he accompanied my grandfather and the princes on a hunt.

Prince Thutmose was the eldest son of Amenhotep and heir to the throne. His mother, Queen Meritamun, had died while he was a boy. His father and mother were also brother and sister. It was not uncommon for

Egyptian royalty to marry their siblings. They believed such intermarriage protected the royal bloodline.

He was about seven years my father's senior and was very accomplished with a bow and arrow. Even though the prince would one day be pharaoh, he did not treat my grandfather like a slave. He treated him with respect – in the same way a student would address his tutor. My grandfather returned that respect by teaching him and his companion the same skills he had been taught as a lad.

Prince Thutmose's companion was Prince Moses. Prince Moses was nine years older than Thutmose – but he was not an elder son or an heir to the throne. He had been adopted by Meritamun while she was still a princess in the palace of her father. I later learned she had gone to the river to bathe one day when she saw a three-month-old baby in a basket caught in the reeds along the shore. His helpless cries touched her heart.

Princess Meritamun, who was childless at the time, rightly assumed he was a Hebrew baby hidden by his parents to protect him from being murdered under the edict of her father. She immediately decided to bring the baby into the palace and raise him as her own son. Her father, Ahmose, had reluctantly permitted his daughter to do so.

By the age of nine, the Hebrew adopted son, Moses, had become the older "brother" to the newborn heir to the Egyptian throne – Thutmose. Despite the age difference, the two soon became constant companions in a relationship that grew closer as the years went by.

On this particular day, these two princes were joining my grandfather – and my father-to-be – on a hunt for gazelle. Large game hunts had only recently become a favored sport of the royals, so pharaoh wanted his princes to be accomplished sportsmen. Several other slaves had been recruited to join them for this particular outing. They were assigned the task of "beaters" – driving the game out of areas of cover by beating the ground with their sticks.

Amenhotep had recently completed building his new palace complex in Thebes. The marshlands were nearby and provided a fertile habitat for much of the large game, including gazelles. My grandfather had sent the beaters on ahead to drive the animals out of their habitat back toward the hunters. As the hunters waited, the herd of gazelle began to swiftly emerge from the high grasses. The hunters carefully took their aim.

Suddenly, another predator – a leopard – also emerged in pursuit of the herd. The big cat saw the hunters a moment before the hunters saw the cat. The leopard changed direction and began to approach his now more sedentary targets – the hunters.

Everything happened quickly – almost too quickly to react. The big cat was within seconds of pouncing on Thutmose, its mouth already poised to kill. But in the blink of an eye, my grandfather drew his knife and placed himself between the leopard and the prince.

The leopard was mid-air when my grandfather thrust his knife into the animal's exposed chest. The two became momentarily entangled before the knife stopped the leopard's heart, causing the big cat to fall away dead.

As the herd of gazelles continued to sprint past the hunters, the sportsmen no longer had any interest in them. Praise be to the Lord God Jehovah – my grandfather, though he received some minor cuts from the big cat's claws, had survived to live another day. And the princes, as well as my father, were completely unharmed.

Amenhotep rewarded my grandfather's bravery and extended his thanks for saving his son by designating him as pharaoh's "master of the hunt."

For the next ten years, as my father grew in age and in stature, the four men would continue to periodically hunt together – not as royals and slaves – but as "equals" – men who together had survived a near-fatal experience.

After that day, my grandfather and father had greater freedom to come and go within the palace complex. My father was very grateful for that freedom when he met a young woman named Miriam. She served as a scullery slave under the supervision of the chief baker in the royal palace. She was a fair-skinned and quick-witted beauty who immediately stole my father's heart.

Jephunneh soon found himself looking for any excuse to go by the palace bakery to catch a glimpse or exchange a word with Miriam. Fortunately, the chief baker was an understanding fellow and enjoyed the gifts of fresh meat the young suitor often brought for him. Eventually, these exchanges in the bakery blossomed into a budding relationship that led to marriage – with the approval and blessing of both sets of parents.

The year my parents married, Amenhotep died and Prince Thutmose assumed his rightful place as pharaoh. Before his father's death, Thutmose married his sister, Ahmose, and they began to raise their family. By the time Thutmose was crowned king, they already had one son and two daughters.

Our family continued to enjoy favor under the rule of our new pharaoh. My grandfather was permitted to enjoy a quieter life in recognition of his faithful service, though he would on occasion still join my father on a hunt. My father, Jephunneh, assumed his father's position as master of the hunt, and my mother became the chief baker's assistant.

"Our favor and position within the royal household blinded us to the hardship that most of our Hebrew brothers and sisters were experiencing at the hands of their Egyptian taskmasters," my father once told me. "The same was true for most of the Hebrews who served in the palace complex – and it was true for the Hebrew Prince Moses as well."

But my father went on to say that one day Prince Moses was outside of the palace alone and came upon an Egyptian who was beating a Hebrew. Moses had seen slaves being beaten before, but never so brutally. And the Egyptian appeared to be enjoying the privilege. This behavior so enraged Moses that he took it upon himself to stop the Egyptian. The man did not recognize Moses as the prince and a fight erupted.

In the heat of the exchange, the Egyptian fell to the ground hitting his head on a rock. He died instantly. Moses panicked! He told the Israelite slave to leave and tell no one what had happened. Then, after looking in all directions to make sure no one was watching, he found a secluded area and buried the Egyptian's body in the sand. The slave who was being beaten was grateful – but he was also confused. Why had the prince killed the Egyptian? He feared he would be held responsible, so he decided to tell one of his taskmasters what had occurred.

The next day, Prince Moses went out again to observe how the Hebrew people were being treated. This time he saw two Hebrew men fighting. *"Why are you beating up your friend?"* Moses said to the one who had started the fight.[6] To which the man replied, *"Who appointed you to be our prince and judge? Are you going to kill me as you killed that Egyptian yesterday?"*[7]

Word about Prince Moses' murder of the Egyptian soon reached the palace. Thutmose was enraged that Moses would do such a thing.

"Is this how he repays the kindness of my mother and my father?" Thutmose shouted. "Has the man whom I have honored as a brother since my birth now become a common murderer? He has made the scent of my household wretched in the nostrils of my people!"

· · ·

Thutmose ordered Moses brought before him to answer for his crime. But Moses was nowhere to be found. He had fled the palace ... and the country.

A cry went up from the heart of Thutmose. His "brother" had betrayed him. This Hebrew had betrayed him! Thutmose determined that he would never again trust a Hebrew.

And life in the palace – and in the nation – was never the same for the Hebrews.

2

So the Egyptians made the Israelites their slaves. They appointed brutal slave drivers over them, hoping to wear them down with crushing labor.[1]

* * *

Soon after Moses fled, King Thutmose's heart was dealt a second blow. His wife, Queen Ahmose, died giving birth to the king's second son, who also did not survive. The king's grief blanketed the palace. Some wondered which was worse for him – his queen's death, his baby son's death, or the loss and betrayal of Moses.

The only person who seemingly eased his pain was Princess Mutnofret. Though the princess was five years younger than the king, she was, in fact, his father's sister. She was a rare beauty, and after a short while her wiles and charms were able to assuage the king's sorrow. Laughter began to return to the palace.

Within a matter of months, a royal wedding was celebrated. Nobles from throughout the land attended. King Thutmose had summoned my father to make arrangements for his honored guests to participate in a royal hunt in celebration of his marriage. Normal life was truly returning to the palace.

A few months later, another cry went up from the slave's quarters within the palace. This time it passed through the lips of my mother, Miriam. She had given birth to a big baby boy with a head full of dark, curly hair. My father proudly declared that my name was Caleb. In Hebrew the name means one who is "faithful, wholly devoted, bold and brave." My father decided it was a name I would always strive to live up to.

The following week my parents received a royal command to present their baby son to the king and queen. It was a rare honor and harkened back to past days when my father had enjoyed a more cordial relationship as a slave to his king.

As my mother and father bowed before the royal couple, Queen Mutnofret proudly announced that she was expecting her first child. Since the king already had a son, twelve-year-old Prince Amenmose, this baby would not be an heir to the throne even if it were a boy. But the king expressed his great joy, nonetheless.

Several months later there was another joyful celebration in the palace – this time it was Queen Mutnofret giving birth to Prince Amenemhat. On the seventh day following his birth, the baby boy was formally introduced to the world during the traditional Sebou ceremony.

As the day began, salt was scattered throughout the palace to ward off the evil eye. The baby was bathed, dressed in a new white robe, and placed in a basket. The king and queen led a procession of family and nobles – all carrying lit candles – from the baby's nursery to the royal great chamber.

There, Prince Amenemhat's grandmother removed him from the basket and shook him from side to side, as was the custom, instructing the baby to always obey his parents. The prince was then presented by his father to the high priest for circumcision.

Next, the baby was presented to the sun god – Ra – who the Egyptians believed created everything. His parents sought the protection and blessing of Ra. As the ceremony concluded, the celebration continued late into the night as the family and the nation together acknowledged this great blessing from their gods.

In the years that followed, I became the prince's primary play companion. But even when we were barely old enough to talk, I knew that though we may be companions, we would never be friends. Amenemhat always made it clear that he was a prince and I was his slave.

King Thutmose long had his eye on the territories of Nubia – to the south of Egypt on the western side of the Nile – and the Levant – to the east of Egypt along the Mediterranean coast. The king, like his father and grandfather before him, believed those lands rightfully belonged to Egypt at the bequest of their gods. Thutmose believed the time was right for him to lead a campaign into those regions to extend Egypt's borders farther than ever before.

The Egyptians were united. Their economy was prosperous. Their armies were well organized, well equipped, and unconquerable. The Hebrew slaves were peaceably laboring to expand the nation's infrastructure. There would never be a better time to expand Egyptian borders.

When the younger prince and I were eight years old, King Thutmose led his army into a campaign to take the Nubian lands. In addition to the added territory, Nubia was a source of gold and other precious resources. The king took his eldest son, Prince Amenmose, now twenty, with him into battle. It would be an opportunity for the people to see the bravery of their current king – as well as their future king. Just like his father, the prince had become very proficient with sword and spear.

. . .

And Prince Amenmose looked very much like his father. They were the same height, same build, and had many of the same mannerisms. The only characteristics that separated them were the wrinkles and weight of leadership worn into the king's face.

The king and his generals formulated their plan to capture the Nubian city of Abu Simbel. Their army pressed forward. Their chariots swept toward the Nubian forces. It looked as if they were going to collide head-on, but at the last moment they turned, running parallel to the enemy line. This allowed the archers to give the Nubians a broadside of archery fire from close range. It also prevented the Egyptians from becoming a stationary target for their opponent as they were protected by the walls of the chariots themselves.

This strategy quickly resulted in enemy troop formations being broken and the Nubians in flight. The battle had been won with minimal Egyptian casualties – with the notable exception of Prince Amenmose. Apparently, he had steered his chariot too close to the enemy line and had been unable to make the turn.

Realizing his mistake, he had quickly dismounted, grabbing his spear and sword for hand-to-hand combat. However, he and the handful of soldiers with him were immediately overtaken by Nubian warriors. He was cut down in the battle within moments.

When King Thutmose received word about his son, his grief reverberated throughout the valley. The victory of battle was quickly drowned out by the sorrow over his son's death. It was a cry heard all the way back in Thebes ... and the nation mourned the death of its crown prince.

Amenmose's death meant that Prince Amenemhat was now destined to become the next pharaoh. I saw him less and less after that. He was now being trained to become a future king. He had less time to play. As the prince got older, the king would occasionally direct my father to take him on a hunt. Though I would usually join them, Prince Amenemhat and I rarely spoke. And each time I saw him, he seemed more withdrawn and distant.

It was around this time I met three boys close to my age. Little did I know the impact those friendships would have on my life.

One extremely hot day after I had completed my chores, I told my father I was going to the river. My father had decided a few months earlier – over the objection of my mother – that I was now old enough to go to the Nile River by myself for an occasional late afternoon swim.

"He is doing a man's work," he had told my mother. "He should be allowed to be treated more like a man than a little boy tied to his mother's skirt. Besides, my father allowed me to go by myself when I was Caleb's age." My father prevailed and thus began my adventures along the bank of the Nile.

On one of those first outings, I came upon an Egyptian boy who looked to be my age, swimming in the river. As I passed by, he called out: "Hebrew, do you know how to swim?"

"Yes," I answered. The other boy responded, "Well then, would you like to race? I am training for a competition and I need someone to race against."

"Sure," I replied, "I'll race with you."

As Sapair and I talked, we discovered we had a lot in common, despite our one glaring difference – free versus slave. We both were twelve years old and, just like me, he was the oldest son of his family. We both were strong swimmers. Both of us had been taught by our fathers not only how to swim, but also to be competitive.

On that first day, he beat me in all of our races. As the days went on, I realized that he was faster than I was at short distances, but I had more stamina for the longer distances. I soon discovered that I could beat him handily in the longer races. We were well matched and our mutual love for swimming soon prompted our competitive natures to meld into a close friendship.

Sapair's father, Rahotep, was the overseer of one of pharaoh's building projects – specifically pharaoh's tomb. King Thutmose was determined his tomb would be grander and more ornate than his forefathers, reflecting his growing accomplishments of restoring Egypt to her past glory and beyond. Rahotep was the architect and overseer of the work. As such, he commanded a multitude of Egyptian craftsmen aided by the sweat labor of a legion of Hebrew slaves.

One day, as we sat along the shore, Sapair told me, "My father does not like the fact you and I have become friends. He says Egyptians are not to be friends with Hebrew slaves. But I told him you are the only boy who can truly compete with me in swimming. We swim as equals ... therefore we will be friends as equals!"

Sapair confessed to me that his father did not treat the Hebrew slaves under his charge with respect. Rather, he directed the taskmasters to treat them harshly. He told me his father's cruelty was driven out of a fear shared by many Egyptians that our number was becoming too great and we would one day overthrow our Egyptian masters.

"But this is your land," I told him. "And one day our God will lead us out of here to our own land."

· · ·

"Perhaps," Sapair said, "but then who will provide the labor needed when you go?"

"We will leave that in God's hands," I said.

Sapair smiled at me and we changed the subject. Even though we were friends, we knew there were some things on which we would never agree.

3

Years passed, and the king of Egypt died. But the Israelites continued to groan under their burden of slavery.[1]

* * *

A few days later I was back at the river, but this time Sapair did not join me. His father was scheduled to have an audience before pharaoh that day and wanted his son to join him.

As I walked along the bank, I came upon two boys lying on their backs staring up at the sky. I overheard one of them say, "My father told me that one day Jehovah God will lead us out of Egypt into our own land – the land He promised to our patriarch Abraham. We will no longer be slaves to the Egyptians; we will be servants to Jehovah God."

"But the Egyptians will never let us leave," the other, smaller boy said. "How can that ever happen?"

. . .

I spoke up and said, "Because God will make a way. Just as He provided the ram to be sacrificed in place of Isaac, He will make a way for us to go. What Jehovah God promises, He will bring about!"

The first boy stood to his feet, smiled, and said, "Yes, He will! Our patriarch Jacob saw angels going up and down on a stairway that reached from earth to heaven, and at the top of the stairway was the Lord, who said to Him, '*I am the Lord, the God of your grandfather Abraham, and the God of your father, Isaac. The ground you are lying on belongs to you. I will give it to you and your descendants. What's more, I will be with you and your descendants, and I will protect you wherever you go. I will someday bring you safely back to this land. I will be with you constantly until I have finished giving you everything I have promised.*'[(2)]

"My name is Hoshea, son of Nun of the tribe of Ephraim, and this doubter is my friend Gaddi, son of Susi of the tribe of Manasseh. You will have to forgive him. He comes by his doubts honestly." Then he added with a laugh, "It stems from the fact that the patriarch Jacob blessed my tribe over his – and they have never gotten over it!"

At that, Gaddi jumped to his feet and pretended to give Hoshea a shove. But it was clear that this was just a joke between two friends.

"My name is Caleb, son of Jephunneh of the tribe of Judah," I said, as I shook their hands. "I have not seen either of you here at the river before. Where do you live?"

"My father is a carpenter and I am his helper," Hoshea responded. We are workmen on the tomb King Thutmose is having built for himself in the Valley of the Kings. We live on the edge of the city near the building site." I realized that Sapair's father was Hoshea's and his father's overseer.

. . .

"My father is an arrow maker," Gaddi spoke up. "We are one of many who keep pharaoh's archers adequately supplied with arrows. My family also lives in the village of Deir el-Medina near Hoshea's family on the edge of the city."

"We aren't able to come to the river very often," Hoshea added.

I explained what my father did and where we lived. Once they heard we lived in the slave quarters of the palace and we knew the royal family, they both started kidding me about being royalty. They continued to mock me by bowing before me.

We spent the remainder of the afternoon swimming in the river and exploring along the shore. As the sun started to show signs of setting, we promised to meet up again soon. Then we each went our way.

As time went on, if I wasn't working or studying, I was either at the river swimming with Sapair or spending time with Hoshea and Gaddi in Deir el-Medina. I had not introduced Sapair to my new Hebrew friends since they had such different interests.

Sapair and I were able to see one another only at the river. His father had forbidden that we meet otherwise. I regretted that my friends were living in two different worlds. For some reason I was able to walk in both of those worlds – but I wondered if that would always be the case.

Several times, I brought my bow and Gaddi brought a few arrows so he, Hoshea, and I could practice shooting at a target together. My father even arranged to take my friends and me out for a hunt one early fall day. I would have liked to include Sapair, but his father would not permit it. Hoshea was the victor that day. He downed a goose and his family ate well for several days!

·   ·   ·

There were nights I stayed at Hoshea's home and other nights he joined me at mine. He and I soon became as close as brothers. Hoshea's father, Nun, was a man of deep faith and trust in Jehovah God. He was a leader within the tribe of Ephraim. Many within their village looked to him for counsel and wisdom. In many ways, he reminded me of my father. God had blessed both Hoshea and me with godly fathers.

When I was fifteen, God blessed our family in another way. My parents had a second child – another son – and they named him Kenaz, which means hunter. My parents told me God had blessed us greatly through hunting and Kenaz was to be a constant reminder of His goodness to us. I was grateful to now have three "brothers" – one (Kenaz) by birth and two (Hoshea and Sapair) by common bond: one whom I could mentor and teach, and two who had become "iron sharpening iron" within my life – even though they were from two different worlds.

Sadly, as time went on, my days at the river with Sapair became more and more infrequent. We were becoming young men with more responsibility and less free time. And our respective cultures were pushing us apart.

Also, as the years continued to pass, we had fewer interactions with the royal family. The king's military campaigns to conquer more of the Nubian and Levant territories were meeting with success. The Egyptian nation's boundaries were expanding.

We, as Hebrews, were no longer the sole slave labor within the kingdom. The Nubians and Levantines were also pressed into service as their lands were conquered. The Egyptian army was becoming the most powerful and feared in the world, and the riches of the nation were multiplying. The king continued to have more to occupy his time and attention.

It had been months since I last saw my childhood companion, Prince Amenemhat. As the heir apparent, he was spending more time shadowing his father so he could learn how to rule. For the most part, King Thutmose was a just ruler. As a military man he was ruthless when it came to his enemies. But he was fair-minded when his enemies became his subjects.

Hopefully, Amenemhat would learn well from his father and model that kind of leadership when he became ruler. But honestly, I had my doubts. There was a cruel and callous side I had seen in the prince when we were young – and I feared it had never departed. Only time would tell!

One day, when I was eighteen, my father sent me on an errand to visit my mother in the palace bakery. When I arrived, I was greeted by a young woman I had never seen before. She was obviously working as a scullery slave in the bakery – apparently under my mother's supervision. She was beautiful!

I had once heard the beauty of another woman described as "whoever sees her is forever thereafter angry with his wife." Whoever said that apparently had this young woman in mind! And her beauty caused me to become completely tongue-tied.

As I tried to introduce myself and ask her where my mother was, my tongue kept tripping over my words. I must have appeared completely foolish! Graciously, she spoke up to rescue me before I swallowed my tongue!

"My name is Rebecca," she said. "You must be my mistress's son. She told me you might come by looking for her. She had to attend to a matter for the chief baker, but she will be back soon. She asked that you wait for her. May I offer you a piece of fresh bread and a drink while you wait?"

Gratefully, I regained my composure enough to nod at her offer of refreshments. I sat on a nearby stool while I waited. We were off to a memorable start!

. . .

Fortunately, my mother returned soon and I was able to fully collect myself. As we talked through the reason for my visit, Rebecca re-entered the room and my mother asked her if I had behaved like a gentleman. She again was gracious and replied that I had. My heart was completely and eternally captivated at that moment. I couldn't help but notice the twinkle in my mother's eye.

I took a page from my father's courting handbook and began to make frequent trips to the palace bakery. The chief baker was again grateful to have a steady supply of the meat I was bringing him as gifts each time I came.

It was quite a while before I learned my father and mother had conspired for me and Rebecca to meet. As time passed and our relationship grew, it became obvious we had the support of both our families.

The day came when I brought a gift – or as we called it the "mohar" – to Rebecca's father to seal our betrothal. Though by tradition I knew my gift was to be equivalent to her value, I knew that even if I had all the riches of pharaoh I would never be able to assemble a gift worthy of Rebecca.

With my meager means, I could only bring the bounty from a hunt. The royal family permitted me to hunt and kill a lion and bring the skin and meat as my mohar. Gratefully, Rebecca's father accepted my gift. Six months later our wedding ceremony took place.

I could not imagine being happier than I was at that moment. But one year later our son, Iru, was born. His name means "thanks" – and I had much for which to be thankful to God.

I was thankful for a healthy son who would follow in my footsteps. I was thankful for a precious wife whom I loved with all of my heart. I was thankful for the gift of my family – my parents who had raised me to seek after God and trust Him in all things, as well as my brother who was growing into a strong young man. I was thankful for my friends – most notably Sapair and Hoshea – whom I knew I could always depend on and they on me.

I was thankful that though we were slaves, our lives were at peace. We were experiencing the pleasure of our king and our Egyptian masters. I was thankful for the everlasting promises of my God. Honestly, if the rest of my life were like these days, I would be thankful and content forever.

But it wasn't long before everything changed! Another cry rang out throughout the palace and throughout the nation – King Thutmose had died! And there was a new pharaoh in Egypt. Prince Amenemhat took his father's name and became King Thutmose II. But the entire nation quickly learned the only similarity between father and son was their name.

* * *

4

———

They cried out for help, and their cry rose up to God.[1]

* * *

Princess Hatshepsut was the eldest daughter of King Thutmose I by his first wife, Queen Ahmose. The princess was two years older than I was. Though I was her younger brother's play companion when we were boys, I only ever saw her from a distance. There was no question that she was beautiful like her mother, and I had heard she was wise like her father.

Her name, which means "foremost of noble ladies," was an accurate description even at an early age. Amenemhat had mentioned to me how she was head and shoulders above the rest. It was said King Thutmose marveled at her courage and cunning. And I had heard whispers in the palace complex that if she had been a son, he would have felt much more confident leaving the rule of Egypt in her hands instead of her younger half brother.

. . .

In the latter years of Thutmose's reign, he often called upon his daughter for counsel concerning affairs of state and always found her responses to be more reliable and discerning than the rest of his nobles. So, it wasn't surprising that as he considered the fate of the nation upon his death, he determined the best solution was for Amenemhat and Hatshepsut to marry. The king believed with Hatshepsut as Amenemhat's queen, his son would have a strong and capable ally as his spouse.

During one of our few times together, in a rare unguarded moment, Amenemhat told me he knew his father's reasons for suggesting the union. He said he resented his father for having such a low opinion of him, and he resented the princess because of the high opinion his father had of her. But he would honor his father's wishes and marry his half sister because he didn't believe he had any other choice.

One of Amenemhat's few joys during his union with Hatshepsut was the birth of their son, Ramses, who was born nine months after their marriage. And King Thutmose appeared delighted not only by the marriage, but also now in the birth of his grandson who would further secure the royal line. While Thutmose still reigned, Hatshepsut gave birth to two additional children – both daughters. Word around the palace was Amenemhat doted on his son but had little to do with his wife or his daughters.

There were many public events to honor King Thutmose when he died. As I watched Amenemhat from a distance, it appeared he felt relief more than sorrow. Ever since the death of his older brother, Amenmose, in the battle with the Nubians, Amenemhat had shared with me that he felt suffocated by his father's control.

During that moment, he told me things had progressed to the point that he didn't want to become pharaoh. He didn't want the pressure or the added expectations. But since his forced marriage to Hatshepsut, he confided he welcomed the opportunity to become pharaoh. He knew at that point he could become the master of his own fate – not his father ... and not his wife.

. . .

I knew his choice to take the name Thutmose II had little to do with respect for his father. He did so as part of his "re-creation" of himself into his own man. He would no longer be Amenemhat – son of Thutmose and husband to Hatshepsut. He would be Thutmose II – his own man and ruler over Egypt, and father of Ramses. He would rule in his own way, and he would be a greater ruler than his father ever thought possible.

Soon we began to see the effects of our new pharaoh's rule. King Thutmose II made it clear the kingdom would become bigger, more powerful, and richer under his rule than it had been under his father's. He escalated the campaigns against the Nubian and Levant territories, pushing the Egyptian boundaries farther into their territories. That effort required more soldiers and more slaves.

He also increased the number of new building projects, further taxing the already overburdened slave laborers. They were required to do more with little increase in the resources they were supplied. Our people felt greatly abused by our Egyptian taskmasters and abandoned by our Jehovah God.

Everyone knew Queen Hatshepsut was ambitious in her own right. Many people wondered out loud whether the changes being made were at her bidding or the king's.

Soon after Amenemhat assumed the throne, he commanded that I come before him. As I approached the royal throne room, I wondered what the reason could be. Upon entering, I bowed before the king and queen.

"Caleb, your grandfather and your father have served my family well," the king said. "I learned much about hunting from your father. You have been a trusted companion and you have honored me in all ways since we were children. Today, I seek to honor your father while at the same time, I honor you. From this day forward by the command of pharaoh, you will now be known as the master of the hunt with all of the responsibilities and privileges of that position.

"And all will know that your father has served pharaoh well these past twenty-eight years and he will be treated with honor. He and your mother will continue to live out their days in their quarters here in the palace complex."

Several months later, God blessed Rebecca and me with a son. We named him Elah, which means "a strong oak." We prayed he would become a mighty man who honors God and honors his family in all things. Two years later, our son Naam was born. His name means "pleasant" and we prayed his life would always bear the pleasant aroma of worship that would be acceptable before Jehovah God.

Then after another four years, God blessed us with our daughter whom we named Achsah, meaning "one who bursts the veil." Our prayer was that in the days to come she would break through the veil to grasp the abundant promises of God, fully experiencing all Jehovah has to offer!

One week after Achsah turned two, the queen gave birth to pharaoh's second son, Wadjmose. His older brother, Ramses, was now thirteen years of age and continued to be the apple of his father's eye. Ramses was handsome and athletic – a natural leader. Wadjmose, on the other hand, was frail and sickly from birth.

The king often directed me to take Ramses on a hunt. The teen demonstrated great skill with the bow, as well as the spear, and became an accomplished hunter – even at a young age. Though the king rarely joined us for a hunt, he routinely called upon me to report on the progress of his son.

. . .

After a particularly successful hunt, I told the king: "Your Majesty, Prince Ramses showed remarkable bravery and skill today. As we stood in the blind in the grassland, a herd of gazelles being pursued by a cheetah swiftly approached us. The prince stood his ground, aimed, and felled the lead gazelle with one straight and true shot.

"He then quickly readied his bow, took aim, and killed the cheetah with a second true strike before the advancing predator even realized we were there. The prince is truly becoming a master huntsman like his father, your highness."

The pride and delight of the king in his son was conspicuous to everyone in the throne room that day.

As I was leaving, I passed Igal and Ammiel waiting to see the pharaoh. Both men were also rising leaders among our Hebrew people.

Igal, son of Joseph, was from the tribe of Issachar. He had risen to his leadership role within his tribe by his uncanny ability to garner favor from Egyptian royalty as well as the taskmasters. On several occasions he had convinced those over the people of Issachar to ease the unrealistic work demands being placed on his tribe.

Over the years, through his growing political alliances, he had amassed enough wealth to free himself and his family from enslavement. This enabled him to enjoy an elevated status in the eyes of the Egyptians. They no longer viewed him as a slave, but neither did they view him as an equal. Even as a free man, he had the remarkable ability to still be respected and admired by his tribe for his achievements. As such, he became a great advocate for his people and was greatly trusted.

Ammiel, son of Gemalli, was from the tribe of Dan. Ammiel had also prospered under Egyptian rule, gaining wealth and position. He, too, had been able to procure freedom for himself and his family. He demonstrated a much more ostentatious and pretentious bearing than Igal. Where Igal continued to reflect his "man of the people" image, Ammiel appeared haughtier. Still, because of his wealth and influence for the betterment of the people, he was respected as a leader by the Danites.

Igal called out to me as I approached and said, "Caleb, again you appear to be the recipient of pharaoh's extraordinary favor. The entire palace is talking about the prince's remarkable accomplishment today. And they say it is all the result of your great tutelage."

"The prince is a quick study and a proficient archer," I replied. "Pharaoh has good reason to be proud of his son, and I am only too grateful to have had some small part in his success. Beyond that, I attribute any favor I have received to the goodness and providence of God."

"Oh, I quite agree," Igal responded before pointedly adding, "but we must continue to take every opportunity to encourage our king to extend his favor to all Hebrews. Most of our people do not partake in the benevolence and favor you and I enjoy. The work conditions for most of our people continue to worsen. More is demanded and less is given."

"Yes, I am quite aware of the conditions of our people," I acknowledged. But I knew there was more I needed to learn. And I knew to whom I needed to turn. Two days later I sought out Hoshea.

"Our people are groaning under the burden," Hoshea explained as we sat outside his unassuming home. Night had set in and the labors of the day were complete. "We have now been slaves in Egypt for more than ninety years. There is no longer a Hebrew living who can remember a time when we were not slaves. It has become our way of life, and in many ways we have come to accept it.

.　.　.

"For the most part, our Egyptian masters provide us with enough to make sure we keep our families fed and have a simple shelter that we can call home. Some of us, like Igal and Ammiel, have actually been granted the opportunity to accumulate wealth and rise out of slavery. And those who work in the palace, like you and your family, enjoy added comforts as trusted servants of the pharaoh. You, as a huntsman, are able to feed your family better than most Egyptians.

"But regardless of the food we eat, or the homes in which we lay our heads, we are still slaves. The Egyptians are our masters. And that is not what our God intended. He created us to serve Him. He created us to worship Him ... and bow to Him alone. He did not create us to be oppressed and serve an earthly master. He created us to work and bring glory to Him through the labor of our hands. He didn't create us to be forced to build monuments to men!

"Caleb, our very hearts cry out to be free from the burden of slavery. Our hearts cry out to be the people God created us to be. We did not set out on this journey that brought us to Egypt to become slaves. We set out as a people of God following Him to the place He had for us to dwell – a place where we would be free to worship Him through everything we do. No matter how good your life may be as pharaoh's master of the hunt, God has something so much greater for you. And in your heart, you know that is true!"

I could not dispute anything Hoshea said. I knew the teachings of the patriarchs. I knew this was not God's intended plan for our lives. And though my family and I enjoyed favor from pharaoh, I knew most of our people were suffering under an oppression I had never truly felt.

I was aware that every day Hoshea and his family, and others like them, were experiencing the whip and oppression of cruel taskmasters like Sapair's father. Each day they were expected to work longer – and yet receive less. The older men and women – and the weak – were dying at increased rates as a result of illness brought on by unjust treatment and poor working conditions. Even the able bodied were dying as a result of accidents that could only be attributed to extreme fatigue. People were being pushed to the point of breaking.

"There is a group of us – representing every tribe of Israel – that has begun to meet in secret to discuss what we must do," Hoshea told me. "Come join us. You can hear firsthand from others what they are experiencing. And perhaps, your favor with pharaoh could be used to an advantage to help our people. Perhaps God has granted you such favor for just such a reason! Will you join us?"

And I knew there was only one answer to the question.

5

God looked down on the people of Israel and knew it was time to act.[1]

* * *

The following week, well after sundown, I journeyed with Hoshea to the sandstone quarry just south of the city. The workers had already left for the day so we did not encounter anyone upon our arrival. On the far side of the quarry, we took a pathway to the entrance of a cave. I followed Hoshea into the pitch blackness and soon heard a familiar voice.

"Caleb, it is good to see you are able to join us tonight. Hoshea told us you would be here."

The man who spoke to me was using a small ember of fire to light a torch for us as we made our way deeper into the cave. As the flame illuminated the man's face, I recognized it was Gaddi. My arrow-making friend was obviously a part of this group, and I was pleased to see another familiar face.

. . .

After exchanging greetings, the three of us hurriedly continued our journey into the cave in silence. Eventually the pathway opened into a large, open space. The area was lit by torches of the other men who had already arrived. Apparently, we were the last ones to get there.

In addition to Hoshea and Gaddi, I also recognized Igal and Ammiel, the men I saw outside the court of pharaoh. They both seemed pleased I had joined them for this gathering.

The man who was quite clearly the oldest of the group spoke first. I would venture that he was in his early eighties. His hair had thinned and what remained was as white as the purest wool. However, he spoke with a commanding voice despite his years. It was obvious he was greatly respected by the rest of the men.

"Welcome, Caleb, son of Jephunneh. We have long awaited the arrival of a son of the tribe of Judah. Hoshea has told us much about you and we are grateful that Jehovah God has chosen to lead you to be a part of this assembly.

"My name is Aaron, son of Amram of the tribe of Levi."

The Levites were our priestly tribe. The pharaohs had all understood the need for us as a people to continue in our religious practices. They knew our strength came from our beliefs – and they had witnessed the power of the Hebrew God. The pharaohs did not want to anger the Hebrew God by forbidding the people to worship Him. They allowed the tribe of Levi to act as our spiritual leaders and be the guardians of our tradition. Though the Levites were never required to provide forced labor, they were still slaves, nonetheless.

·　·　·

As the eldest member of this gathering – and the spiritual leader – Aaron had been chosen to be the convener. I soon discovered he was the one who brought this group together.

"Our reason for gathering is to seek wisdom and direction from Jehovah God," Aaron continued. "We believe God has heard us as we have cried out to Him. And we know He will show us what He would have us do. So, we come together to collectively seek His mind and hear from Him.

"Before we begin, I will ask the other men gathered here, whom you do not already know, to introduce themselves. Shammua, let us begin with you."

A quick scan of the men told me that Shammua was the second oldest of the group. He was about thirty years younger than Aaron, but about five to fifteen years older than the rest of us.

"I am Shammua, son of Zaccur, of the tribe of Reuben," he said. I realized as soon as he spoke that I had heard of him. He had served as a soldier in the Egyptian army. A large number of slaves were recruited to serve as spearmen and in the infantry in the military.

Thirty years earlier when Prince Amenmose was killed in the defeat of the Nubian forces at Abu Simbel, a young soldier by the name of Shammua had distinguished himself. He had bravely come to the aid of the prince as he was being surrounded by the Nubian horde.

Though outmanned, he had fought bravely alongside the prince without regard for his own life. And though the prince had fallen in battle, Shammua had defended the position and prevented the Nubians from desecrating Amenmose's body until the rest of the Egyptian forces came to his aid.

· · ·

King Thutmose I had decreed that all of Egypt honor Shammua for his bravery in battle and for so selflessly defending the prince. Though I was a young boy at the time, I remembered the great honor bestowed on him. Shammua had been made an officer in the army – one of few Hebrews to be so awarded – and had served another twenty years with distinction.

Shammua was greatly admired by all of the Israelites for his bravery and his achievements. He was a leader, not only within the tribe of Reuben, but a recognized leader by all of the tribes.

The next man spoke up. "I am Shaphat, son of Hori of the tribe of Simeon."

I soon learned Shaphat was recognized by this group for his sound judgment. He was highly respected for his wisdom and discernment. Shaphat rarely spoke first, but when he did his counsel was always wise and thoughtful.

The tribes of Reuben and Simeon had a reputation for coming to one another's aid. Though we all were one people, those two tribes seemed to have a unique fraternal bond. Shammua and Shaphat personified that bond, as well. The two of them were inseparable and their gifting complemented one another. Just as the word "brave" described Shammua, the word "wise" described Shaphat.

"From the tribe of Benjamin, I am Palti, son of Raphu," said the next man. Over time I discovered that Palti was a man without fear. He was bold, confident, and self-reliant. But that was his Achilles' heel. Whenever he wasn't in control, his confidence would wane. His self-confidence prompted many within his tribe to view him as a leader, but others who had witnessed him in times of uncertainty did not share that opinion.

. . .

"I am Gaddiel, son of Sodi from the tribe of Zebulun." Gaddiel was the youngest of the group. He was very creative and had a strategic mind. He had the ability to look at challenges or problems and come up with innovative solutions. That giftedness served him well.

As a result, he had been able to amass enough wealth to procure his freedom. His tribe was so awed by his accomplishments at such a young age that they respected him as a leader even though he truly was no longer a slave. Many of them hoped he could obtain for the entire tribe what he had attained for himself.

Sethur, the son of Michael of the tribe of Asher, and Nahbi, the son of Vophsi of the tribe of Naphtali, were next to introduce themselves. They were much alike – in age, in build, and in personality. They were both the strong, silent type, but when they uttered their few words, those words commanded attention. They were both humble men and their lack of pretense had endeared them to their respective tribes.

The last man, whom I didn't know, spoke up: "I am Geuel, son of Maki of the tribe of Gad." I would later see that the tribe of Gad walked in the shadow of the Reubenites and the Simeonites. Geuel reflected that image as he walked in the shadow of Shammua and Shaphat. More like Sethur and Nahbi, he would never become a leader of this group, but he would not be intimidated by the other men, either.

Together with the men I already knew – Hoshea, Gaddi, Igal, and Ammiel – we represented all of the tribes of Israel, including the Levites. I was now being called upon with some frequency to provide leadership within the tribe of Judah. My inclusion with this group was confirming that role. I did not seek a leadership role with my tribe, but I would so serve if that was God's will and the desire of my tribe. I was confident God would enable me to accomplish that which He set before me.

· · ·

With introductions out of the way, Aaron turned our attention to the discussion at hand. "Hoshea, give us a report on the deaths this week during the construction of King Thutmose II's tomb," he directed.

"I am sad to report three men died over these past two days," Hoshea said. "One fell off the front of the edifice out of sheer exhaustion. He couldn't take another step and he lost his balance and fell to his death.

"Another was beaten to death by one of the Egyptian overseers for refusing to go any further. He had become dehydrated, his muscles were seizing, and he was unable to take another step. All he was asking for was a drink of water. But in return he received a beating.

"The third man – whom many of you know – Zimri, son of Azariah from my tribe – was killed as a heavy stone fell on top of him from above. The men who were moving the stone had become so fatigued they lost control of it. But the overseers would not allow them to stop."

"The overseers here at the quarry are making the same unreasonable demands," Sethur the Asherite added. "I overheard the Egyptians talking yesterday and they said pharaoh decided the work on many of the building projects is not going quickly enough so he commanded the work day be lengthened. The overseers push the workers to move even more quickly. One of the Egyptians said some of pharaoh's counselors warned him our workers are beyond the point of breaking, but he appears to be ignoring their advice."

"We must tell our people to cry out to our God with even greater earnest," Aaron lamented. "The same God who saved our father Abraham and his servants from the king of Egypt almost four hundred and thirty years ago[2] is able to save us today. If we will call upon Him, Jehovah God will rescue us from this pharaoh."

. . .

"That is true, Aaron," Shaphat the Simeonite interrupted, "but we must also beseech the king. We must help him understand that his treatment of our people will only hurt his efforts."

Aaron turned to look at Shammua. "You must tell him, Shammua," Aaron urgently pleaded. "You are an honored military officer. You came to the defense of his older brother. Surely he will listen to you."

"His father would have listened to me," Shammua responded. "But I have no favor with this pharaoh. I have never been invited to return to the palace since his father died. No, he will not listen to me."

Igal spoke up. "Ammiel and I have attempted to make our case before King Thutmose II on several occasions. Some of his counselors even nod in agreement when we speak. But each time pharaoh ignores our words and tells us to leave. He will have no part in our counsel. But perhaps our brother Caleb could persuade him. He seems to be in good standing with the king these days. Perhaps the king will listen to him."

All turned to stare at me. Aaron, with pleading eyes, said, "If that is true, you must try, Caleb. Perhaps Jehovah God has granted you favor with the king because you are His means of deliverance. You must speak to him."

I turned and looked at Hoshea. Those were the same words he had spoken to me a week earlier. Had these men been discussing how to convince me to do this? Or was God speaking to me through these men? Or both?

Aaron announced we were all in agreement. I would seek an audience with pharaoh. Aaron led us in prayer asking God to grant me favor as I went before pharaoh. "Open pharaoh's heart to this request and grant us deliverance from the hands of the Egyptians."

. . .

Quietly we left the meeting area two at a time, extinguishing our torches before we exited the cave. Hoshea and I remained silent for the rest of our journey together. I was deep in thought ... and prayer.

* * *

6

"I have certainly seen the oppression of My people in Egypt. I have heard their cries of distress because of their harsh slave drivers. Yes, I am aware of their suffering. So I have come down to rescue them from the power of the Egyptians...."[1]

* * *

In the days that followed the gathering at the cave, I continued to call out to God asking Him to grant me an audience before pharaoh so I could ask for mercy on our people. Since slaves do not request audiences with kings, I had to wait for the king to call for me.

Days turned into weeks, and yet there was still no answer. Until one day, I received a message from the palace manager that the king was summoning me. I quickly went to the throne room.

Queen Hatshepsut was sitting at the right hand of the king's throne. There were also a number of people standing throughout the hall. This was not going to be a private audience.

. . .

As always, their bejeweled thrones sat on an elevated dais at the end of the royal hall. Anyone entering the hall must do so in a subservient posture, keeping their head bowed and their eyes diverted toward the ground. Unless you were a member of the royal family, entry into the hall was only at the bidding of the king; but even then, you must stay twenty feet from the throne. There you waited for permission from the king to draw closer. The king rarely spoke to grant permission but would beckon subjects closer with a motion of his right hand.

After being acknowledged, an Egyptian would bow again and address the pharaoh by saying, "Supreme ruler of heaven and earth, may you live forever." Egyptians considered pharaoh to be a god on earth and the intermediary between the other gods and the people. Pharaoh knew that as Hebrews our faith forbids us from referring to him as a god. So, we were permitted to address him by saying, "Your majesty, may you live forever."

Once I had spoken those words and advanced another ten feet, I remained silent awaiting further word from the king. But instead, it was Queen Hatshepsut who spoke.

"Master of the hunt, we want you to arrange a royal hunt on the occasion of our son Prince Ramses' upcoming eighteenth birthday. The king will also accompany, as will the prince and six other members of the royal household. It will take place one week from today beginning at dawn. Tend to all the arrangements so the hunt is a celebratory start to his high-ness's special birthday. Do you have any questions?"

I had no questions about what I was supposed to do. I had arranged royal hunts many times before. But I also knew this was neither the time nor place to discuss my people's plight. Instead, I would wait for an opportunity to talk to the king in private at the hunt.

• • •

"Everything will be prepared as you have said," I assured the queen. "Thank you, your majesties for allowing me to assist you in such an important celebration. May your majesties and the prince live forever."

The week passed quickly as I made preparations. Two days before the hunt, I visited Hoshea and told him about the upcoming time I would have with the king. I asked him to have the tribal leaders pray to God for His favor during that time. He promised me they would do so.

I arranged to have my eldest son, Iru, now fourteen and quite an accomplished huntsman in his own right, join me on the hunt. I would partner with the king, Iru would partner with Prince Ramses, and six of my most experienced hunters would each partner with one of the six noblemen. A team of proven beaters would go out before us to drive the game toward us. I also enlisted Rebecca's assistance in having the prince's favorite sweetened breads prepared to take with us on the hunt.

As dawn approached, the king, the prince, and the other noblemen joined us. After we arrived in the marshland, the pairs took their place at a hunting stand. We then stood ready and waiting for our prey.

"Caleb, your son Iru is becoming a very capable young man," the king said. "He reminds me of you at that age. You and your wife must be proud of him."

"We are proud of him, your majesty, as you and the queen must be proud of Prince Ramses," I replied. "When the time comes, he will follow you as pharaoh with honor and continue the great work you and your forefathers have begun. You have taught him well."

"Caleb, you of all people know that as a boy I did not want to become ruler of Egypt. I was quite content to live my days as a younger prince, but the gods did not intend for that to be the case. I reluctantly was thrust into this role. But now as I look at Prince Ramses, I see him as my greatest accomplishment. I agree – he will wear the Nemes crown well – and will rule justly."

"But, your majesty, in the meantime may you live forever and rule justly," I responded. I knew this was my moment. "Your majesty, you have accomplished so much. Egypt has never been greater than she is today under your rule. And I would dare to hope your majesty believes the Hebrew people have helped you in your accomplishments. The ancients tell us of a day when a Hebrew prince – Joseph – served alongside of his pharaoh – and they were prosperous days for the Egyptian people as well as the Hebrew people.

"My hope is for the Egyptian people and the Hebrew people to again live and work side by side to serve pharaoh as his loyal subjects, respecting the humanity of one another."

The king looked at me but didn't say anything, so I continued.

"Your majesty, I've heard that many of your Hebrew subjects are suffering and dying at the hands of ambitious overseers who view them more as property than subjects of the pharaoh. You have always treated me and my family with kindness, so I am certain that the ill-treatment of my people is not your wish. I beg you, your majesty, would you have mercy on my people and allow us to be treated with compassion as your loyal subjects?"

Pharaoh's visage instantly changed before my eyes as he angrily replied, "Caleb, you wrongfully receive the kindnesses that my family and I have extended to you as license to lecture your king on how to rule his people. You are a slave! And I am the supreme ruler over heaven and earth. That is what you and your people do not understand. The Egyptian people and the Hebrew people are not equals! We are your masters! The gods have willed it. You live at our pleasure. You work according to our command!

· · ·

"I am leading my people in a mighty enterprise to extend our borders, our riches, and our place in this world. If a few slaves die in the process, that is a small price to pay! How dare you attempt to tell me how to lead my people – or you as slaves.

"Apparently, I have been too relaxed with you! Do not ever speak to me in that way again or I will have you beheaded for being an insurgent! Gather the others from our party – this hunt is concluded! We are returning to the palace now!"

Though pharaoh's reaction shouldn't have surprised me, it did. His response was not that much different from his tantrums as a youngster when I was his playtime companion. He was the ruler and I was the slave! And that would never change.

I immediately went off to gather the other hunters. As I came upon Prince Ramses and Iru, a gazelle leaped through the grasses. Both young men were ready. Their arrows flew and this time it was Iru's arrow that was true. The gazelle responded to the fatal blow and immediately fell.

After I collected the other hunters, the beaters collected the one trophy for the day, and we made our way back to the palace. The other men – Egyptian and Hebrew alike – saw the somberness of pharaoh and fell silent for the rest of our time together. When we parted ways at the palace, pharaoh never looked back. The silence continued. And I knew our relationship would never be the same.

Two days later, I was again summoned to the throne room. This time I knew it would not be pleasant. With great apprehension, I made my way to the royal hall, which was again filled with people. But this time the queen was not present.

. . .

As I eased my way in, I heard a voice speaking boldly to the king. I had never heard anyone speak to him like that. Having just recently experienced the king's wrath, I couldn't help but wonder what awaited this man.

The man was dressed as a shepherd. He was at least twice the age of the king and he carried a staff. Someone was standing beside him, and as I looked more closely, I realized it was Aaron the Levite. I heard some people near me whisper, "Prince Moses has returned...."

Then I heard the one they called Prince Moses say, "*This is what the Lord, the God of Israel, says: Let My people go so they may hold a festival in My honor in the wilderness.*"[2]

"*Is that so?*" retorted pharaoh. "*And who is the Lord? Why should I listen to Him and let Israel go? I don't know the Lord, and I will not let Israel go.*"[3]

But Moses persisted. "*The God of the Hebrews has met with us.* He has told ... *our people* to *take a three-day journey into the wilderness so we can offer sacrifices to the Lord our God. If we don't, He will kill us with a plague or with the sword.*"[4]

Pharaoh replied, "*Moses, why are you distracting the people from their tasks? They must get back to work! Look, there are many of your people in the land, and you are stopping them from their work.*[5]

"See, another one of your people approaches me here even as you speak. My former master of the hunt Caleb attempted to speak to me as you have. And now see what it has gotten him. He and his family will no longer live here in the comfort of the palace complex enjoying the game of my fields. They will now work and live among those who labor in the quarry. He was concerned their lives were too hard and their conditions were too dangerous. Now he will have opportunity to witness those conditions firsthand.

. . .

"Be off with you, Moses and Aaron, and take this former huntsman with you, for he must make haste to leave the palace before I choose a more severe punishment. So have I spoken – and so will it be done!"

Moses and Aaron turned and walked away. They did not bow or offer respect. They walked to me, took me by the arm, and walked out of the hall with me.

When I had asked God for boldness and favor to speak with pharaoh, I had envisioned it going quite differently. My family was now being torn from all they had ever known to enter into a much harder life. But I sensed that all of our people were about to experience a much harder life.

I had often heard that God works in mysterious ways, but His ways were about to get a whole lot more mysterious!

Three nights later, Aaron sent out word for us to gather in the cave at the quarry. All thirteen of us were there. But this time Moses also joined us.

Aaron, as always, was the first to speak: "The Lord God Jehovah has spoken to my brother Moses and said:

'I have certainly seen the oppression of My people in Egypt. I have heard their cries of distress because of their harsh slave drivers. Yes, I am aware of their suffering. So I have come down to rescue them from the power of the Egyptians and lead them out of Egypt into their own fertile and spacious land. Say this to the people of Israel: Yahweh, the God of your ancestors – the God of Abraham, the God of Isaac, and the God of Jacob – has sent me to you. And you, Moses, must lead My people Israel out of Egypt.'[6]

"And the Lord has given Moses these signs to prove these are the words of God." Moses then cast down his staff on the ground and immediately it turned into a snake. All of us except Moses and Aaron jumped back. Moses then reached down and grabbed the snake by its tail and immediately it turned back into a shepherd's staff.

We drew closer as we watched with wonder. Moses then placed his hand inside his cloak and when he took it out, it was as white as snow with a severe disease. But when he placed his hand back inside his cloak and withdrew it again, it was as healthy as the rest of his body. Truly God had sent him to us with His message.

We rejoiced knowing God had heard us, and He had sent Moses. It gave us reason to hope, and yet we knew the days ahead would be difficult. In response to my conversation on the hunt and Moses' demands in the throne room, pharaoh had ordered that our people would no longer be supplied with the resources necessary to accomplish our work.

For example, brick makers would no longer receive straw to make bricks. Now they must gather it themselves but still produce as many bricks as before. And the taskmasters were even harder on all of our people.

Instead of conditions improving they had gotten worse. But still – we had heard the promise of God through Moses – and our hope had been renewed.

* * *

7

"But I know that the king of Egypt will not let you go unless a mighty hand forces him. So I will raise My hand and strike the Egyptians, performing all kinds of miracles among them."[1]

* * *

In the days that followed, our Egyptian taskmasters continued to push our people even more. I was adjusting to working in the sandstone quarry. It was hard, back-breaking work. I had moved my family into a hovel located just outside the quarry. It was a small, squalid, one-room dwelling, about one-quarter the size of our slave lodgings at the palace complex.

And pharaoh's punishment didn't stop with me. He decided my offense also reflected on my father, Jephunneh. Despite promising my parents could live out the remainder of their days in the palace complex in honor of my father's faithful service, they were forced to move with us. My father now worked in the quarry, too.

All of this was quite an adjustment for what was now our family of eight.

. . .

The change was hardest for my dear wife, Rebecca. She had been banished from preparing delicacies in the palace bakery – a job she thoroughly enjoyed performing in a comfortable work environment. Now she had to glean straw in the sun all day to supply the brick makers. The work was difficult, and soon the wear began to show on her delicate features.

She and our daughter, Achsah, had little privacy in our tight living space. Iru was now working alongside my father and me in the quarry. Gone were his dreams of becoming master of the hunt. The younger boys, now thirteen and eleven, were put to work sharpening tools used for cutting and excavating the sandstone.

But through it all, I was proud of my family. They made every adjustment that was demanded without one word of complaint. Iru often spoke on behalf of all four children when he said, "Father, we trust you. You have said that God will deliver us from slavery and bring us into a new land – the land He is giving us. We trust God that what He says He will bring about. We trust Him because we trust you and you trust Him."

Each day, conditions grew worse. When we did not meet our daily quotas, our Egyptian taskmasters whipped our Hebrew foremen. The foremen went to pharaoh and pleaded, *"Please do not treat your servants like this."*[2] But pharaoh replied, *"You're just lazy! Lazy! That's why* Moses says on your behalf, *'Let us go and offer sacrifices to the Lord.' Now get back to work!"*[3]

As the foremen left the palace, they confronted Moses and Aaron, who were waiting outside. The foremen said to them, *"May the Lord judge and punish you for making us stink before pharaoh and his officials. You have put a sword into their hands, an excuse to kill us!"*[4]

Moses replied, "Here is what the Lord God Jehovah has said, *'I am the Lord. I will free you from your oppression and will rescue you from your slavery in*

Egypt. I will redeem you with a powerful arm and great acts of judgment. I will claim you as My own people, and I will be your God. Then you will know that I am the Lord your God who has freed you from your oppression in Egypt. I will bring you into the land I swore to give to Abraham, Isaac, and Jacob. I will give it to you as your very own possession. I am the Lord!" (5)

But our people were becoming more and more discouraged by the growing brutality and pharaoh's unrelenting response; they began to turn a deaf ear to Moses.

Aaron sent out word for our group of leaders to gather the following night in the cave. Sethur the Asherite and I were the first ones to arrive. Now that we were both working in the quarry, I had more opportunity to get to know him. I was able to witness firsthand the great respect the men of the tribe of Asher had for him.

On more than one occasion I saw him stand up to one of our Egyptian overseers in defense of another man. Just that day I had seen him step between a Hebrew man who had fallen from exhaustion and a taskmaster who was preparing to use his whip on the fallen man.

Sethur didn't utter a word. He simply looked at the overseer with his piercing brown eyes and made it clear he was not going to allow the man to be flogged. The Egyptian was quickly intimidated by Sethur and backed away. Sethur reached out and helped the fallen man to his feet.

Moses and Aaron were the next to arrive at the cave, followed closely by the other leaders. After everyone had arrived, Aaron explained that God had spoken to Moses saying: *"Pay close attention to this. I will make you seem like God to pharaoh, and your brother, Aaron, will be your prophet. Tell Aaron everything I command you, and Aaron must command pharaoh to let the people of Israel leave his country. But I will make pharaoh's heart stubborn so I can multiply My miraculous signs and wonders in the land of Egypt. Even then pharaoh will refuse to listen to you. So I will bring down My fist on Egypt. Then I will rescue My forces – My people, the Israelites – from the land of Egypt with great acts of judgment. When I raise My powerful hand and bring out the Israelites, the Egyptians will know that I am the Lord."* (6)

"Moses and I will go before pharaoh tomorrow morning," Aaron continued. "We will do as the Lord has commanded. Be mindful what God has said. He will make pharaoh's heart even more stubborn – which means pharaoh will make the burden even greater for our people.

"And spread the word to all our people to store up water in wooden bowls and stone pots from wells that are not filled from the Nile. For tomorrow Jehovah God will turn water from the Nile into blood.

"You must explain to your tribes what God has said. You must help them prepare for even more burdens leading up to the day God finally delivers us from Egypt. Tell them to have courage and strength. Jehovah God goes before us. Though it will get worse before it gets better, they must trust God. He will neither leave us nor forsake us."

Aaron and Moses continued to assure us of God's promise. Many of the men reported on the worsening conditions among the people – and the fear that was swelling among our ranks. Hoshea described how two Hebrew men had died that day at the site of Thutmose II's tomb. They had both been beaten to death. I saw his distress over what had taken place. Aaron concluded our time by calling on Jehovah God, asking Him to strengthen His people and give us courage for what lay ahead.

As we exited the cave, Hoshea asked if he could come home with me so we could speak. His presence in my home seemed to momentarily brighten the hearts of Rebecca and the children. We had not seen many of our friends since moving to this dwelling, and it was good for them to see a familiar face.

. . .

"Caleb, the overseer who had the two men beaten to their death today was Sapair!" Hoshea exclaimed when we were alone. I could not imagine my friend doing such a thing.

Hoshea explained that over the past few months tensions had continued to grow at the building site. Pharaoh had always placed great pressure on Rahotep to make his tomb grander than any other, and lately he was demanding the project be completed sooner than originally planned. No one understood why he was in such a rush. After all, every Egyptian expected pharaoh to "live forever."

But the added pressure had made conditions even worse for the workers. Pharaoh was demanding the best work in the quickest time from workers who were being physically taxed beyond their limits. All these factors added up to disaster.

Sapair was feeling the pressure, too, since being named Rahotep's assistant. The Hebrew workers were fatigued, fearful, and angered by the unreasonable demands. Tensions were high. Nerves were on edge. Egyptians and Hebrews alike were nearing the breaking point. And now, even Sapair had snapped! I found it hard to believe my friend had done such a thing. But it was a reminder to me that our world had been turned upside down.

The next morning pharaoh was met by Moses and Aaron on his way to the Nile River. No one was permitted to speak with the king unless he first gave permission. However, Moses was still considered a prince of Egypt. Therefore, it was his right. But as soon as the king saw the two men, he became agitated.

"Moses," pharaoh shouted, "do your people still have too much time on their hands? And do you have nothing better to do than waste my time with more of your childish demands?"

. . .

But it was Aaron who replied. "Jehovah God, who is God over all, has commanded that pharaoh release the people of Israel to take a three-day journey into the wilderness to offer sacrifices to Him. He has said that if you refuse, He will bring great hardship upon you and upon this land."

"What power does your God have that my gods are not able to overpower Him?" Thutmose II asked. *"Show me a miracle."*[7]

Moses directed Aaron, *"Take your staff and throw it down in front of pharaoh,* [8] and watch what it becomes."

As Aaron threw the staff on the ground, it instantly became a serpent. The king turned to his magicians and told them to throw down their staffs. They, too, instantly became serpents to the obvious delight of the king. But pharaoh was not prepared for what happened next – the serpent that was Aaron's staff swallowed up the other serpents. Aaron reached for the serpent's tail and immediately it turned back into a staff.

"Your God will need to do more than a magician's trick to make me release His people," pharaoh declared.

Moses replied, *"This is what the Lord says: 'I will show you that I am the Lord. Look! I will turn the water of the Nile to blood. The fish in it will die, and the river will stink. The Egyptians will not be able to drink any water from the Nile.'"*[9]

Moses then – according to the command of the Lord – turned to Aaron and said, *"Take your staff –* the one that turned into a snake *– and raise your hand over the waters of Egypt – all its rivers, canals, ponds, and all the reservoirs. Turn all the water to blood. Everywhere in Egypt the water will turn to blood, even the water stored in wooden bowls and stone pots."*[10]

. . .

Aaron did just as the Lord had commanded and the entire river turned to blood. And there was blood everywhere throughout the land of Egypt. The fish died and all of the waters stank – except the water our people had gathered from wells for their own use.

Pharaoh directed his magicians to do the same. They had water brought to them from a new well and set the container before pharaoh. They called upon their magic and the water turned to blood. But he ignored an important difference. When God turned the waters of the Nile to blood, it included water already stored in basins and pots. When the magicians turned their water to blood, it was only the water in the container before them.

Pharaoh ignored that difference, and again hardened his heart, refusing to allow us to go out into the wilderness. So, for seven days the waters of the Nile remained blood and all of the people dug wells to find drinking water.

* * *

8

"I am the Lord! Tell Pharaoh, the king of Egypt, everything I am telling you."[1]

* * *

On the eighth day, Moses and Aaron again returned before Thutmose II as he was along the bank of the river. Moses declared, *"This is what the Lord says: 'Let My people go, so they can worship Me. If you refuse to let them go, I will send a plague of frogs across your entire land. The Nile River will swarm with frogs. They will come up out of the river and into your palace, even into your bedroom and onto your bed! They will enter the houses of your officials and your people. They will even jump into your ovens and your kneading bowls. Frogs will jump on you, your people, and all your officials.'"*[2]

But pharaoh again refused. So at the Lord's command, Aaron again raised his staff over the waters of Egypt and frogs came up and covered the entire land – with one important exception. The frogs did not enter or cover our households!

Pharaoh called upon his magicians once again, and they were able to conjure up frogs. However, they were not able to make the frogs go away!

. . .

The Egyptians rose up and cried out to pharaoh to deliver them from the frogs. After all, they considered him to be a god – was he not more powerful than the God of the Hebrews? Great turmoil arose among the Egyptians, so pharaoh summoned Moses and begged, *"Plead with your God to take the frogs away from me and my people. And I will let your people go, so they can offer sacrifices to Him."*[3]

"You set the time!" Moses answered. *"Tell me when you want me to pray for you, your officials, and your people. Then you and your houses will be rid of the frogs. They will remain only in the Nile River."*[4]

"Do it tomorrow,"[5] pharaoh said.

"All right," Moses replied, *"it will be as you have said. Then you will know that there is no one like the Lord our God. The frogs will leave you and your houses, your officials, and your people. They will remain only in the Nile River."*[6]

And the Lord did just as Moses had predicted. Frogs throughout the land died and the Egyptians piled them into great heaps. A terrible stench filled the land. But when pharaoh saw that relief had come, for a second time he hardened his heart and went back on his word – again refusing to let the Hebrew people go.

It was about this time I began to see Jehovah God revealing His power over the gods of Egypt one-by-one. His demonstration of power began with the staff that turned into a serpent. The king's magicians had called upon Heka, their god of magic. But he was proven inadequate when the serpents the magicians conjured up were all consumed by the serpent that was Aaron's staff.

. . .

The next time was when God turned the water of the Nile to blood. This time the Egyptian magicians called upon Hapi, the god of the Nile. Though they were able to turn water into blood, they could not turn it back into water. Try as they might for seven days, the magicians were unsuccessful. After they had given up, God restored the water of the Nile. In doing so, He revealed that He alone was God over all – including the Nile. Hapi had no power over the God of the Israelites.

This most recent plague of frogs was a direct affront on the Egyptian goddess Heket. She was considered the goddess of fertility and bore the head of a frog. Again, the magicians were able to call upon their goddess to make the frogs appear. But, when their land and households were infested, they could not make them go away.

When pharaoh again refused to let our people go, the Lord instructed Moses: *"Say to Aaron, 'Stretch out your staff and strike the dust of the land, so that it may become lice throughout the land of Egypt.'"* [7] When he did so, lice infested all of the Egyptians and their animals – but again, our people and our animals were spared.

This time the magicians tried to do the same thing by calling out to their god of the earth – Geb. But they were unable to conjure up any lice. In their humiliation, they could not deny *"This is the finger of God!"* [8] and they admitted defeat to pharaoh.

Despite the infestation of lice remaining on the Egyptian people for several days, the king still would not allow our people to go. His resolve appeared greater with each plague. It was only by the mercy of God that the plague of lice ceased.

But the abatement of their discomfort was short-lived. Early one morning Moses again confronted pharaoh along the Nile and said, *"This is what the Lord says: 'Let My people go, so they can worship Me. If you refuse, then tomorrow I will send swarms of flies on you, your officials, your people, and all their houses. The Egyptian homes will be filled with flies, and the ground will be covered with them.'"* (9)

And the Lord did just as He had said. A thick swarm of flies filled pharaoh's palace, the houses of his officials, and the whole land of Egypt except the homes and regions where our people lived. Just as He had done previously, He defeated the Egyptian god Khepri whom they considered to be their god of creation and who had the head of a fly. Like the lice, the magicians could not recreate this plague, and the oppressiveness of the flies caused chaos throughout the land.

The Egyptian people were beginning to fear us – because they feared our God. Our treatment by our taskmasters was becoming less harsh. Even pharaoh seemed to be backing down. He sent for Moses and Aaron and declared, *"All right! Go ahead and offer sacrifices to your God. But do it here in this land."* (10)

But Moses replied, *"That wouldn't be right. The Egyptians detest the sacrifices that we offer to the Lord our God. Look, if we offer our sacrifices here where your people can see us, they will stone us. We must take a three-day trip into the wilderness to offer sacrifices to the Lord our God, just as He has commanded us."* (11)

"All right, go ahead," pharaoh replied. *"I will let you go into the wilderness to offer sacrifices to the Lord your God. But don't go too far away. Now hurry and pray for me."* (12)

Moses answered, *"As soon as I leave you, I will pray to the Lord, and tomorrow the swarms of flies will disappear from you and your officials and all your people. But I am warning you, pharaoh, don't lie to us again and refuse to let the people go to sacrifice to the Lord."* (13)

. . .

Moses left pharaoh's palace and pleaded with the Lord to remove all the flies. And the Lord did as Moses asked, causing the swarms of flies to disappear from pharaoh and all of his people. Not a single fly remained. But pharaoh went back on his word again and refused to let the people go.

When it became clear pharaoh was going back on his promise to Moses, our people were amazed and discouraged. Amazed that anyone – including this king – would be foolhardy enough to try to stand against the power of our God. But discouraged that what we believed would be our imminent exodus from Egypt into freedom had once again been denied.

That night as we ate dinner at home, Iru asked, "Father, why does God permit King Thutmose II to continue to defy Him? We know that Jehovah God is more powerful than pharaoh. Why doesn't He force the king to release us? Why does He permit pharaoh to try Him again and again?"

"Our Lord has promised us that He will rescue us from our slavery," I replied. "He is our God and we are His people. And He is not slow in keeping His promise as some might understand slowness. He is faithful and He will accomplish His promise in His time regardless of what we may otherwise see."

I looked at my father, there at the end of the table and smiled, before continuing with my answer to my son. "Just as your grandfather taught me when I was your age, we cannot fully comprehend the reason for God's delays, but we can be confident that He will bring it about. Children, remember that truth every day of your lives. Hold on to the faithfulness of Jehovah God."

The next day at the Lord's command, Moses again stood before pharaoh saying, *"This is what the Lord, the God of the Hebrews, says: 'Let My people go, so they can worship Me. If you still continue to hold them and refuse to let them go, the hand of the Lord will strike all your livestock – your horses, donkeys, camels, cattle, sheep, and goats – with a deadly plague. But the Lord will again make a distinction between the livestock of the Israelites and that of the Egyptians. Not a single one of Israel's animals will die! The Lord has already set the time for the plague to begin. He has declared that He will strike the land tomorrow.'"* (14)

The following morning the Lord did just as He had said. All the livestock of the Egyptians died, but the Israelites didn't lose a single animal. Hathor, the Egyptian's goddess of love with the head of a cow, had been unsuccessful in preventing this judgment of Jehovah God. Though the Egyptian people cried out for relief, pharaoh's heart remained hardened, and still he refused to let our people go.

The next morning, I was surprised to receive a message from the king – commanding that I come before him. As I made my way to the palace, I could not imagine what the king wanted. When I entered the royal hall, I immediately saw Queen Hatshepsut sitting to his right and Prince Ramses standing to his left. I also saw Moses and Aaron standing in the hall, but they were not speaking with the king. For some reason they appeared to be waiting.

As I approached pharaoh's throne, he motioned for me to draw closer. "Caleb, we have known one another since we were children," Thutmose began. "Your father faithfully served my father, and your grandfather my grandfather. Until recently you faithfully served me. Our lives have been intertwined for generations. Your family has served mine well, and my family has generously rewarded yours.

"The same is true of all your people. You Hebrews came to us many years ago seeking sanctuary and we have faithfully given it. In return we have expected only that you join us in laboring for greater prosperity. And you and your people have always had a roof over your heads, food to eat, clothes to wear, and a place to call home.

. . .

"Why then have you treated me and my people with such contempt? Why do you permit your God to treat us so severely? Is this how your people repay my kindness and the kindness of my father and grandfather? And Caleb, is this how you repay my kindness?

"Look at Prince Moses standing over there. He was raised as an adopted son of pharaoh. Now see how he repays us! Do you have no appreciation for all we have done? Do you have no honor within your hearts to treat us so poorly?

"It is time for us to put our differences behind us. And as your king I will be the first to take a step toward reconciliation. Today, I am restoring you to your position as master of the hunt. You and your family may return to your rightful home here in the palace complex. All that has passed between us is forgiven. I am granting you mercy and restoration. I am giving you back that which you so rashly threw away.

"What do you have to say to my generosity and gracious leniency? Allow us to take this step together so that your people and my people can be restored to one another as well. We can then all return to life as it once was – before this interloper over here entered back into our presence." As the king made that statement, he glanced scornfully at Moses.

"Let us put all of this behind us," he continued. "What is your answer?"

I would be less than honest if I did not admit I was tempted by the king's proposal. I missed my days as the master of the hunt. I missed enjoying the favor of the king. I missed the comforts of our home in the palace. And I welcomed an opportunity for Rebecca to return to the work she enjoyed in the palace bakery, and my parents to return to the dwelling of comfort they deserved. His offer was quite appealing!

· · ·

But that thought was fleeting. Our God had promised us a land for ourselves. And He had made it clear that now was His time to deliver us into our new land. God was leading us to freedom. Pharaoh was simply offering a less severe form of slavery – and I doubted that was true for most of our people – or if it were really true for any of us.

Throughout our lifetime together, pharaoh had demonstrated he was irrational. He would promise one thing today and do another tomorrow. He was not a man of his word. He would just as easily lie to me as he would tell the truth. But Jehovah God does not lie. And He keeps every promise He makes. There was no question whom I would follow and how I would respond to pharaoh.

"Your majesty," I said, "I thank you for your offer to return me to my former station. And I truly wish you no ill will. But the God of Abraham, Isaac, and Jacob – the God who led us here so many years ago – has said that we are to go. And we can do nothing less than follow Him. Allow us to go where our God leads. Save your people from further suffering and pain. Your majesty, let our people go, that you may live forever."

Pharaoh's demeanor changed in an instant as he flew into a rage shouting: "How dare you again speak to your king like that! This criminal Moses speaks in that way, but he is a prince of Egypt. I am limited as to what I can do to him. But you – you have no such protection. You will be beheaded before the sun falls! Guards, take this worthless slave away from me and out of my sight!"

* * *

9

But even so, pharaoh's heart remained stubborn, and he still refused to let the people go. [1]

* * *

At that moment, Moses spoke up. "Pharaoh, in my hands I hold soot from a brick kiln. Jehovah God has directed me to toss it into the air while you watch. Because of your refusal to let His people go and because of your action toward His servant Caleb, these *ashes will spread like fine dust over the whole land of Egypt, causing festering boils to break out on all of your people and their animals throughout the land.*" [2]

As pharaoh watched, Moses threw the soot into the air, and boils immediately broke out on the people and animals alike. The guards attempting to apprehend me fell to the ground writhing in pain. The magicians were unable to stand before Moses because boils had broken out on them and all the Egyptians. The entire court was in chaos. Even pharaoh's body was consumed with boils. He was no longer showing any interest in me.

· · ·

Moses, Aaron, and I exited the royal hall together. Everywhere we went we saw Egyptian people and their animals in anguish. Their goddess Isis was incapable of alleviating their pain. Another god of Egypt had been defeated and the Egyptian people cried out in exasperation. And yet, despite it all, pharaoh remained stubborn, just as the Lord had predicted to Moses.

The people were still experiencing the pain of their boils when Moses returned before pharaoh a few days later. Moses said, *"This is what the Lord, the God of the Hebrews, says: 'Let My people go, so they can worship Me. If you don't, I will send more plagues on you and your officials and your people. Then you will know that there is no one like Me in all the earth. By now I could have lifted My hand and struck you and your people with a plague to wipe you off the face of the earth. But I have spared you for a purpose – to show you My power and to spread My fame throughout the earth. But you still lord it over My people and refuse to let them go. So tomorrow morning at this time I will send a hailstorm more devastating than any in all the history of Egypt. Quick! Order your livestock and servants to come in from the fields to find shelter. Any person or animal left outside will die when the hail falls.'"* [3]

The word quickly spread among our people and they sought refuge for themselves and for their animals. Many of pharaoh's officials were afraid because of what the Lord had said, and they also quickly brought their livestock in from the fields. But there were many who paid no attention to the word of the Lord and refused to seek refuge for themselves or their animals.

Then the Lord said to Moses, *"Lift your hand toward the sky so hail may fall on the people, the livestock, and all the plants throughout the land of Egypt."* [4]

So, Moses did as the Lord commanded, and Jehovah God sent thunder and hail, and lightning flashed toward the earth. A tremendous hailstorm began to batter Egypt. Never in the nation's history had there been a storm like that, with such devastating hail and continuous lightning. It left Egypt in ruins.

. . .

The hail struck down everything in the open fields – people, animals, and plants alike. The flax and barley were ruined. Even trees and buildings were destroyed or severely damaged. The only places that escaped harm were those where our people were dwelling. God in His mercy had placed His hand of protection over us.

Pharaoh quickly summoned Moses. *"I have sinned and the goddess of the sky – Nut – has failed to protect us from your God,"* he said. *"The Lord is the righteous One, and my people and I are wrong. Please beg your God to end this terrifying thunder and hail. We've had enough. I will let you go; you don't need to stay any longer."*[5]

"All right," Moses replied. *"As soon as I leave the city, I will lift my hands and pray to the Lord. Then the thunder and hail will stop, and you will know that the earth belongs to the Lord. But I know that you and your officials still do not fear the Lord God."*[6]

Moses left pharaoh's court and went out of the city. When he lifted his hands to the Lord, the thunder and hail stopped, and the downpour ceased. And when pharaoh saw the rain, hail, and thunder had ceased, he again refused to let our people leave, just as the Lord had predicted through Moses.

I found myself silently asking the same question my son had asked previously. "Why does God permit King Thutmose II to continue to defy Him?" But I knew the answer had not changed. Our God would deliver us in His time!

Later that day, I decided to walk to Hoshea's home to make certain he and his family were safe. As I approached his village, I met Sapair, whom I had not seen in several years. Much had changed since we had last been together. He appeared to be very distracted. I recognized him first.

. . .

"Hello, Sapair." He looked startled and for a moment appeared not to recognize me. But then his countenance hardened as he said, "Caleb! So, tell me, have you sought me out to inform me how mighty your God is? Have you, like the rest of your people, come to tell me how evil we Egyptians are and that we are only getting what we deserve? Have you come to gloat over the destruction of the building that my father and I have given our lives to build?"

"Sapair, I have not come to rebuke you," I replied. "I did not even come today looking for you. But I am glad to see you. What has happened?"

"Your God has happened!" he answered. "The hailstorm destroyed the king's tomb. There is nothing left but rubble. Many of my kinsman who were there during the storm are dead. Our project has failed. And the king has revoked our commission to rebuild. He has said since we failed the first time, he could not trust us to rebuild the tomb. But we didn't fail! This is all the work of your God and your people!"

"Sapair, I am so sorry for your loss ... and your pain," I began. "It is not my desire – or the desire of any of my people – to see you or your people suffer. Many of us have grown up as friends, not enemies. You and I were almost like brothers. I grieve with you over the death of those you have lost – and I do not rejoice in the destruction of your life's work. There are many of our people who have invested their sweat and toil in the building of the tomb. Some of them are also my good friends. Whether they are slaves or not, they do not want to see the work of their hands destroyed, either.

"The only thing my people have sought to do is be obedient to our God. Surely you understand that, Sapair. We have not brought this pain upon the Egyptian people. The king's refusal to allow us to be obedient to our God has brought this upon everyone. We are not the cause."

. . .

"Would you speak ill of our king?" Sapair asked. "No," I responded. "He is my king, as well. And I know him better than most – yourself included. But he has refused to obey the voice of the one true God. He promised to let us go and then he relented. He has brought this pain down on your people – not us!"

"Pharaoh is our god," Sapair retorted, "and he bows before no other. How could the God of slaves be mightier than our god? You are deceived, Caleb, and perhaps you always have been. You are a slave, and as an Egyptian, I am your master. We cannot be friends, let alone brothers. My father was right, and I was a fool to think otherwise. Off with you, before I turn a whip to you."

I knew I could not dissuade his anger, so with a heavy heart I continued on my journey – mourning the loss of my friend.

I soon arrived at Hoshea's home, pleased to find that he and his family had fared well in the hailstorm. I told him about my encounter with Sapair. He was not surprised. In recent years he had come to see Sapair in a totally different light than I had. He was surprised to learn that Rahotep and Sapair had lost the commission to rebuild the tomb. But Hoshea trusted that would be of little consequence to him and the other workers in the days ahead. Despite our current circumstance, we both trusted God's promise – and we knew that our exodus from this land would soon occur.

The next day, Moses and Aaron again appeared before pharaoh and said, *"This is what the Lord, the God of the Hebrews, says: 'How long will you refuse to submit to Me? Let My people go, so they can worship Me. If you refuse, watch out! For tomorrow I will bring a swarm of locusts on your country. They will cover the land so that you won't be able to see the ground. They will devour what little is left of your crops after the hailstorm, including all the trees growing in the fields. They will overrun your palaces and the homes of your officials and all the houses in Egypt. Never in the history of Egypt have your ancestors seen a plague like this one!'"*[7]

• • •

As soon as Moses and Aaron left the royal hall, pharaoh's counselors approached him and made an appeal. *"How long will you let this man hold us hostage, your majesty? Let the men go to worship the Lord their God! Don't you realize that Egypt lies in ruins?"*(8)

So the king summoned Moses and Aaron to return before him. "All right," pharaoh said, "your men may go and worship the Lord your God. But your women, children, flocks, and herds will remain here."

Moses replied, *"We will all go – young and old, our sons and daughters, and our flocks and herds. We must all join together in celebrating a festival to the Lord."*(9)

"Never!"(10) pharaoh shouted. And with that he had them thrown out of the palace.

Straight away Moses walked to the bank of the river and raised his staff over Egypt, causing the Lord to send an east wind. The wind blew over the land throughout the day and night. When morning arrived, the east wind had brought locusts. They swarmed over the whole land, settling from one end of the country to the other. They devoured every plant and all the fruit on the trees that had survived the hailstorm.

Pharaoh, his priests, and his magicians cried out to Seth, their god of storms and disorder, to remove the locusts. But their pleas again fell on deaf ears. They knew the God of the Israelites was more powerful than any of their gods. He had defeated each and every one of them. They had never experienced such destruction throughout their history as a nation. Pharaoh's counselors and officials again cried out to him. Even the queen was publicly telling him to recant his position and allow the Hebrews to go.

• • •

Pharaoh again summoned Moses and pleaded, *"I have sinned against the Lord your God and against you. Forgive my sin, just this once, and plead with the Lord your God to take away this death from me."*[(11)]

I knew better than most that the king lived in the shadow of his father ... and to some degree his queen. He had vowed to be a better king than his father and to make Egypt greater than it had ever been. And yet, everything he had built – and his forefathers had built before him – was being destroyed. The mightiest nation on earth was being brought to its knees. And he – the ultimate god of Egypt – was being shamed by the God of Hebrew slaves. I knew his plea was again insincere.

But Moses called out to God to take away the locusts. And the Lord responded by shifting the wind to blow from the west, blowing all of the locusts into the Red Sea. But once every locust was gone, pharaoh again refused to let our people go.

So the Lord told Moses, *"Lift your hand toward heaven and the land of Egypt will be covered with a darkness so thick you can feel it."*[(12)] And a deep darkness covered the entire land for three days ... except where our people lived. We continued to have light as usual.

One more time pharaoh summoned Moses. *"Go and worship the Lord,"* he said. *"But leave your flocks and herds here. You may even take your little ones with you."*[(13)] His counselors nodded in agreement. Even the queen and Prince Ramses stood together with the king in making this offer. This had been their recommendation to pharaoh. Surely the God of the Israelites would accept this magnanimous proposal.

"No," Moses said, *"you must provide us with animals for sacrifices and burnt offerings to the Lord our God. All our livestock must go with us, too; not a hoof can be left behind. We must choose our sacrifices for the Lord our God from among these animals. And we won't know how we are to worship the Lord until we get there."*[(14)]

. . .

Immediately pharaoh's heart again hardened and he went into a tirade. *"Get out of here!"* he shouted at Moses. *"I'm warning you. Never come back to see me again! The day you see my face, you will die!"*[(15)]

"Very well," Moses replied. *"I will never see your face again."*[(16)]

The two gods who were considered to be the most powerful by the Egyptians were Ra, god of the sun, and pharaoh himself. The God of the Israelites had now shown that He was more powerful than Ra by plunging the nation into darkness. Only pharaoh himself – considered to be the ultimate power of Egypt – remained. But Thutmose II would never be prepared for what was about to occur.

* * *

10

Then the Lord said to Moses, "I will strike pharaoh and the land of Egypt with one more blow. After that, pharaoh will let you leave this country. In fact, he will be so eager to get rid of you that he will force you all to leave."[(1)]

* * *

Before Moses turned away from the presence of pharaoh, he looked straight into the eyes of the king and said: "Before I go, I have one last word for you from the Lord God Jehovah. *'At midnight tonight I will pass through the heart of Egypt. All the firstborn sons will die in every family in Egypt, from the oldest son of pharaoh, who sits on his throne, to the oldest son of his lowliest servant girl who grinds the flour. Even the firstborn of all the livestock will die. Then a loud wail will rise throughout the land of Egypt, a wail like no one has heard before or will ever hear again. But among the Israelites it will be so peaceful that not even a dog will bark. Then you will know that the Lord makes a distinction between the Egyptians and the Israelites.' All the officials of Egypt will run to me and fall to the ground before me. 'Please leave!' they will beg. 'Hurry! And take all your followers with you.' Only then will I and my people go!"*[(2)]

Then Moses, burning with anger, left pharaoh's presence for the last time.

. . .

Two nights earlier, when darkness had only begun to blanket the Egyptians, Aaron had called for us all to gather at the cave in the quarry. We had little fear of being discovered by our Egyptian taskmasters since they were mourning the deep darkness that covered them.

After we gathered, Moses stepped into our midst and said, "Despite this darkness, pharaoh will again harden his heart and continue to refuse to let our people go. So, here is what the Lord has said: 'Go, *pick out a lamb or young goat for each of your families, and slaughter the animal. Drain the blood into a basin. Then take a bundle of hyssop branches and dip it into the blood. Brush the hyssop across the top and sides of the doorframes of your houses. And no one may go out through the door until morning. For the Lord will pass through the land to strike down the Egyptians. But when He sees the blood on the top and sides of the doorframe, the Lord will pass over your home. He will not permit His death angel to enter your house and strike you down.'"* [3]

Moses continued, "After that, pharaoh will relent and let our people leave this country. In fact, he will be so eager to get rid of us he will force us all to leave. Go and instruct our people to do as the Lord has commanded – because in two nights' time, the angel of the Lord will pass over this land.

"Tell them to be ready to leave. We will not be returning to this place. And tell all our men and women to go to their Egyptian neighbors once pharaoh has given the command for us to leave and ask for clothing and articles of silver and gold. Their neighbors will freely give it to them, just as God promised our patriarch Abraham: '*I will punish the nation that enslaves your descendants, and in the end they will come away with great wealth.*'" [4]

When Moses finished speaking, we all bowed on the ground and worshipped Jehovah God. Though there had been times our hope had grown faint, throughout the advent of the plagues we had seen the faithful hand of God protecting us from His wrath and battling our captors on our behalf. Now, would the one thing we had hoped for all our lives finally be reality? Would we at last be able to leave this place?

. . .

And yet, our hope was mixed with sadness. An angel of death was about to visit the Egyptians. Some of those we had known all our lives were about to experience death at the hand of God. I thought of Sapair – who had once been my close friend. Sapair was a firstborn son. My heart was heavy. It had been one thing for them to experience the plagues of lice, locust, darkness, and the like, but death was quite another.

Then I thought of Prince Ramses. In many ways I had been a part of his upbringing. I had seen him grow into a young man who would one day be a better leader than his father. And now, he would never have that opportunity. Every Egyptian family would suffer the grief of death – even those we dared to call friends. All because of the stubbornness of pharaoh!

So, we lingered as we worshipped our God with thanksgiving and with reverent fear. He was our Deliverer, our Protector, our Light in the midst of darkness, and our mighty Warrior. When we had finished, we left the cave and scattered with urgency to every corner of Egypt to tell our people to get ready.

We all made preparations just as the Lord had commanded. The cover of darkness prevented the Egyptians from seeing what we were doing. Rebecca and I, together with our four children and my parents, gathered in our humble home. We had chosen a young, unblemished goat to sacrifice.

While my youngest son, Naam, and I brushed the goat's shed blood on the top and sides of our home's doorframe, my other sons, Iru and Elah, roasted the meat over a fire under the supervision of my father. Rebecca, my mother, and Achsah prepared the bitter salad greens and bread made without yeast Moses had also instructed us to prepare.

It was the evening of the fourteenth day of Nissan. As we ate our meal, we were mindful of what was about to take place. I recounted to my family the promises of God through our patriarch Abraham and through our new leader Moses. I reminded them we were God's chosen people – set apart by Him for Himself. I instructed them that we would remember this day every year from here on out as a family, and as a people, as the night of the Lord's Passover – the night He protected us and delivered us. We prayed and sang songs of praise to our Lord God.

Our few possessions were gathered by the door, ready for our departure. As we lay down on our mats to rest for the night, we remained fully dressed, even wearing our sandals. Amazingly, by God's grace, a restful sleep quickly came over us.

That night at midnight, the angel of the Lord visited the entire land of Egypt. All the firstborn sons of Egypt were struck down – including those of their livestock. Wailing sounded from every corner of the land. Only our Hebrew homes were silent.

The loudest cry came from the palace. The Egyptian servants came to the king's bed chamber and announced that Prince Ramses had died. Pharaoh's grief was inconsolable. Queen Hatshepsut shifted from moments of deep sorrow to uncontrollable anger – directed toward her husband.

"You did this!" she cried. "Your ineptness in dealing with the Hebrews has caused the death of our son! You alone are to blame. You think you are a god – you are an incompetent fool! Our father looks down upon you and mourns the day you were born. I am ashamed to call you husband!"

Thutmose II strode out of the room. The servants looked away from their sovereign in deference to their king but silently agreed with their queen. Although the king was grief-stricken, he was also overwrought by the hysterical rantings of his queen. He knew he was to blame. And he knew, once again, he had failed as the ruler of his people – and it had cost him his son's life and the devastation of his kingdom.

. . .

As he walked out onto the rooftop of the palace, he heard cries coming from all around him – from the palace to the dungeon and from the sea to the desert. For a moment, pharaoh thought about throwing himself off the roof. And perhaps, if his officials had not interrupted his solitude, he would have done just that.

The officials begged their king to release the Hebrews. And now at the pinnacle of his personal grief and humiliation, he sent for Moses and Aaron. *"Get out!"* he ordered. *"Leave my people – and take the rest of the Israelites with you! Go and worship the Lord as you have requested. Take your flocks and herds, as you said, and be gone."* [5]

But then he surprised even Moses when he added, *"Go! But bless me as you leave!"* [6] Pharaoh no longer stood before Moses as a crazed tyrant; he stood as a broken man. His son was dead. His wife and his people had turned against him. The only place he knew to seek favor was from those he had rebuked, threatened, and despised. But Moses knew that desperation would not last, so he simply turned and walked away.

All of our Egyptian neighbors not only gave us silver, gold, and clothing, they gave us whatever we asked for – and more. They urged us to leave the land as quickly as possible, because they feared if we remained any longer, they would all die!

By the end of that day, our people had begun to make our exodus from Egypt. We went out from every corner of the land – from Rameses to the north, to Goshen to the south, to the capital city of Thebes. It was an amazing sight to watch such a mass exodus from across the land. Moses had instructed us to all travel in the direction of Succoth – east of the Nile, to the land north of the Red Sea. There we would assemble as a people before continuing on to the land God had prepared for us.

. . .

Moses directed Hoshea and the tribe of Ephraim to carry the coffin containing the body of our patriarch, Joseph. As we watched the tribe carry the coffin, my sons asked why Moses had directed them to do so. My father quickly replied, "This was done in accordance with the oath the sons of Israel made to Joseph. He knew that one day God would fulfill His promise and we would leave Egypt. Before he died, Joseph said to his brothers and sons, '*God will certainly come to help you. When He does, you must take my bones with you from this place.'*(7) Today we are fulfilling that promise made long ago."

Words fail me as I attempt to describe how we felt that day. We were somber as we began our journey. The heaviness of all we had experienced in Egypt for hundreds of years weighed heavily on us. Abraham had first visited this land four hundred thirty years earlier – and the promise God had given him then was now being fulfilled. Two hundred fifteen years ago, we had entered this land as a family of seventy people. Today, we were leaving as a family of about two million. Over ninety years ago we had become slaves, but today we had been set free.

Seldom had we allowed ourselves to believe this day would really come. We knew the promises, but we could not imagine the possibility. Our Egyptian masters seemed invincible and the bonds of our slavery unbreakable. And yet, God had shown Himself in might and in power. We had experienced deliverance in a way we never could have imagined. It caused us to begin our journey with a holy hush.

We also understood the unspeakable sorrow of the Egyptian families surrounding us. Most of the families had nothing to do with our enslavement – but most, if not all, had paid the price. They had become not only a grieving people, but a broken people, as well. Whereas we, who had been slaves, had now become free through the price of their sorrow. We knew our joy had come at a great cost to our Egyptian neighbors.

But as we continued our journey and the image of Egypt grew fainter behind us, our hearts began to lighten. Somewhere, someone began to sing. And then another. And another. And soon we all were singing praises to our God as with one voice. The praises echoed throughout the region.

Then soon there was laughter. There was a joy that transcended anything I had ever experienced. It was the joy of freedom. It was the recognition that we were no longer answerable to any master other than our God. We were our own nation – free to go where He led us and free to do whatever He led us to do.

I pulled Rebecca close. My parents were there walking right beside us. Our children surrounded us. My younger brother Kenaz, his wife, and their baby son, Othniel, walked close behind. The tribe of Judah – and all the other tribes – surrounded us. We were free! And nothing had ever felt better!

* * *

11

So God led them in a roundabout way through the wilderness toward the Red Sea. [1]

* * *

The conversations around me began to change as we continued our journey to Succoth. The joy over our escape from slavery began to drift toward concern.

"Where is this land of milk and honey Moses told us about?" someone asked. "And how long will it take for us to get there?" another chimed in. A woman in front of us asked, "Do we know where we will sleep tonight? And what about food? We have enough to last us for a few days, but what will we do if the journey takes longer?"

Then I heard someone say, "At least while we were in Egypt, we always had food to eat!" "And pharaoh's army protected us from invaders," another man added. "Who will protect us now?" "I sure hope Moses knows what he's doing," an older man interjected. "We originally came to

Egypt to keep from starving to death," he continued. "Who will keep us from starving now?"

We had been free only a few hours, and some of our people were ready to go back to being slaves!

I knew it was fear of the unknown. As difficult as our years in Egypt had been, it was all any of us had ever known. Today we were venturing out into uncharted territory. We had no idea what to expect or what we would encounter. At least as long as we had worked in Egypt, we were assured of the food, shelter. and protection of the most powerful nation on earth. Now as we stepped out into this wilderness, we had no idea where we would find food or shelter, or what enemies we might encounter.

Many of our people had built close relationships with the Egyptian people. Not all of the Egyptians had mistreated or abused us. Many had befriended us. And now there was a regret surfacing over friends who would never be seen again. Each step of our journey was taking us another step away from friends we loved.

But I also heard words of excitement and expectancy. One man was telling his family, "We have prayed for this day. We have cried out to God for deliverance. And today He has answered. The path ahead of us is a new beginning! Imagine a land flowing with milk and honey! How wonderful it will be!"

Another man replied, "All our sons and daughters had to look forward to was the threat of the overseers' whips! Now the sweat of their brow will be for their own behalf and not for the benefit of their Egyptian overlords!"

I realized there was a mixture of relief, reservation, regret, and excitement. Everyone was speculating how this new life would impact them. But I also realized there was one problem – they were looking through their own eyes. They were looking at it as a journey that would lead us from Egypt and our escape from slavery, not as a journey that would lead us closer to God. Jehovah God wasn't leading us in order to bring us from a place; He was leading us to bring us to Himself. His purpose was to bring us to a place that would enable us to know Him more intimately.

He is our provision – not Egypt. He is our protector – not pharaoh. He is our shelter – not the hovels we had called home. He would go before us and meet our every need. He had already made sure we received everything from the Egyptians necessary for the journey. That didn't mean we had everything we needed; it meant we had everything God intended to supply through the Egyptians. He would supply whatever else we needed.

And our journey was not going to be a fast one. Two million people – from young to old – together with our livestock and possessions do not move quickly. Our progress would be deliberate but never swift. But I was confident God would accomplish all He intended in our lives through this journey. And we had no idea what that would be!

When we arrived at Succoth, Moses climbed to the top of a hill and declared, *"This is a day to remember forever – the day you left Egypt, the place of your slavery. Today the Lord has brought you out by the power of His mighty hand. On this day in early spring, in the month of Nissan, you have been set free. You must celebrate this event in this month each year after the Lord brings you into the land He has promised.*

"This is what you must do when the Lord fulfills the promise He swore to you and to your ancestors. When He gives you the land where the Canaanites now live, you must present all firstborn sons and firstborn male animals to the Lord, for they belong to Him.

"And in the future, your children will ask you, 'What does all this mean?' Then you will tell them, 'With the power of His mighty hand, the Lord brought us out of Egypt, the place of our slavery. Pharaoh stubbornly refused to let us go, so

the Lord killed all the firstborn males throughout the land of Egypt, both people and animals. That is why we now consecrate all the firstborn males to the Lord.' This ceremony will be like a mark branded on your hand or your forehead. It is a reminder that the power of the Lord's mighty hand brought us out of Egypt." [2]

Moses instructed Aaron to assemble the leaders from all the tribes. Each of us was told to select three additional leaders from our tribe to accompany us to the gathering. Our group of now fifty-two men, not including Moses, came together on the hill where he had spoken to the people.

"The Lord has shown me," Moses began, "that He will not lead us east along the main road that runs through the land of the Philistines, even though that is the shortest route to the Promised Land. God has said, *'If the people are faced with a battle, they might change their minds and return to Egypt.'* [3] Instead, He will lead us south along the western shore of the Red Sea."

Those of us who understood the geography of this region were surprised by the direction. But we had seen the way God directed us out of Egypt and we were not about to question Him now.

Moses continued, "Tomorrow we will break camp and leave Succoth. The Lord God will go before us and guide us by day with a pillar of cloud. At night, He will provide light with a pillar of fire. When the pillar moves, we will move. When the pillar remains in place, we will stay in place. The pillar of cloud and pillar of fire will be a constant reminder that our God goes before us to direct our steps. Tell the people, we will rest for the night and follow the Lord's pillar of cloud in the morning."

The next morning, the pillar of cloud began to move, and we followed. I smiled as I saw our people pointing to the cloud and rejoicing that Jehovah God was going before us. We could clearly see His hand leading us and guiding us in our journey. There was no question He was making the way. There was no question He was ordering our steps.

Two days later we arrived in Pi-hahiroth. We were on the west bank of the Red Sea, between Migdol and the sea. It came to be known as "the place where the reeds grow" because of the tall grasses growing at the edge of the water. The grass attracted a large number of hummingbirds and butterflies – which further fostered the atmosphere of safety and sanctuary we all felt in this place.

It truly was a good place to rest and be refreshed. The cool breezes off the sea soothed our souls. Was God giving us a glimpse of what He had in store for us in the land He was giving us? Our people were overflowing with excitement, contemplating the blessings awaiting us in the Promised Land.

The next morning the pillar of cloud remained in place. It was the Sabbath, so we settled in to enjoy this beautiful place and rest. God was permitting us to wait before Him and be renewed. Children's laughter rang throughout our encampment as they ran and played. Mixed in were the sounds of gentle breezes blowing in off the sea and the quiet chirping of sea birds.

Men and women who had had little cause to be happy were chuckling and teasing one another. It was as if we no longer had any cares or concerns. Our God had delivered us. He was leading us. We were in His care.

Little did we know our feeling of freedom would soon be replaced by panic and fear.

"Your majesty," the officials reported to pharaoh, "the Hebrew people are not showing any signs of returning. It has been five days since they left to go into the wilderness to offer sacrifices to their God. Moses told you they would only be in the wilderness for three days. He dared to lie to the mighty pharaoh!"

"What have we done, letting all those Israelite slaves get away?"[4] pharaoh asked no one in particular. His question was actually a reminder to his officials that they were the ones who urged him to let the Hebrews go.

"Your majesty, the gods have apparently caused the Israelites to become confused," another official announced, "because they have camped on the western shore of the Red Sea and are now trapped! They are still within the grasp of pharaoh. They cannot escape you! If we go after them, we can easily bring them back to Egypt."

So pharaoh ordered his chariot harnessed and all his troops called up. "I will lead my troops," he said, "to capture those ungrateful Hebrews and bring them back to Egypt to pay for all the death and destruction they have caused. And I will show them once and for all the gods of Egypt are greater than the God of the Israelites!"

All the forces of pharaoh's army advanced on the Hebrews – all his horses, chariots, charioteers, and troops. Never had such an army advanced against an enemy!

Meanwhile in Pi-hahiroth, just before sunset, Moses called the leaders together. "The Lord has told me," he said, "that we are to remain camped in this place. Once again God has hardened pharaoh's heart, and he and his army are now advancing toward us. Jehovah God has allowed this in order to display His glory through pharaoh and his army. Our God will defeat them, and once and for all the entire Egyptian nation will know that Jehovah alone is the Almighty God!"

At that moment, we heard shouts coming from our people as they pointed to the horizon. A mighty cloud of dust was approaching from the north.

Soon we could hear the thunderous galloping horses and the shouts of an advancing army. Our people began to panic and cry out in fear.

One lone chariot advanced quickly ahead of the others. We could tell by the glimmer of gold on the chariot this was pharaoh himself. He was leading the army to overtake us!

As if with one voice our people cried out to Moses, *"Why did you bring us out here to die in the wilderness? Weren't there enough graves for us in Egypt? What have you done to us? Why did you make us leave Egypt? Didn't we tell you this would happen while we were still in Egypt? We said, 'Leave us alone! Let us be slaves to the Egyptians. It's better to be a slave in Egypt than a corpse in the wilderness!'"* [5]

Our oasis was now an obstacle as our enemy approached, threatening a merciless attack. The Red Sea lay before us and defeat threatened us from behind. We had no way to defend ourselves against the mightiest army on earth! Most of our people began to question whether God had abandoned us. We were never going to taste the blessings God had for us. And even worse, it appeared that God had forsaken us.

But as I surveyed our situation – we were defenseless in this place where the reeds grow – I was reminded of an important lesson.

The reed is not known for its strength or beauty. It is a tall, coarse grass with few distinguishing features. But a master craftsman can do much with a reed. He can turn it into a musical instrument that makes beautiful melodies of praise. He can turn it into an arrow that defeats his enemy or carries his message to others.

He can take that reed together with other reeds and weave a beautiful tapestry. Left to its own devices, the reed can do nothing, but in the hands of a master craftsman – like Jehovah God – the reed can become an instrument of His glory. And He alone determines how and when the reed will be used.

God had brought us to Pi-hahiroth – the place where the reeds grow. He had us right where He wanted us – even as the army approached! Maybe we weren't quite as defenseless as we thought!

12

As pharaoh approached, the people of Israel looked up and panicked when they saw the Egyptians overtaking them. They cried out to the Lord.[1]

* * *

*M*oses called out to the people, *"Don't be afraid. Watch the Lord rescue you today. The Egyptians you see today will never be seen again. The Lord Himself will fight for you. Just stay calm."*[2]

As we watched, the pillar of cloud moved abruptly and now stood between us and the approaching Egyptians, whom we could no longer see. They were dwarfed and completely eclipsed from our sight by the sheer magnitude of the cloud. The shouts and cries from our people began to subside as our fear of the Egyptians turned to a reverent fear of our ominous God. Even the most faithless among us knew our God had just stepped between us and our enemy. The Lord truly was fighting for us!

As darkness fell, the cloud turned to fire. As ominous as the pillar appeared when it was in the form of a cloud, it couldn't compare to its form as a pillar of fire. On our side, the pillar looked like a guiding light to illuminate our path. It was a light in the midst of our darkness. But we could tell from its outer contours that the other side of that pillar looked very different. It was a consuming fire capable of destroying everything in its path. We could no longer see pharaoh and his army, but we knew they were being kept at bay by the mighty power of our God.

Just then I saw Moses walk to the water's edge. I told my family and those around us to watch what he was about to do. Slowly, our entire camp turned toward Moses. No one spoke. The only sound was some young children crying because they were frightened by the pillar of fire. Their parents were quietly consoling them.

Moses raised his staff over the sea. It reminded me of the day God turned the water of the Nile to blood and the dust of the earth to lice. As he did, a strong wind began to blow from behind us. The sheer force of the wind began to part the sea. But miraculously, it had no effect on us or our animals. Our clothing didn't even stir in the breeze.

Then suddenly, two mountainous walls emerged as the water parted, creating a wide pathway right through the middle of the sea. As the wind continued to blow, the seabed became dry land.

There was an audible gasp throughout the camp as we looked at this extraordinary sight. Moses called for me to lead the tribe of Judah through the pathway to the far side. We would lead the way. Everyone began to look apprehensively at the walls of water. What if they came crashing down on us when we got to the center of the sea? We would perish! We knew that God had made the path – but did we trust Him enough to walk through the sea?

I knew my family and I needed to show our people we trusted God. Slowly we stepped off the shore onto the pathway. Initially the walls of water were only a few inches high, but as we continued farther into the seabed the walls quickly became taller than we were – soon approaching the height of the pyramids of Egypt. The strong winds continued to blow at our backs, not only parting the sea, but now also gently helping us pick up our pace as we made the journey.

Though the pathway was dry, it was also rocky. The large boulders that usually rested at the bottom of the sea now sat in the midst of our route. We were grateful for the light from the pillar of fire to help us navigate around them.

"Papa, look at the fish!" my youngest son exclaimed. He pointed at the walls of water that were like windows through which we could see the fish swimming. I was carrying my daughter, who had buried her head in my shoulder. But Naam's comment caused her to raise her head to see her brother's discovery.

The remainder of our tribe followed closely. Our eyes darted from side to side looking at the magnificent wonders, while also carefully watching our step around the rocks and trenches in the dry seabed. Some people had placed their possessions in carts when we started our journey but had to abandon them when the wheels became damaged by the uneven terrain.

The other tribes began to follow. "Continue to keep moving," Moses called out. "We must all cross over to the other side before the sun rises!"

Some of our flocks and animals were more afraid of the walls of water than our people and required a lot of coaxing. It was easier to carry the smaller animals in order to keep moving.

After a while my family and I saw the bank of the eastern shore. We soon began to emerge from the deepest parts of the path. We all let out a collective sigh as we stepped onto shore and then moved out of the way of those behind us.

.   .   .

For several hours my family and I remained on the shore watching as the rest of our people completed their journey across the sea. The final tribe to emerge was the Levites. Aaron, his wife, Elisheba, and their four sons led their tribe. Moses, his wife, Tzipora, and their two sons were the very last to emerge. Jehovah God had enabled us all to safely cross the sea without even getting our feet wet!

The sun was just beginning to rise as we stood on the eastern bank and looked back toward the western shore. Even as the last of our people were emerging from the dry seabed, we could see the pillar of fire returning to the form of a cloud. The cloud had moved from between us and the Egyptians and was now before us, ready to lead us on the rest of our journey.

To our dismay, pharaoh and his army were now rapidly approaching. The pathway through the sea was still there. God had not closed it! Did He intend for the Egyptians to pass as well? Had we crossed the sea to now die on its eastern shore?

Concern appeared on the faces of our people and quickly turned to fear and angst. With the aid of their horses and chariots, the Egyptians would soon be upon us! They were now halfway across the sea. What should we do? Again, we began to call out ... to Moses ... and to God.

Just as we did, the Egyptians' progress stopped. They appeared confused about the direction they should be heading. The wheels of their chariots began twisting on the rocky seabed. Their horses were panicking. Some of the chariots turned around and were attempting to go back, but they began to collide with the chariots that were still advancing. Their forces were in total confusion.

We could hear the screams of pharaoh trying to bring order to his army. But it was to no avail. His soldiers were now shouting, *"Let's get out of here – away from these Israelites! The Lord is fighting for them against Egypt!"* [3]

• • •

At that moment, Moses raised the staff in his hands over the sea, the winds stopped, and the walls of water collapsed – washing over and eliminating the pathway. Water began to violently crash down upon the Egyptians. For a moment, I saw King Thutmose II with his arms outstretched as if he were trying to stop the water.

I quickly thought back to when he and I were children playing along the edge of the rushing waters of the Nile River. Young Prince Amenemhat had tried to command the water that day to stop flowing. He had shouted at the river, "I am a prince of Egypt – the son of pharaoh – and I command you to be still." He had quickly learned he had no power over the rushing waters … then … or now.

The hysterical cries of the soldiers were soon silenced. Within moments, there was no sign a pathway ever existed. The waters covered everything and everyone. We strained to see if anyone emerged on the western shore. But no one did. In a matter of moments God had utterly destroyed pharaoh and the greatest army on earth.

Soon we began to see the bodies of soldiers and their horses wash up on shore. In the past several hours, we had witnessed God's deliverance of us without one person being harmed, and the complete destruction of our enemy without one person surviving. We had witnessed power beyond our comprehension. We had seen the laws of nature overturned. We had witnessed the mighty hand of an Almighty God!

We stood gazing at the sea in stunned silence, marveling at how God had saved us by making a way and then destroying the enemy that pursued us. Our terror was gone, our enemy was gone, and the night was past. Nothing was left but the stillness of a shocked people at daybreak. Finally, we collectively exhaled.

• • •

One by one, we began to worship our Almighty God. Some of us fell to our knees in awe and others stood with outstretched arms. We were now truly free!

A wave of emotions passed over me as I stood there. I felt sorrow for the death of Amenemhat, Ramses, Sapair, and so many others. I wept for the soldiers who were only obeying orders. However, I was equally overcome with relief. Our people had escaped the threat of the invading force. We had escaped death. And we had witnessed a miracle by the hand of God.

As I was praising God, I thought about the important truths I had just learned and knew I must hold onto forever.

- Whenever I am in a difficult place, I must remember Jehovah God either placed me there or, in His providence, allowed me to be there for reasons perhaps known only to Him. God had directed us to a place where we appeared – from our vantage point – to be in imminent danger. But in reality, it was a place where we would witness the splendor of God's power and deliverance.

- God never fretted about the outcome at the Red Sea. He knew He could – and would – provide an escape route for us. This was never about our relief; it was always about Him bringing glory to His name. I knew in the days ahead I must be faithful to remain focused on His glory – not my relief.

- God enveloped us in His presence. He led us as He went before us; He protected us as He went behind us; and He comforted and assured us as He walked beside us. And He always will.

- God would always use our current crisis to build our faith for the future. As hard as it was to imagine we would ever encounter a crisis like this one again, I knew we probably would. But I knew He would be faithful. From here on, I must always place my faith in our God … and my trust in His servant Moses.

Then Miriam, Moses' and Aaron's sister, took a tambourine and began to sing:

> *"I will sing to the Lord, for He has triumphed gloriously;*
> *He has hurled both horse and rider into the sea.*
> *The Lord is my strength and my song;*
> *He has given me victory.*
> *This is my God, and I will praise Him –*
> *my father's God, and I will exalt Him!*
>
> *The Lord is a warrior;*
> *Jehovah is His name.*
> *Who is like You among the gods, O Lord –*
> *glorious in holiness,*
> *awesome in splendor,*
> *performing great wonders?*
> *You raised Your right hand,*
> *and the earth swallowed our enemies.*
>
> *With Your unfailing love You lead*
> *the people You have redeemed.*
> *In Your might, You guide them*
> *to Your sacred home.*
>
> *You will bring them in and plant them on Your own mountain –*
> *the place, O Lord, reserved for Your own dwelling,*
> *the sanctuary, O Lord, that Your hands have established.*
> *The Lord will reign forever and ever!"* [4]

And for the remainder of the day we remained there on the eastern shore praising our Deliverer.

* * *

13

Then Moses led the people of Israel away from the Red Sea, and they moved out into the desert of Shur.[1]

* * *

My, how things can change in just a few days!

We had followed the pillar of cloud for three days through the desert of Shur. On Sunday, we were singing His praises – *"Who is glorious in holiness like You – so awesome in splendor, performing such wonders?"*[2] But now on Wednesday we had turned against Him. Instead of focusing on pleasing God, my people's main concern was "What will we eat?" and "What will we drink?" That's what happens when you take your eyes off Him!

On Sunday we had experienced one of the greatest miracles of God, but by Wednesday we were again losing hope. Earlier in the week we had walked through walls of water without even getting our feet wet. By Wednesday we were crying out in dismay that we had been left here in the desert to die of thirst.

. . .

The name "Shur" means walled enclosure. God had led us through a walled enclosure of water, and then for the next three days He had led us through a walled enclosure of wilderness. He had allowed the Egyptian army to enter the walls of water through the Red Sea that they might be defeated for His glory. And now He had allowed bitter waters to enter our way through the wilderness for that same purpose.

When we arrived today at the oasis of Marah, we had traveled for three days through the desert without water. A single day in the wilderness without water is tolerable, two days is difficult, but three days is beyond endurance – particularly for children and animals. And now the water before us was bitter and undrinkable.

Was the God who led us through one trial on Sunday able to overcome this trial on Wednesday? Wasn't the God who had proven Himself to be our God – who had promised to redeem us, deliver us, and lead us – able to see us through any and every hardship or trial? Didn't that include the bitter waters of Marah?

And yet, how quickly we forgot and lost heart! The people began to complain, and I had come to realize our people never did that quietly! *"What are we going to drink, Moses?"* [3] they began to shout.

It amazed me how our people always looked to Moses to solve our problems. It had started back in Egypt and had only gotten worse during the past week. Had Moses parted the Red Sea? Had Moses defeated the Egyptian army? Could Moses really give us good water to drink? We had not yet learned to take our concerns to the One – the only One – who could really solve them!

Moses stood before us and cried out to the Lord for help saying, "Lord, hear the cries of your people for we thirst, and the waters of this oasis are bitter." The Lord directed Moses' gaze to a nearby piece of wood and directed him to throw it into the water. Afterward, God said, "Now, have the leaders of each of the tribes drink the water!"

Each of us approached the water's edge – some more apprehensively than others. Hoshea and I were the first to kneel. Though we trusted Moses, our confidence was in God. We knew the God who could part a sea of water was able to heal a spring of water and make it pure.

We looked at each other, smiled, cupped the water in our hands, and drank it. As we expected, the water had no hint of bitterness. It was sweet! The rest of the men followed our lead and soon everyone was gathering sweet water from the spring.

After people had received their fill, Moses again stood before us saying, *"Thus says the Lord: 'If you will listen to My voice and do what is right in My sight, obeying My commands and keeping all My decrees, then I will not make you suffer any of the diseases I sent on the Egyptians. For I am the Lord who heals you!"* [(4)]

As the pillar of cloud began to lead us farther south, I prayed our people would listen and do what was right. But we had already shown that our memories were short, and our obedience was fleeting. Later that day we arrived at the oasis of Elim, where we found twelve springs and an abundance of palm trees. The cloud stood still, and we remained there for two weeks experiencing the refreshment of the Lord for both body and soul.

This was the first time we were able to talk as a family – without fear of retribution or the haste of travel – about all we had seen God do over the recent weeks.

One night as we sat around our campfire, Naam asked, "Papa, why did all of those children need to die in order for us to leave Egypt? Many were babies – or boys younger than I am. What did they ever do that caused God to kill them? I understand that we were saved because of the goat's blood you and I brushed on our doorframe. But the Egyptian fathers didn't know to do that. Why did their sons have to die?"

It was a sobering question – perhaps a question too few of us had stopped to ask. I had thought about Ramses, Sapair, and others I knew, but I had not stopped to think about the young children. I looked around the campfire and saw my father, my family, and some of our friends and neighbors sitting with us. All eyes had turned to me.

Slowly I began. "Naam, do you remember why we had to move from our home in the palace complex to the hovel in the quarry?"

"Yes, papa," Naam replied, "pharaoh was punishing you for what you said to him."

"That's right," I answered. "But the punishment didn't only affect me, did it? You and your brothers and sister, as well as your mother and grandparents, were punished for what I had done.

"There are consequences for the choices we make. In my case, I chose to stand up for what was right before pharaoh. I believe I was honoring Jehovah God and our people, but pharaoh did not like what I said, and he chose to punish me in a way that punished all of you.

"Our Jehovah God is a righteous God – unlike pharaoh, or any of us for that matter. God had clearly told pharaoh through Moses to let His people go. And yet pharaoh repeatedly refused. God extended mercy and grace to pharaoh many times. Pharaoh could have chosen to obey God numerous times – but He did not! And as a result, God said, 'That's enough!' And the punishment that God chose to extend to pharaoh affected all the people.

. . .

"The punishment God chose to inflict was actually determined by Thutmose II's great-grandfather. Eighty years ago, King Ahmose executed all the male Hebrew babies – not because of anything our people had done. It was an evil act that was abhorrent in the eyes of God. But God chose to delay His punishment until this generation. And when King Thutmose II chose to again disobey God, the punishment of his grandfather's actions fell on the firstborn male children several generations removed.

"It was never God's desire that the Egyptian children die at the hands of the angel of death. That happened because of the sin of the father and the father's fathers, going back generations. Our God had been merciful and long-suffering for generations, and yet the leaders had continued in their sin. Yes, our God is merciful, but He is also just – and He will not ignore disobedience.

"That's why we must seek to obey Him in all things – and when we fail, we must seek His forgiveness. Because the consequences of our sin – our failure to do what He says – can affect not only ourselves but those we love. Our wrong choices can result in harm for those we love, just as pharaoh's wrong choices resulted in the death of the firstborn sons of the entire nation.

"Now, Naam, let me ask you a question? Why did we brush the blood of the goat on our doorframe?"

"Because that is what God told us to do," Naam answered.

I couldn't help but smile at my son as I replied, "That is exactly the reason! God told us to do it. And we must always do what God tells us to do, even if we don't understand His reason. Don't ever forget that!

. . .

"Also, the goat was a sacrifice we offered to God as He told us to do," I continued, "so the shed blood of the sacrifice would cover our sins and keep us from experiencing death at the hands of the angel of death. It was God's way of extending His mercy and His grace to us."

"I think I understand, papa," Naam said. "I don't think I ever understood how important it is to obey God until now. I don't think I realized how much it hurt God to see the Egyptian sons die or the Hebrew babies. He wasn't the cause – sin and disobedience were the cause. Papa, I don't want to sin or be disobedient."

"Unfortunately, you will sin," I explained. "All of us do. What is important is that we seek God's forgiveness when we do. And if we truly seek His forgiveness with all of our heart, He has promised to forgive us. But never forget – God desires obedience more than He desires sacrifice. We must set in our hearts to obey Him and follow Him in all things."

As I looked around, all those listening to our conversation were nodding their heads in agreement. But I feared that Naam may have understood what I said more than many of our people. Would we as a people truly obey our God in all things? Would we follow Him as He leads – and trust Him all the way – even when we didn't completely understand? It wasn't long until the answer to that question became apparent.

The next morning the pillar of cloud began to move, and we left the oasis of Elim. Moses told us God was leading us to the mount called Sinai. God had told Moses He was leading us to worship Him there before He would lead us to take possession of the Promised Land.

Our path to Sinai was through the wilderness of Sin. "Sin" is the Egyptian name meaning "moon god" and was a reminder of the many false gods Egyptians worship and the false beliefs they hold in opposition and in disobedience to the law of God.

• • •

Opposition and disobedience were the very things Naam and I had been discussing last evening. Isn't it interesting that God's name for those attitudes and actions is "sin?" And here we were journeying through that wilderness. But the good news was if we kept our eyes on God and followed Him obediently, we would make it through that wilderness intact!

* * *

14

Then the whole community of Israel set out from Elim and journeyed into the wilderness of Sin, between Elim and Mount Sinai. They arrived there on the fifteenth day of the second month, one month after leaving the land of Egypt.[1]

* * *

One month had passed since we left Egypt. We had repeatedly seen God's miraculous protection and provision. But the people again began to complain against God.

"If only the Lord had killed us back in Egypt," they moaned. "There we sat around pots filled with meat and ate all the bread we wanted. But now He has brought us into this wilderness to starve us all to death."[2]

That evening after we stopped for the day, Moses and Aaron assembled the people. Then Moses said, "In the morning you will see the glory of the Lord, because He has heard your complaints. The Lord will give you meat to eat this evening and bread to satisfy you in the morning. Then you will know that He is the Lord your God."[3]

. . .

That evening a flock of quail – beyond anything we could count – descended on us and covered the camp. The sheer number of birds blotted out the remaining sun! It didn't require any hunting skill to capture them. They literally came right up to us to take.

There were more than we could ever need. And each bird was large and plump. That night we ate our fill of quail meat. Those who gathered a lot had nothing left over, and those who gathered only a little had enough. Each family had just what they needed.

My father had taught me a little bit about quail, just as he had about all the prey we hunted. They are a migratory bird. They begin their migration from equatorial Africa in the spring of each year. Based on the average flying speed of quail, it would have taken them approximately three days to travel from Africa to where we were now. God had promised us we would have meat to eat that evening. That means He had already set in motion the events to deliver the quail to us at least two days prior to giving us His promise – even before our people had begun to complain.

Also, the wilderness of Sin actually lies east of the migratory corridor of the quail, which means that God shifted the prevailing winds during their migration to deliver them right to our camp. God was again showing us He will literally move heaven and earth to accomplish His purpose and fulfill His promise.

We had never tasted meat so good or in such quantities as God provided that night. It was truly a feast beyond anything we could have imagined.

After that meal, our people could hardly wait to see what God was going to do in the morning. He had promised us bread! We could almost smell the fragrant aroma of fresh bread baking. We had long ago exhausted the supply of bread we brought with us from Egypt. So, we already had a praise on our lips based on our anticipation.

•   •   •

Some people were too excited to sleep that night. Many of us chose to rise a little earlier than usual so we could be among the first to partake of God's provision. As the sun appeared on the horizon, people began to look for God's morning delivery of bread. Some looked to the sky to see if God's bread was falling from the ovens of heaven just as the quail had the night before. Some looked to the coal fires we used to roast the quail to see if God had delivered bread to those same fires to bake.

But everywhere we looked, we didn't see bread. All we saw was the wet morning dew – and we had seen that every morning of our journey. What was going on? God had promised! God had always been faithful to accomplish what He promised. Where was the aroma? Where were those fresh loaves of bread?

Bewildered, our people looked to Moses and Aaron for an explanation. Had they heard God correctly or had they misunderstood? It was morning and there was no bread. Then Shammua, son of Zaccur the Reubenite, said, "Yes, but morning isn't over. Morning goes until noon – and God is always right on time and never late! Watch and see. It just hasn't arrived yet."

As the morning passed, we continued to watch and wait. The dew began to disappear. Someone noticed that where the dew had evaporated, there remained a thin, white layer of crust. No one had ever seen anything like it before. One neighbor pointed it out to the next and pretty soon their curiosity got the best of them, so they walked toward it to investigate.

Someone reached down and broke off a piece. It didn't feel like anything we had ever felt before. Someone smelled it; it didn't smell like anything we had ever smelled before. Then someone was brave enough to taste it, and it didn't taste like anything any of us had ever tasted before. It was white like coriander seed, and it tasted like honey wafers.

. . .

Then the people asked Moses, *"What is it?"* [4] And Moses said, "It is the food that God has promised you."

"Oh no," they responded, "this can't be God's provision! It doesn't look, smell, taste, or feel anything like we thought it would. This isn't what we expected. Surely this isn't God's provision!"

But Moses responded, *"It is the food the Lord has given you to eat. These are the Lord's instructions: Each household should gather as much as it needs. Pick up two quarts for each person in your tent."* [5]

After we got over the shock that this "white, flaky substance" was God's bread for us, we set about the process of gathering what was needed for our households. Some of our people gathered a lot, some only a little. But when we all measured it out, everyone had just enough. Those who gathered a lot had nothing left over, and those who gathered only a little had enough. Each family had just what they needed.

Moses also told us, *"Do not keep any of it until the next morning."* [6] But some of our people did not listen and they kept some. The next morning a putrid smell filled the camp.

"What do you have in your tent?" I asked one family. "My wife put away some of the manna so we would have it in case there wasn't any today," the man replied. "But when we awoke, it was crawling with maggots. We had to remove everything that was near it and bury it out in the clearing. But we can't get rid of the smell."

Apparently, this family wasn't the only one trying to stockpile the manna. The smell permeating the camp was overwhelming. It was definitely a sin that could not be hidden!

· · ·

Moses expressed his anger and the Lord's anger with them, but the stench in their tents was sufficient punishment to keep them from ever doing it again. From then on, the people gathered only the amount of bread needed for that day. And as the sun became hot, the flakes that had not been picked melted and disappeared.

On the sixth day, Moses commanded us to gather twice as much as usual – four quarts for each person instead of two. He explained, *"This is what the Lord commanded: The seventh day will be a day of complete rest, a holy Sabbath day set apart for the Lord. So bake or boil as much as you want today, and set aside what is left for tomorrow."* [(7)]

So, we put a portion aside for the following day, just as Moses instructed. And in the morning the leftover food was wholesome and good. Moses said, *"Eat this food today, for today is a Sabbath day dedicated to the Lord. There will be no food on the ground today. You may gather the food for six days, but the seventh day is the Sabbath. There will be no food on the ground to gather on the Sabbath day."* [(8)]

Again, some of the people disregarded Moses' instruction and went out anyway on the seventh day, but they found no food. So, they went without that day. These people were just like those who earlier in the week had disobeyed God by trying to hoard some for the next day. Both groups believed they knew more than God – and chose to disobey His commands.

The Lord asked Moses, *"How long will these people refuse to obey My commands and instructions? They must realize that the Sabbath is My gift to them. That is why I give them a two-day supply on the sixth day, so there will be enough for two days. On the Sabbath day they must each stay in their place. They are not to go out to pick up food on the seventh day."* [(9)]

Eventually, our people learned they could not gather food on the seventh day. We called this food manna – which means "what is it." It became a basic staple of our daily diet.

. . .

God commanded a sample of manna, the "bread of heaven" as we would later describe it, be set aside and forever kept as a memorial and a reminder to all future generations. It would be a testament of God's faithfulness to us and His provision for us.

Where there was nothing, He had provided. No matter where we were, He had provided. And He promised that wherever He leads, He will provide. We could do nothing to make manna. We could do nothing to earn manna. We could do nothing to save manna. It was an expression of God's grace to His people. We were to keep it and remember it as a treasured memorial.

Some of my people were slow to learn that God's provision is sufficient for the day and for the need. It is not the result of our merit or our deservedness, it is a condition of His faithfulness. He is our provision – and He will be sufficient for this day and every day.

But regrettably, many of us had short memories.

* * *

15

———————

*At the Lord's command, the whole community of Israel left the wilderness of Sin
and moved from place to place.*[1]

* * *

Soon the Lord led us to continue our journey through the wilderness
of Sin. We traveled south along the peninsula, first making camp at
Dophkah and next at Alush. But each morning, no matter where we
camped, the manna was always there waiting for us when the dew dried.

Rebecca, like many of our women, learned to become creative when
preparing the manna. My wife and mother used their skills with season-
ings and sauces acquired through their years of service in the palace
bakery to add a new and different taste to our daily portion of manna! I
was now very grateful they had been insistent about the quantity of spices
we carried with us from Egypt.

Eventually, we camped in a fertile part of the peninsula called Rephidim.
The name means "place of rest." We were thankful to have a respite from

the arid regions of the wilderness through which we had been traveling. And Rephidim appeared to be very similar to Elim. However, we quickly discovered that Rephidim did not possess the springs of sweet water we had enjoyed in Elim.

Word spread quickly throughout the camp there was no water. It didn't take long for concern to become panic. An impromptu group of representatives was chosen to seek out Moses to demand: *"Give us water to drink!"* [2]

"Quiet!" Moses replied. *"Why do you continue to test the Lord?"* [3]

But instead of receiving Moses' correction, they continued to argue with him: *"Why did you bring us out of Egypt? Are you trying to kill us, our children and our livestock with thirst?"* [4]

Several of the men picked up stones. Surely, they didn't plan to stone Moses! How could these people again forget how faithful God had been to us? I started making my way toward Moses to come to his aid. A short distance away, I saw Hoshea starting to do the same.

Before we were able to reach him, I heard Moses cry out, *"Lord, what should I do with these people? They are ready to stone me!"* [5]

A hush fell over everyone as we heard a thunderous rumble from heaven. Moses was looking upward intently as he heard the voice of God: *"Walk out in front of the people. Take your staff, the one you used when you struck the water of the Nile, and call some of the elders of Israel to join you. Strike the rock, and water will come gushing out. Then the people will be able to drink."* [6] We couldn't understand what God had said, but we knew He had just spoken to Moses.

· · ·

As Hoshea and I approached, Moses called out to us to join him on the rock. As we did, Moses struck the rock with his staff and water began to cascade from it. The people hurriedly brought their jars, their pitchers, their basins, and their sheepskin water containers to collect all the water they could carry.

While Moses, Hoshea, and I watched, the water gushed from the rock for hours until everyone had gathered all they could use. Then the water stopped. Our God had again supplied all that was needed!

Moses declared to the people, "Henceforth this place will be called Massah, meaning "test," and Meribah, meaning "arguing," because you have argued with me and tested the Lord your God. And yet again, He has proven Himself to be faithful. Do not continue to test the Lord your God."[7]

Moses turned to Hoshea and said, "Hoshea, from this day forward, you will be called Joshua, meaning 'Jehovah is generous.' Because today you have again witnessed the generosity of our God. May your name be a reminder to all of us from this day forth of what we have seen the Lord our God do!"

I had always believed in my heart that God would use Hoshea in great ways. Today it had been confirmed – and I knew the one I would now call Joshua would not only continue to be my dearest friend, like a brother, but I also believed he would one day become my leader. I would follow him, just as together we now followed Moses, as we all followed God – with a grateful heart!

The next day, the pillar of cloud did not move, so obviously neither did we. As the day progressed, we saw a large army of warriors approaching from the north. This was the first time we had encountered any other people since the defeat of the Egyptian army. These warriors were on foot

– not in chariots. Their weaponry consisted of swords, spears, and clubs. They did not advance with the precision of the Egyptians; but rather, with the fierceness of a horde.

The bulk of the force stopped some distance away while a handful continued to approach us. Joshua and I, together with a few of our other leaders, joined Moses and Aaron as they walked out to meet the men.

This group was obviously being led by one particular man who stood head and shoulders above the rest. As we came near, he spoke to us with a booming voice: "My name is Eliphaz. I am a leader of the tribe of Amalek. You are approaching our land. What business do you have here?"

Moses replied, "My name is Moses. We are the people of Israel – the brother of your ancestor, Esau. We are the people of Jehovah God – who has led us out of bondage in Egypt. He has led us out into this place to worship Him."

"Yes, we have heard how your God defeated the army of Egypt," Eliphaz responded. "It is said that your God is leading you to conquer the lands to the north – including ours. We have come to tell you that neither you, nor your God, is welcome in our land. Turn around and go elsewhere or you will feel the full wrath of the people of Amalek!"

"We can only do what our God tells us to do," Moses answered. "And we can only go where He leads us to go. He has led us to this place, and He will lead us onward. We wish you no harm, but if you stand in our way, our Almighty God who overpowered the great army of Egypt will defeat you! Return to your homes and let us travel in peace. No harm will come to any of you."

Eliphaz replied, "We will not return to our homes and we will not let you travel in peace. You are not welcome here. This is our land, and tomorrow you and your God will feel the full wrath of the people of Amalek!" Then, he and those with him turned and walked back to rejoin their army.

Our people were the descendants of Jacob, the grandson of Abraham, whom God had renamed Israel after he had wrestled with God one night by the Jabbok brook. The Amalekites were the descendants of Amalek, the grandson of Esau, the brother of Israel and also a grandson of Abraham. It had been over three hundred years since the families of Esau and Israel had last met.

During the ensuing years, while our people inhabited and were later enslaved in Egypt, the descendants of Esau, the Amalekites, had established their territory in the southern part of the land promised to Abraham. That promise was passed on to Isaac, and through him to our father, Israel. Esau had in fact given up that birthright; he had been stripped of his blessing – all in exchange for a bowl of lentil stew.[8]

The land the Amalekites now inhabited had become our birthright, and the Amalekites knew that all too well. They knew God was leading us to occupy that land. But the Amalekites were determined to fight for what they had lost. Their warriors had come to defeat and destroy us.

Their army went about setting up camp for the night. As their campfires flickered in the dark, we heard loud howls and taunts. If their noise was intended to unsettle our people, they succeeded.

But as I lay awake, I couldn't help but think about the arrogance of the Amalekites. God had defeated the most powerful army in the world – the Egyptians. He had moved heaven and earth to defeat them. He had revealed His power and His glory to a watching world. He had firmly established His reputation that there was none like Him. He had clearly shown Himself to be the Sovereign and Almighty God, and that we belonged to Him.

. . .

The Amalekites' threat against us was actually a feeble shaking of their fist at the Lord God Jehovah and a declaration of war against His throne. It wasn't so much they had chosen the wrong people to engage in battle, they had chosen the wrong God!

Early the next morning we watched the Amalekites form their battle lines. Some among us wondered out loud: "How is God going to annihilate this army? We saw how He defeated pharaoh and we can't wait to see how He's going to do it this time. I wonder if He's going to rain down fire from heaven or bury them in the sand? I wonder if He will lead us up to the hilltop so we can clearly witness His mighty power like He did last time?"

Naturally, we were surprised when Moses commanded Joshua to call us to arms to fight the army of Amalek. I, along with all our men of fighting age, assembled behind Joshua. Then Moses called on his brother, Aaron, and his brother-in-law, Hur, to go with him to the top of the hill overlooking the battlefield ... the field where the descendants of Abraham – Israelite and Amalekite – would battle one another.

As we assembled for battle, some of our men were still asking questions. "This wasn't how God defeated the Egyptians. Why doesn't He have Moses stand on the top of the hill holding up the staff that parted the Red Sea – and brought the sea back together – and supernaturally defeat them?"

But this time, we were to be face to face with our enemy in battle; and we would see the blood of friends and family spilled on the field.

God directed Moses to stand at the top of the hill with the staff of God upraised in his hands over the field of battle. He was going to defeat the Amalekites through the staff, but it wasn't how our people imagined. God promised that as long as the staff remained upraised, our people – His chosen people – would have the advantage in the fight. God assured us of victory if we followed His instruction.

• • •

God knew Moses would not be able to keep his hands upraised by himself, so He provided brothers to stand on either side to help him. God also knew Joshua could not defeat the army of Amalek by himself, so He provided an army of brothers to fight alongside him.

We quickly realized the advantage during the battle kept going back and forth – and it was determined by the position of the staff. When the staff was upraised, we prevailed; God was giving His people victory. Though He had required us to take up arms, the victory was no less His.

The Amalekites fought with unrelenting brutality. But, as Moses' hands held steady until sunset, we were able to resoundingly defeat them. Their defeat was so absolute that those few who remained quickly retreated out of our sight.

Moses instructed us to build an altar on the hill where he had stood throughout the day. He named the altar "Jehovah Nissi," which means the Lord is my banner. It was a reminder that God would continue to go before us as our banner – even to defeat our enemies – if we would faithfully follow Him.

Moses declared, *"The Amalekites have raised their fists against the Lord's throne, so now He will be at war with Amalek for generation after generation."* [9]

The next morning as the pillar of cloud began to lead us from that place, I was mindful that God had kept us in Rephidim so we would witness His defeat of the Amalekites. Their attack had not come as a surprise to God. He knew their plan. But more importantly, He used their plan to bring further glory to His name. No matter what they attempted, He defeated them. Word spread quickly that the God of Israel had not only defeated pharaoh and his mighty army, but He also had defeated the Amalekite warriors.

. . .

As we continued our journey to the mountain of God, I prayed we would hold onto that truth and trust Him unwaveringly in the days ahead no matter what – or whom – we encountered.

* * *

16

Moses' father-in-law, Jethro, the priest of Midian, heard about everything God had done for Moses and His people, the Israelites.[1]

*** * ***

As we camped near the base of the mountain of God, known as Mount Sinai, Moses told us how he had been shepherding his father-in-law's flock on this very mountain the day God spoke to him through a burning bush. God said He was preparing to deliver His people from the bondage of slavery and that Moses should return to Egypt. God instructed Moses, *"When you have brought the Israelites out of Egypt, you will return here to worship Me at this very mountain."*[2]

As we rested in camp, a caravan approached from the east. When they drew closer, I recognized Moses' wife, Tzipora, and their two sons, Gershom and Eliezer. After the defeat of the Amalekites, Moses had sent his family to deliver a message to Tzipora's father about the miraculous ways God had delivered His people.

• • •

Tzipora and her father, Jethro, were Midianites. The tribe of Midian dated back to another son of Abraham. After Abraham's wife, Sarah, died, he had married a woman named Keturah who bore him six sons in his old age. One of those sons was Midian. He was not a son of the promise through Isaac. Abraham had given Midian and his descendants the land to settle along the shores of the Gulf of Aqaba – land that was separate from what God promised for His people. That land included the area where we were now camped.

The Midianites were known for their shrewdness in business. It was a group of Midianite tradesmen who bought our patriarch, Joseph, from his brothers for twenty shekels of silver and then were used by God to provide him with transportation to Egypt. There they sold Joseph for a profit to Potiphar. These same "cousins" who were unknowingly instrumental in helping our people get to Egypt, were now some of the first to greet us upon our exodus from that land.

The caravan reflected Jethro's flamboyant nature. Compared to the simple clothing of Hebrew slaves, Jethro and his entire party boasted colorful attire. Their camels and beasts of burden were also draped in fabrics of many colors. Even Tzipora and the boys were wearing bright robes. From a distance we could hear them singing and laughing as they approached.

The acts of the God of the Israelites had become notorious throughout the region. The leaders of the Midianites had no interest in provoking Him. They decided it would be wise to warmly greet their Israelite cousins. So, as a noble prince of the people of Midian, Jethro was sent to Sinai to greet the Israelites as their ambassador of goodwill.

But he had other important reasons for coming to greet Moses. Moses had faithfully served his father-in-law by tending his flocks for forty years. Having heard how God blessed Moses' efforts and how He had moved on behalf of His people, Jethro was proud of what Moses had accomplished. So, Jethro came to Sinai to express his great pleasure and affection toward his son-in-law.

. . .

Jethro was also the priest of the people of Midian. He was their religious leader. Though he believed in the God of Abraham, he also believed in many gods. But Jethro could not deny that the God of Abraham, Isaac, and Jacob had rescued this people from the hands of the Egyptians in mighty ways.

This feat made Jethro realize there was no other God like this one. So, he traveled to Sinai to prepare and present a sacrificial offering, entering into fellowship with Jehovah God and His people.

We all watched as Moses went out to greet his father-in-law with an embrace. As Rebecca and others went out to welcome Tzipora, Joshua and I joined several other men in Moses' tent as he talked with Jethro. After providing his father-in-law with refreshment, Moses began to recount everything the Lord had done on our behalf. He described the hardships we had experienced along the way, but he was quick to recite all God had done to deliver us from the hands of the Egyptians and the Amalekites – and how He provided for our every need.

Those of us gathered in the tent would periodically inject a hearty word of agreement. *"Praise the Lord!"* Jethro responded after Moses had finished. *"The Lord has rescued you from the Egyptians and from pharaoh. Yes, He has rescued Israel from the powerful hand of Egypt! I know now that the Lord is greater than all other gods, because He rescued His people from the oppression of the proud Egyptians."*[3]

"We must prepare a burnt offering and sacrifices in thanksgiving and praise to Jehovah God," Jethro continued.

Later, as we all ate that sacrificial meal in the presence of God, I realized something. Jethro was not just giving an offering as the priest of Midian, he was offering it personally. He was declaring his personal allegiance to

Jehovah, the God of his son-in-law, Moses, and now his own God. Before our very eyes, he was confessing his faith and entering into God's holy presence. Oh, how I wished that all our people would see God through those same eyes of faith!

The next morning, Moses took his seat among the people to hear their disputes against one another. He had started doing this on the days the pillar of cloud did not move. From morning until evening, an endless line would form before him in order to bring their complaints or disagreements for adjudication. It was exhausting! Moses would spend the entire day listening to constant bickering and trivial complaints.

But, he saw this as his responsibility as our leader. *"The people come to me to get a ruling from God."* Moses explained to Jethro, *"I am the one who settles the case between them. I inform the people of God's decrees and give them His instructions."* [4]

But in reality, he was allowing his time to be consumed by trivial matters instead of truly leading us as a people. And the people were quite content for him to do so.

If anyone could offer advice to Moses it was Jethro. Not only was he Moses' father-in-law, but the two also had a lot in common. Both had been groomed as princes of their people. They were also experienced as shepherds leading their flocks from place to place. And they both served as priests of their people. Besides sharing great affection for one another, they also greatly respected each other.

After observing Moses for a few days, Jethro came to him privately and said, *"This is not good! You're going to wear yourself out – and the people, too. This job is too heavy a burden for you to handle all by yourself. Now listen to me, and let me give you a word of advice, and may God be with you.*

. . .

"You should continue to be the people's representative before God, bringing their disputes to Him. Teach them God's decrees, and give them His instructions. Show them how to conduct their lives. But select from all the people some capable, honest men who fear God and hate bribes. Appoint them as leaders over groups of one thousand, one hundred, fifty, and ten. They should always be available to solve the people's common disputes, but have them bring the major cases to you.

"Let the leaders decide the smaller matters themselves. They will help you carry the load, making the task easier for you. If you follow this advice, and if God commands you to do so, then you will be able to endure the pressures, and all these people will go home in peace." [5]

Moses heeded Jethro's advice and chose approximately three hundred men from all our tribes and appointed us as leaders over the people to help settle disputes. He divided our people – a total of about three hundred thousand families – into three hundred groups of one thousand families with a leader over each group. Those groups were then broken down into smaller groups of one hundred, fifty, and ten families.

This system worked well. Disputes were settled quicker and the responsibility that Moses had needlessly shouldered on his own was now being shared by many. Again, God had proven Himself faithful by bringing Jethro to our camp at just the right time to speak wisdom into a process that had become burdensome. His word of counsel enabled Moses – and all of us – to be the leaders of our people that God had called and equipped us to be.

God had also used Jethro's visit to transform *his* life. He had arrived as the priest of Midian, but he departed as Reuel, the friend of God.

When Reuel left Sinai to return to his people, he left his son, Hobab, to stay with us while we camped in Sinai since it was part of the Midianites' territory. Hobab could help quell any conflict that might arise with other Midianites in the area, and perhaps help our people work through the challenges of living in the wilderness.

Hobab, which means "beloved," was Reuel's only son, and Reuel had awaited his birth for many years. Hobab had been a young boy when his sister, Tzipora, married Moses. We could all see that Moses and Hobab were as close as brothers. But we also understood Reuel was making a great sacrifice by leaving his only son with us.

It was a sacrifice that demonstrated not only Reuel's great love for Moses, but also his love for Jehovah God's chosen people. And Hobab was a provision from God to His people. In the days ahead, Hobab's presence would be of great benefit to us – and he would be a reminder that God does not leave any details to chance.

The next morning Moses announced he was going to climb the mountain to appear before God. The whole camp was buzzing with excitement. It had been exactly two months since we left Egypt, and we were certain God was going to give Moses final instructions on entering our Promised Land. Our journey would soon be over!

I stood there at the base of the mountain with Joshua and several other men as we watched Moses make his climb. He was almost out of view when my oldest son, Iru, came running toward me. "Papa, you must come quickly!" he exclaimed as he caught his breath. "Something has happened to savta! Mother says you must come quickly!"

I immediately began to run toward our tent. When I arrived, I saw my wife and my father leaning over my mother. She was lying still on her sleeping mat – and both of them were sobbing. Rebecca looked up at me and said between tears, "Eema did not stir this morning. I thought she must be needing more rest, so I did not disturb her. But when I came to look in on her a little while ago, I saw that she was not breathing, and her skin had turned cold. I have sent Naam for a midwife, but he has not yet returned." All the while my father just held my mother's hand and spoke softly to her as he sobbed.

As my wife was speaking, Naam arrived with the midwife. The midwives and the priests of Levi had become the practitioners of medical care among our people. They had learned much about the healing arts from the Egyptian magicians. The midwife immediately came to my mother's side, but it took only a cursory examination for her to confirm my mother was dead.

My father continued to hold my mother's hand and speak softly to her. The midwife took charge and told us the desert heat meant we would need to make burial arrangements without delay. She told the rest of us to gather around my mother and say our goodbyes. Afterward, the midwife asked us to leave the tent so she could wash and prepare my mother's body for burial. She used some of the myrrh and aloes we brought with us from Egypt.

The news of her death spread quickly throughout the camp. Soon, as we waited outside of our tent, friends came to offer their sympathy and grieve with us. I couldn't help but notice that my father's sullenness went beyond the grief I would expect. It appeared as if his own life had been taken away, and he began to take on an ashen appearance.

Soon after midday, my brother Kenaz, my sons, and I carried my mother's body into the desert outside of camp. My father, together with Rebecca and Kenaz's wife, walked in front of the procession, led by a Levite priest. A large gathering of friends followed. It was quite a noisy spectacle as many of the women wailed loudly and threw dust into the air. We buried my mother's body deep in the ground to protect it from scavenging animals.

As my father and I walked back to camp, I couldn't help but think about how excited my parents had been – like all of us – about entering the

Promised Land. My mother would no longer be making that journey with us. But I trusted Jehovah God had something much more special in store for her. I tried to engage my father in conversation as we walked, but to no avail. The life had gone out of him when my mother took her last breath.

I grieved for myself and for my family – but I ached for my father. Even the hope of the Promised Land did not assuage my sorrow. And little did I know that one week later my family would again make a trip into the desert – this time with the body of my father – lifeless as the result of a broken heart.

* * *

17

The Lord called to Moses from the mountain and said....[1]

* * *

The day after my mother died, Moses returned from meeting with God on the mountain and called the elders together to give us this report.

"Jehovah God has given me this directive," he said. "_Give these instructions to the family of Jacob; announce it to the descendants of Israel: 'You have seen what I did to the Egyptians. You know how I carried you on eagles' wings and brought you to Myself. Now if you will obey Me and keep My covenant, you will be My own special treasure from among all the peoples on earth; for all the earth belongs to Me. And you will be My kingdom of priests, My holy nation.'_"[2]

We responded together, "_We will do everything the Lord has commanded._"[3]

As those words echoed in my ears, I couldn't help but wonder if we all truly understood what we were saying. Were we really prepared to do everything the Lord commanded? Were we capable of doing all that He commanded? I feared that just like in our past, our future actions would not bear witness to our words.

Moses declared, "God has said, *'Go down and prepare the people for My arrival. Consecrate them today and tomorrow, and have them wash their clothing. Be sure they are ready on the third day, for on that day I will come down on Mount Sinai as all the people watch. Mark off a boundary all around the mountain. Warn the people to be careful! They are not to go up on the mountain or even touch its boundaries. Anyone who touches the mountain will certainly be put to death. No hand may touch the person or animal that crosses the boundary; instead, stone them or shoot them with arrows. They must be put to death. However, when the ram's horn sounds a long blast, then the people must gather at the foot of the mountain.'"* [4]

We did as God commanded through Moses. We had become accustomed to seeing God go before us as a pillar of cloud, but now that cloud was going to descend upon Mount Sinai!

We would hear His voice and experience His presence. This very ground was about to become holy ground because of the presence of the Lord God Jehovah. And worship would be our response to entering into God's presence and experiencing Him.

But before we could enter into that holy place, we had to prepare ourselves. God told us we could not enter into His presence the way we were. We must be purified. Our preparation was so important that He left nothing to chance.

In order to hear the heart of God, we must be cleansed of all impure affections, disquieting passions, and any other worldly concerns. God knew a few moments of prayer was not going to prepare our hearts. He instructed us to take two days to do nothing. We were even to abstain from sexual relations. We were to be wholly devoted to making preparations to enter into His presence. He wanted to ensure there would be nothing to distract us from Him.

Also, we were to wash our clothing. We were preparing to enter into God's presence and that involved *all* of our person – physically, emotionally, intellectually, and spiritually. We must be prepared and cleansed in every respect.

Then God told us to anticipate His arrival on the third day. He clearly wanted us to have hearts prepared to encounter Him, hearts singularly focused on Him, and hearts attuned to Him.

In addition, He instructed us there would be a boundary line beyond which we could not pass. We were not even allowed to touch the boundaries or we would die. He established the boundary as a "safe zone," so we could experience His presence without seeing His face.

On the morning of the third day, thunder roared, lightning flashed, and the cloud descended on the mountain. There was a long, loud blast from a ram's horn. We could see, hear, smell, taste, and feel that God was there. He left nothing to our imagination. He left no doubt as to His presence. And we trembled in reverence and awe! Moses led us out from the camp to the foot of the mountain. The blast of the ram's horn grew louder and, as Moses spoke, God thundered His reply.

When our people saw and heard everything that was happening, they trembled with fear. They cried out to Moses, *"You speak to us, and we will listen. But don't let God speak directly to us, or we will die!"* [5]

"Don't be afraid," Moses replied, *"for God has come in this way to test you, and so that your fear of Him will keep you from sinning!"* [6]

• • •

At the Lord's command, Moses reminded us that we were not to cross the boundaries. Then he climbed the mountain and disappeared into the cloud. As I stood there watching, I was mindful that as we draw closer into God's presence, we will no longer be seen. Only He will! And I prayed that I would walk with God in such a way that He is seen and not me!

My father died while Moses was still in God's presence up on the mountain. All of us were anticipating Moses' return. All of us looked at the cloud with great anticipation. Like so many, my father had looked forward to the fulfillment of this promise all his life – and now it was here! But he had thought he and my mother would enter into that promise together. And now she had taken a different path.

In the days since her death, his longing to be with her eclipsed his longing for the Promised Land. So, on that day – exactly one week after my mother took her last breath – my father took his. He followed his wife of forty-two years, as well as the patriarchs who had gone before him. Throughout his lifetime my father had walked by faith. And he had kept his eyes on God to the end.

I was now the patriarch of our family. That responsibility weighed heavily on me in the midst of my grief. No matter what I encountered, I had always been able to turn to my father. He always had a word of wisdom and a word of encouragement. He had taught me to walk uprightly before God – and man.

He had shown me to trust God with all my heart. He had shown me what it meant to love God and to love my family. He was my hero – and I couldn't imagine what it would be like to continue on without him. But I knew I needed to because my family was looking to me – and I knew my father would tell me I needed to look to God. So that's what I did.

. . .

Moses returned to the base of the mountain two days after my father died. While Moses had been in His presence, God had given him the commandments of the covenant that would exist between God and His people. These were the commandments that we had already sworn to honor. When Moses returned to the foot of the mountain, he carefully wrote down all that God told him in a Book of the Covenant. Having done so, he repeated all the commandments and instructions God had given him.

The Lord had said to Moses: "*Say this to the people of Israel,*

'*I am the Lord your God, who rescued you from the land of Egypt, the place of your slavery. You must not have any other god but Me.*

You must not make for yourself an idol of any kind or an image of anything in the heavens or on the earth or in the sea. You must not bow down to them or worship them, for I, the Lord your God, am a jealous God who will not tolerate your affection for any other gods.

You must not misuse the name of the Lord your God.

Remember to observe the Sabbath day by keeping it holy. You have six days each week for your ordinary work, but the seventh day is a Sabbath day of rest dedicated to the Lord your God.

Honor your father and mother. Then you will live a long, full life in the land the Lord your God is giving you.

You must not murder.

You must not commit adultery.

You must not steal.

You must not testify falsely against your neighbor.

You must not covet your neighbor's house. You must not covet your neighbor's wife, male or female servant, ox or donkey, or anything else that belongs to your neighbor.'"[7]

Through Moses, God also gave us detailed instructions as to how we were to worship Him through our sacrifices, through our relationships with one another, and through three annual festivals He was establishing so we would never forget all He had done for us. God concluded those instructions with a promise. He promised that He would always go before us to bless us with food and water and protect us from illness. He would meet every need. He would defeat every enemy. He would give us the land He had promised our patriarchs.

All we had to do was obey His commandments and His instructions. Again, our people said in unison, *"We will do everything the Lord has commanded."* [8]

Having made that declaration, Moses then announced to us that God had instructed Aaron and seventy-two elders to climb the mountain with him to meet with God. Though I was still grieving my parents, I trembled with awe as Moses told me I was to be one of those elders. I knew this was an invitation I could not refuse. God knows the timing of all things. What better way to honor my parents than to honor the God they had taught me to worship?

Early the next morning Moses arose and built an altar at the foot of the mountain. He set up twelve pillars, one for each of the twelve tribes of Israel. Then he sent some of our young men to present burnt offerings and to sacrifice bulls as peace offerings to the Lord. Moses drained half the blood from these animals into basins. The other half he splattered against the altar.

Then Moses took the blood from the basins and splattered it over all of us, declaring, *"Look, this blood confirms the covenant the Lord has made with you in giving you these instructions."* [9]

· · ·

Moses, Aaron, and the rest of us then set off to climb the mountain. Joshua and I walked side by side as we kept our eyes on the path before us and our hearts attuned to the God who awaited above us.

* * *

18

There they saw the God of Israel....[1]

*　*　*

hen we reached a summit on the mountain, Moses instructed us to go no farther. Above our heads we saw what looked like the underside of pavement made of brilliant sapphire. It was as clear and bright as the sky. And resting on that pavement appeared to be a massive throne. All we could see was its underside as well, but it sparkled with the beauty of every jewel imaginable. And we saw what could have only been the soles of God's feet. We could not see Him, but we were witnessing a hint of His glory and we knew we were in His presence.

It was a moment we wanted to last forever. We each experienced a unique combination of emotions – fear, awe, joy, reverence, elation, and peace – just to name a few. Moses told us to remove our sandals because we were standing on holy ground. Then he directed us to sit around a table that had been prepared before us.

· · ·

There we ate a meal. In our culture, a meal eaten together was a mark of friendship and agreement. This meal was a symbol of the covenant between us and Jehovah God – for us to be His people and for Him to be our God. Jehovah God who is infinitely holy and almighty was condescending to sup and fellowship with us!

After we concluded the meal, the Lord said to Moses, *"You come up further to Me on the mountain. There I will give you tablets of stone on which I have inscribed the instructions and commands so you can teach the people."*[2]

Moses told Joshua to accompany him. Then before leaving, he said to the rest of us, *"If anyone has a dispute while I am gone, consult with Aaron and Hur."*[3]

As Moses and Joshua disappeared into the cloud, we remained on the summit for a while before starting our journey back down the mountain. As we approached the base of the mount, our families and the rest of the people were there to greet us.

"What did you see?" one asked. "Did you see God?" "What did He look like?" another inquired. Everyone was asking questions all at once without giving us time to respond.

Aaron waited for the crowd to quiet down before he responded, "We have been in the presence of Jehovah God! His glory was all around us. We could not see Him like you can see us. We merely saw a glimpse of the soles of His feet and the underside of His throne. But what we saw was more magnificent than words could ever adequately describe! Everything shimmered like gold – the brightest and the purest of gold.

"He set a table before us and we ate in His magnificent presence. We felt an indescribable peace and calm, but at the same time a reverence and awe. The meal affirmed our covenant with Him and His with us. We are

His people, and He is our God. There is no other like Him! He alone is able to part the sea. Only He can command water to issue forth from a rock. He is the only One who commands the quail to fly into our camp or the manna to appear every morning. He has all power and all might."

Just then someone asked, "Where is Moses?"

"God directed Moses to come farther up into the mountain," Aaron replied. "God is inscribing His instructions for us on stone tablets He will give to Moses. Moses had Joshua accompany him. I would expect they will return in a few days just like the last time Moses went up into the mountain."

I embraced Rebecca and my children. My emotions were overflowing. The awe of having been in the presence of God combined with the weight of my sorrow over my parents' deaths was taking its toll – emotionally and physically. I took my family back to our tent so we could have time alone. The others began to scatter as well. Soon the sun set for the day. And what a day it had been!

Each day at camp we had food to eat and water to drink. Our God was protecting us and providing for our every need. The days soon turned into weeks and some of our people were beginning to become concerned.

"What has happened to Moses?" they asked. "Why is he away so long?"

And each time Aaron would respond, "I do not know why he is away so long. But I know that when God is ready for him to return, he will return. Until then we will wait patiently and delight in God's provision."

But when Moses had been gone more than thirty days, the people became belligerent and anxious over his absence. Despite assurances from Aaron and the elders, the people were on the edge of rebellion. *"Look,"* they said to Aaron, *"make us some gods who can lead us. We don't know what happened to this fellow Moses who brought us here from the land of Egypt."*[(4)]

"Moses, did not bring us here!" I shouted. "Jehovah God delivered us from the hand of Egypt and brought us here. Thirty days ago, we all vowed to honor Him and obey Him. We vowed we would never make an idol or bow down before anyone other than Jehovah God! And yet today you would go back on that promise – dishonoring yourselves and dishonoring our God! You must not do this!"

I was further disheartened when one of our elders shouted back at me, "But that was before God took Moses away from us! God has left us to fend for ourselves. He has taken away our leader. We are now at the mercy of this wilderness and our enemies who seek to destroy us. If God is so concerned about us, where is He and where is Moses?"

Then another added, "We must have a god we can see and one we know will always be with us!"

Then the first elder exclaimed, "Aaron is now our leader. Moses left him in charge. We don't care what you think, Caleb! We need a god to lead us and Aaron, you are our leader. Make us a god who can lead us!"

The crowd began to shout in agreement. The noise was deafening. How easily our people could turn their hearts from God!

The crowd was pressing against Aaron, and I could see he was beginning to panic. Some of the men had picked up stones and were making ready to stone him. My heart sank as I heard Aaron shout, "Alright! *Take the gold rings from the ears of your wives and sons and daughters, and bring them to me!"*[(5)]

. . .

"Aaron, you can't do this!" I pleaded. "You can't make this idol. It is an abomination to God. We entered into a covenant with Him. Moses will return. We must keep the people from doing this!"

"I have no choice, Caleb," Aaron responded with a mixture of sadness and resignation. "The people will not listen to us. They have already decided to go their own way. I must keep them from rioting. Hopefully, Moses will return before any real damage is done."

"Any REAL damage?" I asked incredulously. "You're agreeing to help them abandon their God. The damage cannot be any more real than that!"

"Perhaps," Aaron replied. "But Moses left me in charge. We will do as I have said."

Soon the people brought baskets upon baskets heaping with gold jewelry of all types before Aaron. He took the gold and, with the help of several other Levites, melted it down and began to mold it into the shape of a calf. I watched with horror as the image of the Egyptian god Hapi began to take shape.

Hapi supposedly represented eternity itself and the balance of the universe. We had all seen this image displayed in Egypt. It was but another one of the powerless man-made gods of Egypt. And yet, here was Aaron forming an idol in that same image to be our god!

This was the first time since my father's death that I was glad he was not here. I was thankful he would never see this. Our people were turning their backs on the one true God and turning to an idol of Egypt!

My stomach turned as the people began to exclaim, *"O Israel, these are the gods who brought you out of the land of Egypt!"* [6]

. . .

But I was unprepared for what Aaron did next. Seeing how excited the people were, he built an altar in front of the calf and announced, *"Tomorrow will be a festival to the "lord"!"*[7]

The people rose early that next morning. The golden calf Aaron had formed stood in their midst. Many of our people slaughtered animals from their flocks and offered them as burnt sacrifices and peace offerings to this idol of Egypt.

They sat around it to eat and drink. They played around it, bowed to it, and brought offerings to it of every kind. They laughed, they sang, and they danced around it. They indulged in the pagan revelry we had left behind in Egypt as they shouted, "This is our god, O Israel, who brought us out of the land of Egypt!"

Some of the people remarked they had never enjoyed this much pleasure. Even some of the few who had been against forming this golden idol were now being drawn into the celebration by the euphoria of the crowd. They hadn't set out to disobey God, but they were lured by the excitement and the attraction of pleasure.

As the noise became more feverish and the activity more frenzied, the people became more and more blinded to their disobedience. What had begun as deception had escalated into debauchery.

As the day was drawing to a close, I looked up and saw two men walking toward us from a distance. I immediately recognized Moses and Joshua. Moses was carrying two large stone tablets. As they entered the camp, Moses saw the people dancing – and then he spied the golden calf.

. . .

Moses threw the stone tablets to the ground, smashing them into pieces. I knew those tablets contained the commands of our covenant with God – and now they were broken. But we had already broken the covenant!

The revelers gasped as they saw Moses, and everything came to a halt. They knew their sinful behavior had been discovered. Gone was the rebelliousness of the day before. Some of the people began to scatter as if to distance themselves from their sin. Others looked around to see who they could blame. A few in the group started to come up with excuses to justify their sin. Some tried to deny they had any involvement. But most just stood there feeling ashamed.

The cauldron Aaron had used to melt the gold was still sitting atop a flame. Moses and Joshua picked up the golden calf and threw it into the cauldron. No one attempted to stop them. Everyone stood and watched in shame, fearful of Moses's anger.

As the calf burned down, Moses took a nearby pestle and ground the gold into powder. Then he cast the powder into the nearby spring and commanded the people to drink it. No one objected. No one attempted to raise a hand to stop him. In their shame and embarrassment, everyone drank from the spring.

Next he turned to Aaron and demanded, *"What did these people do to you to make you bring such terrible sin upon them?"*[8]

"Don't get so upset, my lord," Aaron replied. *"You yourself know how evil these people are. They said to me, 'Make us gods who will lead us. We don't know what happened to this fellow Moses, who brought us here from the land of Egypt.' So I told them, 'Whoever has gold jewelry, take it off.' When they brought it to me, I simply threw it into the fire – and out came this calf!"*[9]

. . .

Moses realized Aaron had let our people get completely out of control. So he stood at the entrance to the camp and shouted, *"All of you who are on the Lord's side, come here and join me."*[(10)]

My family and I moved to stand beside Moses, as did many of our tribe. The Levites and many others gathered around him, as well. As a matter of fact, most of the people stood on his side. But there were some who remained on the other side of him. Their shame had turned into defiance.

Moses turned to the Levites beside him and said, *"This is what the Lord, the God of Israel, says: 'Each of you, take your swords and go back and forth among the people on the other side. Kill everyone – even your brothers, friends, and neighbors.'"*[(11)]

The Levites obeyed Moses's command, and about three thousand men died that day.

Then Moses told the Levites, *"Today you have ordained yourselves for the service of the Lord, for you obeyed Him even though it meant killing your own sons and brothers. Today you have earned a blessing."*[(12)]

The next day Moses announced to the people, *"You have committed a terrible sin, but I will go back up to the Lord on the mountain. Perhaps I will be able to obtain forgiveness for your sin."*[(13)]

So, Moses returned to the Lord and said, *"Oh, what a terrible sin these people have committed. They have made gods of gold for themselves. But now, if You will only forgive their sin – but if not, erase my name from the record You have written!"*[(14)]

But the Lord replied to Moses, *"No, I will erase the name of everyone who has sinned against Me. Now go, lead the people to the place I told you about. Look!*

My angel will lead the way before you. And when I come to call the people to account, I will certainly hold them responsible for their sins."[(15)]

Then the Lord sent a great plague upon our people because they had worshipped the golden calf. Many died as a result, and many wished they would die. Some survived but were left with lingering symptoms as a continuing reminder. They experienced the divine consequence for their disobedience.

Some of the people were truly repentant before God and sought His cleansing and forgiveness. Others were merely remorseful before God and sought a second chance. Some were stubborn and sought neither forgiveness nor grace.

Aaron's disobedience was not his own death, but rather living with the knowledge that his sin had led to the death of thousands. He also bore the responsibility that generations to come would bear the scars of his disobedience. Moses interceded to God on Aaron's behalf, and in God's sovereign plan, He chose to spare Aaron's physical life. However, He did not spare him from the grief and anguish he was forced to endure for the remainder of his life.

When Moses and Joshua climbed the mountain, Moses had left both Aaron and Hur in charge of the people. Hur didn't oppose the making of the calf but had stood by silently. As a result, Hur died in the plague.

I wondered which one had paid the greater price for his faithless disobedience – Aaron enduring years of grief and anguish, or Hur experiencing physical death. I'll leave that to you to decide.

* * *

19

The LORD said to Moses, "Get going, you and the people you brought up from the land of Egypt....[1]

* * *

After the plague had passed, Moses assembled us together to hear these words from God. "Here is what the Lord has said to me," Moses began. *"'Go up to the land I swore to give to Abraham, Isaac, and Jacob. I told them, 'I will give this land to your descendants.' And I will send an angel before you to drive out the Canaanites, Amorites, Hittites, Perizzites, Hivites, and Jebusites. Go up to this land that flows with milk and honey. But I will not travel among you, for you are a stubborn and rebellious people. If I did, I would surely destroy you along the way. Remove your jewelry and fine clothes while I decide what to do with you.'"*[2]

After hearing those stern words, we all went into mourning. Most of us were mourning the actions that had so grieved the heart of God. However, some were mourning the fact they could no longer wear the jewelry they brought out of Egypt – at least the portion they still possessed after the collection for the fabrication of the golden calf.

. . .

Moses went on to say, "We will set up a tent of meeting outside our camp. I will go to the tent to meet with our God and bring our requests before Him."

As we watched Moses enter the tent, the pillar of cloud descended and hovered at the entrance. As the cloud covered the tent, we bowed in reverence before the glory of Jehovah God.

Later, Moses told us about the conversation he had with God.

"LORD, You have been telling me to take this people up to the Promised Land," Moses recounted. "But You haven't told me whom You will send with me. You have told me that You look favorably upon me. If I have found favor in Your sight, please show me now Your ways, that I may know You in order to find favor in Your sight. Consider too that this nation is Your people. If Your presence will not go with me, do not bring us up from here. For how then shall it be known that I have found favor in Your sight – I and your people? Is it not in Your going with us, so that we are distinct, I and Your people, from every other people on the face of the earth?"[3]

And the Lord replied to Moses, "This very thing that you have spoken I will do, for you have found favor in My sight."[4]

The Lord continued, "Before we leave this place, chisel out two stone tablets like the first ones. I will write on them the same words that were on the tablets you shattered. Be ready in the morning to climb up Mount Sinai and present yourself to Me on the top of the mountain. No one else may come with you. In fact, no one is to appear anywhere on the mountain. Do not even let the flocks or herds graze near the mountain." [5]

Early the next morning, Moses climbed Mount Sinai carrying the two stone tablets. Later he told us that when he reached the top of the mountain, the Lord had come down in a cloud saying:

"I AM Yahweh! The LORD!
The God of compassion and mercy!
I am slow to anger
and filled with unfailing love and faithfulness.
I lavish unfailing love to a thousand generations.
I forgive iniquity, rebellion, and sin.

"But I do not excuse the guilty.
I lay the sins of the parents upon their children and grandchildren;
the entire family is affected –
even children in the third and fourth generations." [(6)]

Moses had immediately fallen prostrate on the ground and worshipped the Lord saying, *"LORD, please forgive our iniquity and our sins. Claim us as Your own special possession."* [(7)]

Moses remained on the mountain before the Lord for forty days and nights. During that time, he ate no bread and drank no water. God again wrote the terms of the covenant between Himself and His people – the ten commandments – on the tablets of stone.

When the time concluded, Moses returned to us. As he approached the camp, Moses was unaware the shekinah glory of God's presence radiated from his face. But the light did not originate from within Moses; it originated from God. Moses was displaying the glory of the Heavenly Father.

Most of our people were afraid to come near Moses because they weren't sure how to act around him. God's holiness demands reverence and awe. But Moses called us over and told us of God's instructions. This time, we received God's commands appropriately.

After Moses spoke, he humbly covered his face with a veil so the radiance would not bring him attention. He removed the veil only when he went into the tent of meeting to speak with the Lord. Moses wanted nothing to distract the people from God.

During Moses' initial meeting with God (when the people rebelled), he was given specific instructions for the building of a tabernacle. As Moses explained, *"This will be a sacred residence where God can live among His people."*[8]

The Lord had not only given instruction regarding the tent itself, but also all of the elements and utensils that would be used in the tent – as well as the establishment of a priesthood, their role, and their special clothing. He issued specific instructions regarding the offerings to be presented and the incenses and oils to be used.

God had directed that Aaron and his sons would serve as priests of the tabernacle. Somewhat surprisingly, God did not change that decision after Aaron's role in the blasphemy of the golden calf. He also decided the tribe of Levi would serve as stewards of the tabernacle with responsibility for its assembly, function, disassembly, and transport.

Now, after Moses returned from his second meeting with God, he assembled our people to tell us God's instructions.

"Take a sacred offering for the LORD. Let those with generous hearts present gifts to the LORD."[9]

God had provided us with all the resources required to construct the tabernacle before we left Egypt. He had entrusted us to carry them for His purpose.

It was time for those resources to be gathered. I couldn't help but notice that Moses did not command our people to bring gifts. Only those with generous hearts who wanted to help in the work were to present offerings. This was a freewill offering –returning to God what He had already provided for the building of His tabernacle.

As I looked around our camp, I thought about the different amounts of wealth represented among former servants and ex-slaves. Some, like Igal and Ammiel, had accumulated significant wealth. Others, like me, had enjoyed the generosity of our Egyptian masters over the years. But most of our people had very little. And yet, God was giving each of us an opportunity to be part of His work.

It saddened me when some among us chose to have no part in the offering. Instead, they clenched His provisions in their fists and declared them as their own. I wondered if they realized they were not only robbing God of His provision, but also robbing themselves of the joy of giving.

These people picked up God's manna every morning but chose not to bring a love offering to Him. They rationalized it. They tried to justify it. But the reality was they just didn't love God enough to give.

As Moses shared these instructions, I was struck by two things. Our disobedience as a people with the golden calf had cost us greatly. It had cost us the displeasure of our God. It had cost the lives of many among us. It had cost further delay in our journey to the Promised Land. We would have been ready to build the tabernacle two months' earlier if we had not been delayed by our disobedience. And it had cost a squandering of the resources God had provided for the building of His tabernacle. Resources that should have been used for the tabernacle were wasted on the sculpting of a golden calf.

God had not only provided the physical resources we needed, He had chosen men among us who were uniquely qualified for this work. God called them, He chose them, and He set them apart.

. . .

God called Bezalel to be the lead builder. Bezalel was the grandson of Hur and Moses' sister, Miriam. But more importantly, he had been equipped by God with every skill necessary to complete the work. God had given him great wisdom, intelligence, and skill. God also called Oholiab to be Bezalel's assistant, having also given him the necessary skills to accomplish his assignment. And God had given them both the ability to teach their skills to others.

Though God had given Moses the detailed plan, He had given Bezalel the responsibility of managing the work. Bezalel was entrusted with this job because of his willingness and obedience to God's call. Moses demonstrated wisdom and discernment in letting go and allowing God to work the way He intended.

I knew God could have supernaturally built His tabernacle. He could have easily spoken it into existence, the same as He spoke the earth, the sun, and the stars into being. He did not need the resources we carried or the skills of our craftsmen to accomplish the work – anymore than God needed a people to make His name known.

But God chose to use us. He chose to set us aside as a people unto Himself. But now the question for us all was – were we willing? Did we have the generous and willing hearts to present our gifts … and present ourselves? The answer to those questions remained to be seen.

* * *

20

"The people have given more than enough materials to complete the job the LORD has commanded us to do!"[1]

* * *

Almost one year had passed since we left Egypt. Roughly three hundred of those days had been spent camped at the base of Mount Sinai. The grumbling, complaining, and disobedience of our people along the way proved our hearts were not fully turned toward God. We had repeatedly displayed selfishness and self-centeredness that rivaled that of the Egyptian taskmasters who had enslaved us.

It had been about eight months since my people had disobeyed God with the idol of a golden calf. Since then, we had experienced the discipline of God in a way we never had before. Thousands of our number died both by the sword and as a result of the plague. It was a painful learning lesson, but the people began to understand that though God was merciful, He was also just, and He would by no means ignore our guilt.

• • •

But there were also those among us who received unwarranted mercy. As a result, we all began to more clearly see our Lord God Jehovah through eyes of reverence and awe, with fear and with trembling. We had learned that walking in fear of the Lord is walking in the awareness of His love, His grace, and His mercy, and it is also walking in the awareness of His might, His power, His righteousness, and His justness.

We had also been willingly giving an offering out of reverence for God. And one day, the word was sent out throughout the camp: *"Men and women, don't prepare any more gifts for the sanctuary. We have enough!"*[2]

The fabrication work under Bezalel's leadership was now complete and had been done just as God commanded. Bezalel and the craftsmen brought the entire tabernacle to Moses. They had crafted the sacred tent with all of its furnishings, all of the elements and utensils that would be used in the tent, as well as the priestly garments, oils, and incenses.

It was on the first day of the first month of the second year, the tabernacle was erected in the center of our camp as a reminder that the Lord God Jehovah was to be at the center and focus of everything we would ever do.

Once the tabernacle was in place, the pillar of cloud settled over it and the glory of the Lord filled it. Only Aaron, as high priest, and his sons were permitted to enter the tabernacle – and only then as they followed God's specific instructions. Even Moses was not permitted to enter while the glory of God filled the tabernacle.

God's presence had gone before us since the journey began, but on this day His presence filled us. And throughout the rest of our journey, when His Spirit led, we would continue on our journey; when His Spirit inhabited the tabernacle, we would remain in camp.

. . .

Though our journey was far from over, we had come to a place where, no matter what, we dwelt in the presence of God because He dwelt in our midst. We dwelt in the shelter of the Most High and in the shadow of the Almighty. A journey that had begun to escape the slavery of Egypt had become a journey into the very presence of God.

But why had Lord God Jehovah chosen to dwell among us? Was it our obedience each and every step throughout our journey? No, because we had repeatedly demonstrated we were disobedient people. Was it our faithfulness to worship Him and Him alone? No, we had rebelliously created a golden calf to worship. Was it our walk of faith and our trust in Him? No, at each crossroad of faith on our journey, we had demonstrated a faithlessness in the God who went before us, often ignoring and denying His presence.

We had done nothing to merit God's favor. We did not deserve to have the God of heaven dwell among us. He had chosen us to be His people; we had not chosen Him to be our God. He promised to bless all the nations through us; and He had been faithful, even though we had broken every promise we had made to Him. He continued to demonstrate His love for us, even when we were unlovely.

Even now we were anxious about continuing our journey. God had promised us a land flowing with milk and honey. He had not said we would spend an eternity camped in front of a desolate mountain. We were growing impatient – but we were learning that our God is a God of order and there were still further preparations He wanted us to make before we left this place.

The fourteenth day of this first month of the second year was the one-year anniversary of the night the angel of death passed over our homes in Egypt. So, at twilight we gathered as families in our tents to remember the Passover – just as we had that night one year earlier. And just as they had one year ago, Rebecca and Achsah prepared the bitter herbs and unleavened bread while my sons and I prepared the Passover lamb.

• • •

As we gathered in our tent that night, we remembered God's deliverance and faithfulness. But we were also mindful of my parents' absence from around our table. One year ago, we had eaten this meal together in awe and anticipation. We had experienced God's deliverance together. Now, we must continue the journey without them, leaving their burial place behind us.

Two weeks later, on the first day of the second month of the second year, the Lord God directed Moses saying, *"Take a census of all the congregation of the people of Israel, by clans, by fathers' houses, according to the number of names, every male, head by head. From twenty years old and upward, all in Israel who are able to go to war, you and Aaron shall list them."*[3]

The Lord Himself chose a leader from each of our tribes to oversee the task of administering the census. Nahshon, son of Amminadab, was chosen to oversee the task within our tribe. Nahshon was Aaron's brother-in-law – his sister, Elisheba, was Aaron's wife. He was a contemporary of my father's but had not shown himself to be a leader while we were in Egypt. However, he had distinguished himself once we began the exodus.

He was a good choice to lead our tribe. He and his family had been the first to follow me and my family the day we crossed through the Red Sea. He had demonstrated a courageous faith and trust in God when many were still reluctant to do so.

And after his family had safely crossed the sea, he had remained in the dry path to help people climb the embankment onto shore. Even while we remained here at Sinai, he had demonstrated his faithfulness to God by leading his family to be the first to bring their gifts for the fabrication of the tabernacle.

• • •

Nahshon, together with the assistance of several other men and myself, began the process of having every man aged twenty and older register by family and by clan. When the process was complete, we learned that the tribe of Judah was larger than any of the other tribes. We numbered seventy-four thousand, six hundred men. With women and children, we were about one-quarter million people.

When the counts were collected for all of our tribes, the able-bodied men who were 20 and older numbered more than six hundred thousand. That number did not include our Levite brothers who were charged with the care of the tabernacle, as well as guarding it. From then on, the Levites' tents were pitched in a way that immediately surrounded the tabernacle on all four sides.

God also assigned the rest of the tribes specific locations to set up camp surrounding the Levites. Can you imagine the quarreling if it had been left up to us to determine who camped where in relation to the tabernacle? Or which clan and tribe got to lead out when we continued our journey?

I realized God in His wisdom did not delegate that assignment to Moses. He knew the grief the people would give Moses if he chose the order, so God Himself made the assignments.

The Lord divided us into four groups of three tribes each. The first group was led by our tribe of Judah. Issachar and Zebulun were Judah's two younger brothers, also sons of Leah. As such, these two tribes joined us on the east side of the tabernacle, facing the rising sun.

The second group camped on the south side of the tabernacle and was led by the tribe of Reuben, the firstborn of Jacob, together with the tribe of Simeon, the second born of Jacob, and the tribe of Gad. Though their blessing had been given to Judah, their birthright as sons of Jacob earned them this position.

. . .

The third group camped on the west side. These were the sons of Rachel, the favored sons of Jacob. These were led by the tribe of Ephraim, followed by Manasseh and Benjamin.

The fourth and final group camped on the north side and was led by the tribe of Dan, the eldest son of Jacob by Rachel's maidservant, Bilhah. The military prowess and feats of the tribe of Dan were displayed when we defeated the Amalekites. Their fighting ability, together with the size of their fighting force, made them an appropriate choice for this last group. They, together with the tribes of Naphtali and Asher, the remaining sons of the maidservants, became the rearguard.

Each group carried a banner for identification, which also served as a rallying point for our people. The banners carried an emblem that represented the lead tribe of the group. Our group bore the likeness of a lion, the second bore the likeness of a man, the third bore the likeness of an ox, and the fourth bore the likeness of an eagle.

"Papa, why do the banners bear those images?" Achsah asked.

"The banners are to serve as a reminder," I replied, "that we are God's chosen people formed for His purpose. When our patriarch, Jacob, blessed his sons soon after they arrived in Egypt, he used those symbols to convey his blessing. The image of the young man should serve as a visual reminder to us that we are God's people – created in His image in order to follow Him and worship Him. As we follow Him into the land of His promise, we are to walk in His way with the courage of a lion, the steadfastness of an ox, and soar with the strength of an eagle."

"Papa, I want to soar like an eagle!" my daughter exclaimed. "You will, little one," I assured her. "I know that you will!"

. . .

Everything was in order. We had our assignments. We knew our places. Now we waited on the Lord God. Then on the twentieth day of the second month of the second year, the cloud lifted from the tabernacle. It was time for our journey to continue.

* * *

21

So the Israelites set out from the wilderness of Sinai and traveled on from place to place until the cloud stopped in the wilderness of Paran.[1]

* * *

W e had been camped at Mount Sinai for almost a year when we began to travel again. It was a three-day journey to the wilderness of Paran. Moses had reminded us Paran was where Hagar and Ishmael found refuge when Sarah told Abraham to send them away. The wilderness was bounded on the north by southern Canaan, the Promised Land. We were in the fourteenth month of our journey and we were now nearing our destination!

We left Sinai very different people from when we arrived. We started as a ragtag multitude following the promises of God. We left as an ordered people following the presence of God.

Prior to Sinai we had experienced God's provision and protection, but at Sinai we experienced His presence dwelling in our midst. We arrived in Sinai with a self-centered view of God, His promises, and His purpose. We left Sinai as the recipients of His law and His covenant, with a better understanding of His purpose and His plan for our lives.

We left Sinai not only having experienced God's presence but also having experienced His wrath and His judgment following our rebellious worship of the golden calf. Prior to Sinai we had seen God's power directed against our enemies, but now we had seen God's power directed against us as a result of our disobedience. We had learned to live in reverence and awe of the Almighty God.

As we left Sinai, the mount was behind us, but the Ark of the Lord's covenant was before us. Though we would never return to the mount of the Lord, the Lord of the mount would continue to go before us.

The Ark, which had been crafted while we were at Sinai, contained the two stone tablets of the law – God's covenant with us, as well as the golden pot of manna – a testimony to our future generations of God's faithful provision. On the top of the Ark was the mercy seat, the place where God spoke to Moses in the wilderness tabernacle – the visible symbol of His gracious presence. The Ark represented the presence and the promises of God that went before us.

We arrived in Sinai carrying riches from Egypt. While there, God transformed those riches into His wilderness tabernacle – His earthly dwelling place. Yes, we arrived in Sinai led by God. But we now left fully surrounded by His presence – shaded, protected, and bounded by His limitless power and grace.

As we journeyed farther from Sinai, Moses' brother-in-law, Hobab, came to Moses and said, "*I must return to my own land and family.*"[2]

Hobab had completed the task his father Reuel had given him. He had stayed with us in Sinai and had endured the rebellion of our people as well as the consequences. He had not needed to quell conflict with any Midianites; rather, our conflict had all come from within. He had watched patiently for over ten months as the tabernacle was being built and then erected. He had demonstrated he was an obedient son and a loyal brother-in-law. He had seen us at our worst and had not abandoned us.

But, more importantly, he, too, had seen our God up close and personal. He had seen Jehovah's righteousness and justness displayed through the Levites' swords and the plague in response to our rebellion. He had seen the glory of Jehovah displayed through His presence and His radiance on Moses' face. And He had seen the faithfulness of our Lord through His abiding presence, His daily provision, and now His leadership as we continued in our journey.

"Please don't leave us," Moses pleaded. *"You know the places in the wilderness where we should camp.* You know where the green pastures are. You know the location of the quiet waters. Help guide us in the path in which God leads us. *Come, be our guide and we will share with you all the good things that the Lord does for us."* [3]

As I listened to their conversation, I realized we didn't need Hobab to tell us where to march or where to camp. God would do that! But Hobab's knowledge of the land was invaluable as we made decisions about moving from place to place. It occurred to me that Hobab was as much God's provision for us as His cloud and everything else He had placed in our path.

I also was aware of God's promise to bless all the nations through our people. Hobab represented one of those nations. God wanted to bless Hobab – a Midianite. And I for one was grateful when Hobab agreed to continue on with us. Together, we would continue to experience the blessings of God!

. . .

Regrettably, not all of the other "foreigners" in our midst were like Hobab. A murmuring was stirring in the midst of the foreigners who were traveling with us. These people were not part of any of our specific tribes. They were people from other regions – like the Nubians and the Levantines – who had also been enslaved in Egypt. Some of them saw our exodus as their opportunity to escape from slavery, so they had joined us.

This group also included some who were the offspring of marriages between the children of Egypt and the children of Israel. Having never felt, nor been treated like they were truly Egyptians, they joined us in the exodus from Egypt. But since we had organized into clans, families, and tribes as we were leaving the wilderness of Sinai, they no longer felt a part of Israel, either. They had no place under one of our banners. They remained on the outskirts of our camp and had begun to question whether they had made the right choice. They were craving the things of Egypt they had left behind. But the murmuring did not stop with them. Soon that same murmuring was extending among all our people.

Our diet in Egypt had been almost exclusively fish, particularly during the hot months of April and May. It was now that time of year, and many of our people were craving the fresh fish we used to eat. These were some of the same people who complained about always eating fish when we still lived in Egypt! They were remembering the fish, the cucumbers, the melons, the leeks, and the onions and garlic – and everything else they used to eat "for free!"

Somehow, our months in the wilderness had erased from their memories that we were slaves in Egypt. They seemed to have forgotten their labor, their toil, their taskmasters, and the sting of the whip on their backs. They had forgotten that nothing in Egypt was free; it came at great price!

I was amazed at all we had seen God accomplish on our behalf. And yet, many of my people were longing to be back in slavery. They had left their hovels seeking the blessings of the Promised Land, but their hearts were still in bondage. They sought after the trappings of their enslavement and ignored its cost and its consequences.

And their discontent began to infect others. A little leaven permeates the whole lump! Leaven is a heart in bondage to the sin and slavery of Egypt, yet seeks its own fulfillment in the Promised Land. It is the heart that seeks the trappings of sin but has grown cold to the fruit of faithfulness. It is a heart that has never truly been transformed but one that goes through the motions.

There is only one sure way to destroy leaven – fire! The Lord's anger blazed and He sent a purifying fire to destroy the complainers in the outskirts of camp. This rabble had not turned to Him, and now He would turn from them, purging them from His people. He allowed them to go through fire in order to remove the impurities, the leaven, and the sin in the camp that had rendered this group unusable for His purpose.

Moses cried out to the Lord for the fire to stop – and it did. But not until the leaven had been purged. I do not know what that place was called prior to that day – but from that day forth it was called Taberah, which means the place of burning.

Unbelievably, the murmuring still continued within the camp! Now people were complaining about the manna God supplied us with each day. Apparently, most of the women were not as creative as my wife when it came to using the manna to prepare bread and pastries. The people complained that it was tasteless. Each night they would stand in the doorways of their tents and whine about it – to the point it began to weigh heavily on Moses.

The people grumbling were dishonoring God. But they were directing their criticism toward Moses, and unfortunately he took it to heart. The load he took upon himself was becoming too heavy to bear. At that point, the service God had placed before Moses ceased to be a blessing and became a burden. He cried out to God to be taken out from under the burden. But God taught Moses that service to Him was never intended to be overwhelming.

Moses said to the Lord, *"Why are You treating me, Your servant, so harshly? Have mercy on me! What did I do to deserve the burden of all these people? Did I give birth to them? Did I bring them into the world? Why did You tell me to carry them in my arms like a mother carries a nursing baby? How can I carry them to the land You swore to give their ancestors? Where am I supposed to get meat for all these people? They keep whining to me, saying, 'Give us meat to eat!' I can't carry all these people by myself! The load is far too heavy! If this is how You intend to treat me, just go ahead and kill me. Do me a favor and spare me this misery!"* [4]

As I overheard Moses crying out to God, I realized there were lessons for anyone God chooses to be a leader among His people.

First, we are under a burden God never intended when we overvalue our own performance in God's work. Moses said, *"I can't carry all these people by myself!"* [5] As if he were carrying us at all! Who had parted the Red Sea? Who had defeated the Amalekites? Who provided for our every need? Moses hadn't accomplished any of it. God had chosen to accomplish it *through* Moses. Moses had stepped into a trap we all struggle with – he had overvalued his part in all of this.

Secondly, Moses said to God, *"If this is how You intend to treat me, just go ahead and kill me."* [6] Part of the pressure he felt was because he failed to appreciate the honor God had given him. Moses had been chosen by the Lord God Jehovah to lead us out of Egypt to the Promised Land. God didn't need to honor Moses, and Moses did not deserve to be honored. God chose to honor Moses.

The same is true of me. God has given me rights and honor as His child, not because I am worthy but because He chooses to do so. And what God has given value, no man can take away. With God's value comes the enablement and the empowerment to finish the task. The Lord God was showing Moses – and all of us – to not undervalue what God has valued – and to not allow others to do so, either.

Thirdly, Moses lost sight of the fact this was God's assignment. God's assignment will always be far greater than anything we can do ourselves. God's work results in God's glory. If Moses – or any of us – could do it, who would get the glory? I, like Moses, will find myself under a load that is far too heavy when I overestimate my own ability or underestimate God's ability. God was reminding Moses there is nothing He has placed before him that He does not have the strength to complete. And conversely, there is nothing God has placed before Moses that Moses has the strength to complete apart from God. The lesson was that Moses was supposed to always give his load to God.

Lastly, we must always be aware of those with whom God has surrounded us to be co-laborers in His work. Most often, God has not called us to go it alone. The Lord said to Moses, "*Gather before Me seventy men who are recognized as elders and leaders of Israel. Bring them to the Tabernacle to stand there with you. I will come down and talk to you there. I will take some of the Spirit that is upon you, and I will put the Spirit upon them also. They will bear the burden of the people along with you, so you will not have to carry it alone.*"[7]

I was one of those leaders. God had placed us here for just this purpose. Just as He had placed Hobab in our midst for His purpose. Yes, Moses nominated us, but it was God who qualified us. He had prepared us, and He had gifted us. Now the Lord was preparing to fill us with His Spirit so we would be fully equipped to accomplish His purpose. The Promised Land was just ahead and how well we all learned these lessons would determine if we were going to enter into that promise!

* * *

22

Now the LORD will give you meat, and you will have to eat it.[1]

* * *

M oses stationed our group of seventy elders around the outside of the tabernacle. Afterward, the Lord came down in the cloud and descended upon the tabernacle.

As His Spirit came upon us, we all began to prophesy – speaking the truth of God, under the anointing of God, with the power of God. To this point, our people had heard only Moses and Aaron speak with that kind of authority. They marveled at the boldness with which we now spoke.

God showed us that day He does not operate under our limitations or our restrictions. God's Spirit will fill whomever He chooses, wherever He chooses, and whenever He chooses.

Moses even lamented to Joshua, *"I wish that all the LORD's people were prophets, and that the LORD would put His Spirit upon them all!"*[3]

. . .

It was an admonition to those sitting in our camps and complaining instead of being filled with His Spirit and focused on His mission as champions of His kingdom!

Our group of elders, anointed to share Moses's burden, returned with him to the camp where he told the people, "The LORD has said, '*Purify yourselves, for tomorrow you will have meat to eat. You were whining and I have heard you. I will give you meat and you will have to eat it. It won't be for just a day or two, or for five or ten or even twenty. You will eat it for a whole month until you gag and are sick of it. For again you have whined and rejected the LORD.'*"[4]

Even Moses had questioned how the Lord would bring that about. How could there be that much meat for an entire month – even if we butchered all our flocks and herds or caught all the fish in the sea?

It had been a year since God had provided the quail that night in the wilderness of Sin. He had delivered it fresh to the doorways of our tents and nothing had ever tasted so good. Now our people craved meat again. But this time they didn't crave the meat of God, they craved the meat of Egypt. Their craving was so strong that they were standing in front of their tents weeping.

The excitement on the faces of our people was palpable when that great sea of quail began to descend upon our camp. I can't begin to describe the multitude of birds. For miles in every direction they were flying about three feet above the ground. We went out and caught quail all that day and throughout the night and all the next day. Not one of our six hundred thousand men gathered less than fifty bushels. That meant we had more than thirty million bushels of quail!

Immediately, we stoked the cooking fires and prepared to dine on this feast of quail. But while we were gorging ourselves, a severe plague broke out among us. And those who had craved the meat from Egypt fell dead and were buried in that place.

"What is wrong with wanting meat?" my son Iru asked me.

"Nothing is wrong with wanting meat," I replied, "if it is the meat of the Lord. The problem is our people weren't asking for the meat of the Lord, they were murmuring for the meat of Egypt. And what did Egypt hold for us? It was a place of bondage and death. And the meat of Egypt brings with it that bondage and death."

So, unknowingly, many of our people received exactly what they had been murmuring about. Did all of our people die? No, only those who craved the meat of Egypt. But there were many others who experienced the sickness that the meat of Egypt can bring. They hadn't craved it, but they had eaten it. And from that day forward we called that place Kibroth-hattaavah, which means "the graves of gluttony," as a permanent reminder of God's judgment.

After we buried our dead, the pillar of cloud led us to Hazeroth. While we were camped there, Moses' sister, Miriam, and Aaron chose to publicly criticize their brother for marrying Tzipora the Midianite.

When Moses fled from Egypt and settled in the land of Midian, God knew he would need help in leading our people. Moses would need to know how to be a shepherd, a husband, and a father. God had given Moses a companion, a helpmate – her name was Tzipora, meaning "little sparrow." Jethro had given Moses his firstborn daughter because of the bravery, faithfulness, and loyalty Moses displayed in those early days in Midian.

The sparrow, though humble in stature, is a resilient little migratory bird. It is a species that stays its course regardless of what it encounters. It was that kind of faithful determination we had witnessed in Tzipora's life. She was not timid. She and her sisters had bravely tended their father's flocks before Moses came to Midian. They routinely competed with other shepherds for watering rights for their flocks. Though they often were bested, the women did not shrink from their adversaries.

When Moses returned home from his time before the Lord at the burning bush, he announced to Jethro and Tzipora what God had told him to do. Tzipora, along with her sons, packed up to leave the only home she had ever known to follow her husband on his mission from God. Tzipora was preparing to journey to Egypt as the wife of a fugitive of pharaoh. She had no idea what fate would await them. She had heard no word from God – but her husband had. And she proceeded to walk alongside her husband in his obedience to God.

I had heard Moses tell this account on a number of occasions, including how his faithfulness to God was tested along the route to Egypt.

God was angry with Moses because he had failed to circumcise his second son, Eliezer. Tzipora's people did not practice circumcision, so she had asked Moses to refrain from doing so. She had endured the circumcision of their firstborn, Gershom, but she considered the practice barbaric. However, she did not realize what Moses's disobedience was about to cost him.

One day during their journey, God sent an angel to slay Moses. He could not use Moses to bring about the deliverance of His people if Moses continued to be disobedient. His boy must be circumcised now; but Moses, standing at the precipice of his own death, was unable to do it.

Putting her own fear aside, Tzipora stepped forward with knife in hand and circumcised their son. Although she didn't attempt to hide her displeasure and disdain for the practice, she did what was needed to save her husband.

. . .

As their journey as husband and wife continued, Tzipora came to know our God as the Lord God Jehovah – the one true God. She began to follow Him – just like her father and brother would do. As a result, this little sparrow, with faithful determination, became an invaluable helpmate to Moses as he led the people. She also was an encouragement to all those around her. As our journey unfolded, she walked in a position of respect and influence as Moses's wife.

I was surprised when we arrived in Hazeroth that Miriam and Aaron chose to publicly criticize Moses about his marriage instead of discussing it in private. And why had they chosen now as the time to do so? In fact, Miriam's thorny words and mean-spirited criticisms reminded me of the landscape surrounding us.

Hazeroth was an encampment in the wilderness of Paran, characterized by stone enclosures that had become entangled by thorny acacia branches with needle-like spikes. These enclosures formed an impenetrable hedge around the tents and cattle in our settlement. Miriam's rhetoric was no less pointed than those acacia needles.

As Miriam and Aaron continued to complain, it became obvious their real issue was that Moses had not consulted them before selecting the seventy elders. Miriam was jealous that Moses had sought the counsel of his wife instead of her. As for Aaron, he was again demonstrating that he was easily swayed by others. So, when Miriam became critical of Moses, he went along with her. But they forgot there was one other Person listening, and He wasn't going to sit idly by while they found fault with His anointed.

God had called Moses to his position of leadership, and He had provided him with a helpmate. He had entrusted Moses with a people to lead, a position and a responsibility to heed, and a path he must follow. He allowed Moses to hear His voice, to speak with Him, and to see His face. That calling and that anointing did not come without accountability, but that accountability was to God. It was an accountability the rest of us did not have.

God made it clear to Miriam, Aaron, and all of us that if you attack His anointed, you are also attacking the Lord God Jehovah. And you will not win that battle! Moses, in his humility, was prepared to overlook the criticism, but God Almighty was not.

The Lord descended in the pillar of cloud at the entrance to the tabernacle and called out to Aaron and Miriam in a voice that we could all hear and understand: *"Listen to what I have to say. Of all this house, Moses is the one I trust. I speak to him face to face – clearly, and not in riddles! He sees the LORD as he is. So why were you not afraid to criticize My servant Moses?"*[5]

The Lord's anger was conspicuous. As the cloud moved away from the tabernacle, Miriam's skin turned white as snow with leprosy. Again, God chose not to punish His high priest Aaron. But when Aaron saw what had happened to his sister, he cried out to Moses, *"Oh, my master! Please don't punish us for this sin we have so foolishly committed."*[6]

Moses, in his compassion, began to intercede on Miriam's behalf, but God Almighty was not ready to remove the consequence of her sin so quickly. His decision to afflict Miriam with leprosy underscored how seriously He took the criticism of His servants. When a person contracted leprosy, they were sent away from our camp. Because of their disfigurement and disablement, they were considered unclean – rejected and excluded from the rest of society.

Miriam's selfish ambition for greater inclusion in Moses's leadership decisions resulted in her exclusion from the people. Her critical rejection of Moses caused her to be rejected by the people. God kept all of us in that place of needles and thorns and permitted Miriam to suffer from leprosy for seven days. She and every one of us now knew God would not take criticism of His servants lightly.

. . .

One night as my family was gathered in our tent in Hazeroth, Iru asked me, "Papa, why did God treat Miriam so severely?"

"He wants all of us to understand we are not to criticize those whom God has placed in authority over us," I explained. "We are to encourage them and afford them the honor that is due them. When disagreements or misunderstandings arise, we are to approach them with all of the respect they are due as God's anointed."

"But what if the leader is being disobedient to God?" Iru continued.

"Then we should approach the leader respectfully and prayerfully," I replied. "Remember, this is God's anointed; if discipline is needed, God will make sure that it is administered – rightly, justly, and swiftly."

After seven days, God led us farther into the wilderness of Paran.

* * *

23

"Send men to spy out the land of Canaan, which I am giving to the people of Israel."[1]

* * *

Two days later we arrived in the northernmost part of the wilderness of Paran. We were just south of Canaan; our Promised Land was in sight! Our long-awaited hopes and dreams were about to become reality. As the pillar of cloud stopped, you could feel the excitement as we set up camp.

The Lord told Moses to send one leader from each of our twelve tribes. Moses chose to send those who had gathered with Aaron almost two years earlier in the cave at the sandstone quarry in Thebes. Our group of leaders had expanded since then, but it seemed fitting that we, who had met in secret seeking the Lord's deliverance from Egypt, would now quietly enter into Canaan to spy out the land of His promise.

Our group was comprised of:

- Joshua of the tribe of Ephraim – my best friend, and now Moses' trusted aide

- Gaddi of the tribe of Manasseh – my childhood "arrow-making" friend

- Shammua of the tribe of Reuben – the brave soldier who had distinguished himself by standing with Prince Amenmose at the battle of Abu Simbel, the eldest of our group

- Igal of the tribe of Issachar and Ammiel of the tribe of Dan – the two who had earned their freedom from slavery in Egypt and stood before pharaoh to advocate for our people

- Sethur of the tribe of Asher – whom I had learned to respect greatly for his bravery and defense of our people when we worked together in the sandstone quarry

- Shaphat of the tribe of Simeon – who had always demonstrated sound wisdom and discernment

- Palti of the tribe of Benjamin – who was known for his boldness and self-confidence

- Gaddiel of the tribe of Zebulun – who had also amassed enough wealth to earn his freedom from Egyptian slavery through his creativity and wit, the youngest member of our group

- Nahbi of the tribe of Naphtali and Geuel of the tribe of Gad – both of whom were humble and quiet servant leaders

- Me, representing the tribe of Judah.

Having known and served with these men, I was humbled to be counted among their number. We were all honored to go on behalf of our people.

. . .

Moses gathered us together and gave us these instructions before he sent us out to explore the land: *"Go up into the Negev and go up into the hill country, and see what the land is, and whether the people who dwell in it are strong or weak, whether they are few or many, and whether the land that they dwell in is good or bad, and whether the cities that they dwell in are camps or strongholds, and whether the land is rich or poor, and whether there are trees in it or not. Be of good courage and bring some of the fruit of the land."*[2]

The day we went out from camp was during the latter part of spring – the beginning of the harvest of the first grapes. Though we came from different backgrounds, had different personalities, and possessed different gifts, we traveled today as a band of brothers – united with one purpose. We were excited and filled with anticipation.

We would be the first to see this land flowing with milk and honey. We had heard about it all our lives. We had longed for it. Truthfully, we had begun to wonder if our generation would pass without seeing it, as had so many generations before us. We had imagined by faith what it would be like. And now we had the opportunity to be the first to see it in person.

But also, the responsibility weighed heavily on us. Moses had specifically told us where we were to explore. We were being sent northward out of the wilderness of Paran through the hills into southern Canaan. We were being sent to explore the closest entry point into the Promised Land.

Up until now, God had led us on a circuitous route out of Egypt. He had done so to bypass the land of the Philistines, and to deliver us from the Egyptian army through the Red Sea to the glory of His name. He had brought us through Mount Sinai so we would worship Him in that place according to His promise. But now He was ready to lead us directly into the Promised Land. It was to that entry place chosen by God that we were first being sent.

· · ·

Moses had also told us what we were to explore. We were to spy on and report on the inhabitants and their encampments, as well as the land and its crop production. How many people lived there? What were their demographics? Did they live in fortified cities or unprotected encampments? Was the land fertile or fruitless? What could we anticipate as we entered into the land? What kind of life and livelihood would the land provide?

Our instructions were to bring back samples of what a "land flowing with milk and honey" produces so the people could see for themselves. We were to quickly explore the land and bring back our report.

We were never tasked with evaluating the feasibility of inhabiting the land. That was never the question. God had said, "I will bring you into the land; and I will completely destroy your enemies." Our assignment was not to evaluate how – our mission was solely to explore where and what. We weren't even tasked with researching when we should enter the land – God had already determined the time.

The challenge for this group of gifted men was to not become distracted by our own abilities and wisdom or attempt to formulate our own plans. Our God had already formulated the plan. Our role was simply to follow Him.

We spied out the land from the wilderness of Zin to Rehob near Lebo-hamath. From there we went up into the Negev and came to Hebron, where our patriarchs Abraham, Isaac, and Jacob, together with their wives, were buried. It was in Hebron that some of the men began to express concerns.

Hebron was a walled city surrounded by a barrier that was twelve feet thick and thirty feet high. It was built using huge rocks – some up to six feet in diameter. Many of us had built large structures in Egypt, but the size and weight of these rocks surpassed anything we had ever seen. The men who had built this wall clearly had superior strength.

. . .

Throughout our travels, we made every effort to not call attention to ourselves. We spoke quietly and dressed so we would blend in. We limited our interaction with people. But in Hebron that did not happen.

When we found the cave where our patriarchs' bones were buried, we were overcome with emotion. We fell to our knees and wept. We thanked God for their faithfulness to Him, and we thanked Him for His faithfulness to them. Here we stood on the brink of receiving the very promise God had given them centuries before. Our emotional outburst drew unwelcome attention and people began to realize we were foreigners.

As a result, a race of giants – who were the descendants of Anak – began to show great interest in us. They were suitably named because the word "Anak" means "long-necked." These men were formidable and towered over us at about nine feet tall. They obviously controlled the city. Even the fighting men in our midst like Shammua couldn't help but be awed by their size. The giants quickly began to quiz us – who we were, where we were from, and why we were here.

Joshua replied, "We come in peace. We are traveling through your land having come from the land of Egypt. Our ancestors inhabited your land many years ago as friends and neighbors. We have come to pay our respects to their memory."

The giant who was obviously the leader of this group said, "We know of your people. Your speech and your interest in those who are buried in this cave tell us who you are. And we have heard how your God defeated the army of Egypt and the Amalekites. We have heard that you believe your God has given you this land. And we have heard that you intend to drive us out of our land.

"You men have obviously been sent to spy out this land. We have decided to allow you to live so that you can take this message back to your people. Tell them that we are not like the Egyptians, nor are we like the

Amalekites. Your God cannot defeat us. If you attempt to cross into our land, every one of your men will die. We will enslave your women and your children. Every one of your possessions will become ours.

"Be gone from this place. If we see you again, we will kill you without any further warning. Do not test us in this. We will destroy you!"

There was no question that in our own strength we would be physically incapable of defeating the Anakim. After we departed the city, we began to discuss what we had seen and heard.

"Look at the size of those men!" Gaddiel exclaimed. "How could we ever possibly defeat them? They are not only large of stature; they are obviously warriors trained for battle. We all heard what they said. If we attempt to enter into this land, they will oppose us. And we will be defeated!"

"There is no question," Palti added. "For the most part, we are not trained warriors. We are farmers and laborers and field hands. With the exception of a few of us like Shammua, we know nothing about battle – particularly with men like these giants!"

"What about the Amalekites?" Joshua interrupted. "Our God defeated the Amalekites handily and sent them scurrying."

"True," Sethur responded. "But they were not giants like these men! Their stature and fierceness did not compare with the Anakim. We were more evenly matched with our distant cousins the Amalekites."

"Have we forgotten how our God defeated the Egyptian army – the most powerful army on earth?" I asked. "Have we forgotten how utterly He destroyed them without our even raising a hand?"

. . .

"Yes," Gaddi said. "You are right! But there is no sea near here where God can drown the Anakim. I agree with Gaddiel and Palti. We know how to make weapons, but we do not know how to wield them against warriors like the Anakim."

Igal joined in. "Perhaps there is another way into this land – or another portion that we can inhabit – and avoid entering into battle with this tribe. There must be a diplomatic solution that can avoid unnecessary bloodshed."

"Hear, hear!" Ammiel agreed. "We will simply report to Moses and the people that we need to find another path and establish our homes in areas that are not currently controlled by the Anakim. I don't believe they lived in this region when God promised the land to Abraham. If they had, He surely wouldn't have included this land in the promise. All we need to do is make a minor compromise. Don't you agree, Shammua?"

Every eye turned to Shammua. Though we all knew Joshua was being groomed by Moses to become our future leader, most of our group viewed Shammua as the leader of our band of spies.

Shammua paused for a few moments before he replied. "If our God directs us into battle with the Anakim, I will stand shoulder to shoulder with our fighting men and fight bravely. God has equipped me to be a warrior. But I have fought in battles where one side was woefully unprepared and ill-equipped to enter into battle.

"And I believe if we enter into battle with the Anakim, we will be the ones who are woefully unprepared. Therefore, I do not believe God would direct us into battle with them. I agree that He must have sent us to spy out this land in order to direct us to find a better way to enter into the land."

. . .

Immediately, those who hadn't yet voiced their opinion agreed with Shammua.

Joshua spoke up. "Obviously we have differing opinions. Caleb and I believe we should proceed as God has already directed, while the rest of you believe we should find another way. Fortunately, we have not been charged with making that decision on behalf of our people. Our commission was to explore and report – and that is what we will do. I trust the Lord will lead Moses and all of our elders to do as He leads. Let us continue on with our journey."

We walked to the Valley of Eshcol and cut down a branch with a single cluster of grapes. The grapes were so large and lush that it required two of us to carry them on a pole. We also brought pomegranates and figs.

We traveled about five hundred miles during our forty days in the land of Canaan. We didn't discover anything God hadn't already told us we would find.

The land was occupied by the Kenites, Kenizzites, Kadmonites, Hittites, Perizzites, Rephaites, Amorites, Canaanites, Girgashites, and Jebusites just like God had told Abraham over four hundred years earlier. He hadn't listed the Anakim specifically, but He had included the Rephaites who were also a race of giants. These inhabitants really posed no obstacle to us – as long as we looked down at the giants from God's perspective and not up from our perspective.

There was no question this was a good and rich land flowing with milk and honey. We were bringing back incredible fruit for our people to taste and see.

. . .

We had even seen the burial sites of our patriarchs and been reminded of the legacy of faith they had passed on to us. God had promised them, and He had promised us, that He was giving us this land. Everything we had seen during our forty days aligned with God's promise – and every detail of His promise had been accurate.

He promised us victory. He would go before us and scatter His enemies. All we needed to do was follow Him by faith. And He had repeatedly proven to us He was faithful; we simply needed to trust and obey.

Our people greeted us enthusiastically as we returned to camp in Paran. They marveled at the sight of all we carried. Our families ran to embrace us. Some had become fearful because we had been gone so long. But now we had returned – and the people were anxious to hear our report!

24

At the end of forty days they returned from spying out the land.[1]

* * *

S hammua was the first to speak. "It is indeed a magnificent country, a land flowing with milk and honey. It is everything God has promised it would be. Its fruit is better than anything we have ever seen and greater than we could ever have imagined. Look at the size of these grapes that Nahbi and Geuel are holding! And have you ever seen such luscious pomegranates and figs!"

"It is indeed a bountiful land," Shaphat added, "rich and fertile valleys surrounded by majestic hills and mounts."

"We saw the burial sites of our patriarchs Abraham, Isaac, and Jacob," Igal reported. "And we were reminded of our rich heritage as their descendants. From one has come many – wherever we have been."

. . .

This was the report our people had hoped for, and they could hardly contain their excitement. Everything the men were saying was exactly what God had promised – and in a matter of days it would belong to them!

But then the report took a dramatic turn when Gaddiel spoke. "*But ... the people living there are powerful, and their cities are large and fortified.*"[2]

"*We even saw giants there, the descendants of Anak!*"[3] Ammiel added. "The people are stronger than we are. We are like grasshoppers compared to them. If we go there, the land will swallow us up. It would be better for us if we went back to Egypt."

Palti spoke up saying, "*The Amalekites live in the Negev, and the Hittites, Jebusites, and Amorites live in the hill country. The Canaanites live along the coast of the Mediterranean Sea and along the Jordan Valley. All the people we saw were huge!*"[4]

But it was Shammua who delivered the crushing blow when he added, "*We can't go up against them! They are stronger than we are! The land we traveled through and explored will devour anyone who goes to live there.*"[5]

Shammua was a military hero. He was older and wiser. People in the crowd began to exclaim, "If Shammua says we can't go up against them, it must be true!"

I tried to reassure the crowd. "Joshua and I saw the exact same things that these other men saw. We all saw the richness of the land. And yes, we saw the size of the people and the strength of their fortifications. But what these men saw as giants, we saw as defeated foes. What they saw as obstacles that could not be overcome, we saw as opportunities for God to demonstrate His power.

.   .   .

"Don't you remember what God did at the Red Sea? It looked like we were about to be slaughtered by pharaoh and his army. And then God made a way where there appeared to be no way and defeated our enemy. *Let's go at once to take the land. We can certainly conquer it!*"[6]

All the way back to camp, Joshua and I asked ourselves: "How could the other men have seen things so differently from us? How is it they saw overwhelming defenses while we saw glaring vulnerability? How could we have such different opinions when we were all looking at the exact same things?"

But then we realized the other men were looking through the eyes of fear, and Joshua and I were looking through the eyes of faith. Eyes of fear will always look up at obstacles from man's perspective; eyes of faith will always look down at obstacles from God's perspective. Eyes of fear gaze out from under the circumstances; eyes of faith look over the circumstances in light of God's promises. Eyes of fear are blinded by the visible; eyes of faith are illuminated by the unseen assurance of God.

As the people heard our reports, they could see the leaders of the twelve tribes were divided ten to two. An eighty-three percent majority was advising that we not enter the Promised Land – at least through this path. It was an overwhelming majority – a landslide vote. Their argument was compelling. And this report was coming from men who were highly respected.

The people began to murmur. "If these men don't think the land should be entered, then who are we to disagree with them? If ten out of twelve of the men say we shouldn't enter the Promised Land, surely that is the right decision. God gave these men wisdom and the ability to think, didn't He? Walking by faith doesn't mean we do not use the wisdom God has given us. God must not have clearly seen the circumstances that await us in the Promised Land. Or perhaps that fellow Moses simply misunderstood what God said."

. . .

So, the people accepted the opinion of the majority. Our entire community began to weep. Their voices rose in a great chorus of protest against Moses and Aaron.

"If only we had died in Egypt, or even here in the wilderness!" they complained. *"Why is the Lord taking us to this country only to have us die in battle? Our wives and our little ones will be carried off as plunder! Wouldn't it be better for us to return to Egypt?"* (7) Then some of the men began to incite the crowd saying, *"Let's choose a new leader and go back to Egypt!"* (8)

Moses and Aaron fell face down on the ground before all the people. Joshua and I tore our clothing and fell on our knees. Joshua cried out, *"The land we traveled through and explored is a wonderful land! And if the Lord is pleased with us, He will bring us safely into that land and give it to us. It is a rich land flowing with milk and honey. Do not rebel against the Lord, and don't be afraid of the people of the land. They are only helpless prey to us! They have no protection, but the Lord is with us! Don't be afraid of them!"* (9)

But the whole community began to talk about stoning Joshua and me.

Just then the glorious presence of the Lord appeared before all the Israelites at the tabernacle. And the Lord said to Moses, *"How long will these people treat Me with such contempt? Will they never believe Me, even after all the miraculous signs I have done among them? I will disown them and destroy them with a plague. Then I will make you into a nation greater and mightier than they are!"*(10)

But Moses replied to God, *"What will the Egyptians think when they hear about it? They know full well the power You displayed in rescuing Your people from Egypt. Now if You destroy them, the Egyptians will send a report to the inhabitants of this land, who have already heard that You live among Your people. They know that You have appeared to Your people face to face and that Your pillar of cloud hovers over them. They know that You go before them in the pillar of cloud by day and the pillar of fire by night. Now if You slaughter all these people*

with a single blow, the nations that have heard of Your fame will say,
'The LORD was not able to bring them into the land He swore to give them, so He
killed them in the wilderness.'

"Please, LORD, prove that Your power is as great as You have claimed. For You
have said, 'The LORD is slow to anger and filled with unfailing love, forgiving
every kind of sin and rebellion. But He does not excuse the guilty. He lays the sins
of the parents upon their children; the entire family is affected – even children in
the third and fourth generations.' In keeping with Your magnificent, unfailing
love, please pardon the sins of this people, just as You have forgiven them ever
since they left Egypt." [11]

Then the Lord said, *"I will pardon them as You have requested. But as surely as*
I live, and as surely as the earth is filled with My glory, not one of these people
will ever enter that land. They have all seen My glorious presence and the miracu-
lous signs I performed both in Egypt and in the wilderness, but again and again
they have tested Me by refusing to listen to My voice. They will never even see the
land I swore to give their ancestors. None of those who have treated Me with
contempt will ever see it.

"But My servants Joshua and Caleb have a different attitude than the others. They
have remained loyal to Me, so I will bring them into the land they explored. Their
descendants will possess their full share of that land. Now turn around, and don't
go on toward the land where the Amalekites and Canaanites live. Tomorrow you
must set out for the wilderness in the direction of the Red Sea." [12]

God had repeatedly told us He was bringing us into the land and He
would defeat our enemies. He told us before we left Egypt.[13] He told us
as we were leaving Egypt.[14] He told us at Sinai before many of our
people chose to worship the golden calf.[15] And He told us again at Sinai
after the golden calf had been destroyed.[16] God had left no margin for
doubt about His intentions. He had clearly given us a promise.

. . .

The majority of the spies – and the majority of our people – had made a grave error. They were looking at God's promise to us in light of the circumstances they saw. That caused them to feel overwhelmed and discouraged, and they began to distrust God. Instead, they should have looked at our circumstances through God's promise knowing that He would use the circumstances ahead to fulfill His purpose while He fulfilled His promise. We should have learned that lesson once and for all at the Red Sea.

We were God's chosen people. We were the ones He had delivered from the bondage of Egypt so that through us He might reveal His name and His glory to the nations. We were the people with whom God had made the covenant: *"If you will obey Me and keep My covenant, you will be My own special treasure from among all the nations of the earth; for all the earth belongs to Me. And you will be to Me a kingdom of priests, My holy nation."* (17) And yet, time and again since we left Egypt, our people had forgotten God's promise, doubted His promise, or rejected His promise.

Here we were on the cusp of receiving the land God had promised us. It was everything He told us it would be. He had led us here. He had defeated our enemies along the way. He had provided for our every need. He had repeated His promise, revealed His presence, and redeemed His people. And now, on the eve of what could have been the greatest day of our lives and our history as a nation – the day we were to enter God's Promised Land – our people had chosen to reject God once again.

Turning their back on God would cost the people dearly. It wasn't God who turned us back to the wilderness, it was the people themselves because of their disbelief. Those who despised the promise of God would be kept from it. However, God in His faithfulness would preserve His promise for their children.

God had set our faces toward the Promised Land with every step in our journey, and He had prepared us for what lay ahead. But now, our faces were set back toward the wilderness – a place of judgment. My people had brought God's sentence on themselves by their very own words.

Since they placed their trust in the testimony of ten men instead of God, they were now destined to wander in the wilderness for forty years. Instead of inheriting the Promised Land, this entire generation, except for Joshua and me, would be buried in the wilderness.

* * *

25

Then the LORD said to Moses and Aaron, "How long must I put up with this wicked community and its complaints about Me?"[(1)]

* * *

As the Lord's glorious presence continued to fill the tabernacle, Moses stood before the people and said: *"'As surely as I live', declares the LORD, 'I will do to you the very things I heard you say. You will all drop dead in this wilderness! Because you complained against Me, every one of you who is twenty years old or older and was included in the census will die. You will not enter and occupy the land I swore to give you. The only exceptions will be Caleb son of Jephunneh and Joshua son of Nun.*

"'You said your children would be carried off as plunder. Well, I will bring them safely into the land, and they will enjoy what you have despised. But as for you, you will drop dead in this wilderness. And your children will be like shepherds, wandering in the wilderness for forty years. In this way, they will pay for your faithlessness, until the last of you lies dead in the wilderness.

. . .

"'Because your men explored the land for forty days, you must wander in the wilderness for forty years – a year for each day, suffering the consequences of your sins. Then you will discover what it is like to have Me for an enemy. I, the Lord, have spoken! I will certainly do these things to every member of the community who has conspired against Me. You will be destroyed here in this wilderness, and here you will die!'" (2)

When Moses finished delivering this message, the ten spies who had brought the negative report to the people were struck dead by God. Of the twelve spies, only Joshua and I remained. I grieved for these men and their families. They had become like brothers to me. I thought of the excitement we had shared six weeks ago as we began our journey to explore the land. If only they had trusted God, they would be alive today. And if only they had trusted God, today would have been a very different day for all of us.

When the people saw the ten men struck dead, they became fearful.

Many began to protest. "I did not want to turn back. I agreed with Joshua and Caleb. We need to trust God and follow Him." But their declarations were too late. Not one of them had spoken up until now. Even if they truly believed what they were saying, they had been indicted by their silence.

But still the people rose early the next morning and said, "Let's go. We realize that we have sinned, but now we are ready to enter the Land the LORD has promised." (3)

Moses looked at them incredulously. "Why are you now disobeying the Lord's orders to return to the wilderness? It won't work. Do not attempt to go up into the land now. You will only be crushed by your enemies because the Lord is not with you. When you face the Amalekites and Canaanites in battle, you will be slaughtered. The Lord will abandon you because you have abandoned the Lord." (4)

. . .

But just as the people had ignored God's promises, they now ignored Moses's warning. The majority of our men defiantly pushed ahead toward the land of Canaan. The pillar of cloud did not go before them. Neither did the Ark of the Lord's Covenant nor the tabernacle. All of that remained in camp.

Moses and Aaron, together with their families, as well as all the Levites remained in the camp. Joshua and I, our families, and some of our fellow tribesmen remained as well. Regardless of what others may do, we would obey our God.

"God does not go before them," I explained to my sons. "And if He does not go before them, they cannot prevail. If only they had believed that when God goes before us, we cannot be defeated – today would have looked very different."

As our people crossed into the land of Canaan, they were met by the Amalekites and Canaanites who came down from the hills. Their attack was swift. The ranks of our men broke quickly. Many were slaughtered and those who survived were chased out of the land.

The survivors returned to our camp defeated, dejected, and disgraced. They finally realized what their disobedience had cost them. In many respects our people had returned to a captivity of their own making – the captivity of the wilderness. They were now destined to wander in this wilderness until they died. Hope had become hopelessness because their faith had become faithlessness. And that hopelessness now settled heavily over the entire camp.

The Lord continued daily to give us instruction through Moses on how we were to act and what we were to do when we finally settled in the Promised Land. I looked at the sadness on the faces of the adults, I could see that even the instruction was a constant reminder of their fate. And their sadness and hopelessness soon gave birth to rebellion.

. . .

The ringleader was Korah, son of Izhar of the tribe of Levi. Korah was the cousin of Moses and Aaron. His father, Izhar, was the brother of Amram, the father of Moses and Aaron. The tribe of Levi was subdivided into three clans – the Gershonites, the Kohathites, and the Merari. Moses, Aaron, and Korah were all descendants of Kohath. The Kohathites were responsible for caring for and transporting the Ark of the Lord's Covenant as well as the furnishings and utensils of the tabernacle. The Ark represented God's presence wherever we went, and as a Kohathite, Korah was charged with bearing the Ark.

But Korah had a greater ambition. He decided he and his sons had as much of a birthright to the priesthood as Aaron and his sons. Korah also resented the fact his cousin Elzaphan had been chosen by Moses as the leader of the Kohathite clan. Korah was no longer content to serve simply as a "minister of the Ark" but demanded he was entitled to a position of greater authority.

Korah craftily enlisted two hundred fifty other leaders – all prominent members of our assembly – to stand with him in his rebellion. They joined him as he stood before Moses and Aaron and publicly declared, *"What right do you have to act as though you are greater than anyone else?"* (5)

Apparently Korah and the others had forgotten how God had responded to Miriam just a few months earlier when she made a similar accusation. Aaron – and most of the rest of us – remembered all too well.

I knew what Korah was really saying was, "What right do you have to act as though you are greater than I am?" Korah was not seeking position for others; he was seeking out his own interest to satisfy his own unholy ambition.

. . .

Two of the leaders he enlisted were Dathan and Abiram, the sons of Eliab, from the tribe of Reuben. He thought enlisting others to join with him – and particularly those from other tribes – would lend credence to his complaint and overshadow his own selfish motive. I knew firsthand that Dathan and Abiram were upset our tribe of Judah had been given the place of honor in camp.

They had voiced their displeasure to me on more than one occasion since Shammua's death. They felt as the firstborn of Jacob that the privilege rightly belonged to the tribe of Reuben. Shammua had kept that jealousy in check, but now there was no one within their tribe to squelch their selfish ambition.

With the Kohathites and the Reubenites camped beside one another on the south side of the tabernacle, it didn't take much for pride and selfish ambition to escalate into this rebellion against Moses. Though they were already leaders within their respective tribes and clans, they wanted even greater position and prestige.

Korah had also enlisted On, the son of Peleth, who was also from the tribe of Reuben, to join his rebellion. I had gotten to know On through Shammua. Over the years, the two men had become good friends. Shammua had become the younger man's mentor and influenced him greatly. When Shammua was stricken dead for leading the people to rebel against God, On had become very bitter against Moses … and against God.

Though I believe he resented the fact that Joshua and I survived, he also knew the great affection we had for Shammua – and he had for us. A few days before Korah declared his rebellion, On came to me. "Caleb, my spirit is in turmoil and I need to seek the ear and the wisdom of someone who will speak honestly with me. Now that Shammua is gone, I have no such friend. I believe you and Joshua are men who have the wisdom I need to hear. But Joshua is too close to Moses. Can I speak with you?"

· · ·

"You honor me, On," I replied. "I pray Jehovah God grants me the wisdom you seek."

"I am certain He will," On said.

As we sat in my tent, On confessed his feelings toward Moses and the Lord regarding Shammua's death. He attempted to justify his anger and bitterness. Then he told me about his conversations with Korah, and how he thought such a rebellion was justified.

But then he said, "But I do not have a peace that I am right. I have justified all of this in my own mind, but I still do not believe it is the right thing to do. Caleb, what would you say to me?"

On was about the age of my younger brother, Kenaz, so I decided to speak to him as I would my brother.

"On, you know I loved Shammua as I did all my brothers as we spied out the land. I looked up to Shammua for his selfless bravery and his wisdom. And I have grieved for his death – and miss him greatly. But Shammua was wrong. He gave counsel to our people to distrust and disobey God. He relied on his own understanding and discredited the promises of Jehovah God. His sin caused the death of many men in the failed attempt to enter the land of Canaan – and it will cause the rest of us to wander in this wilderness for forty years.

"If Shammua were here with us today, he would now readily admit he was wrong. His blindness to the truth led to his sin. But today he would speak as one who is not blinded – and he would admit his sin.

"Korah is blinded by his own selfish ambition. He does not seek the welfare of our people. He seeks only his own personal interest and prestige. If Shammua were here today, he would speak as one who can now see – and he would say, 'Do not pursue this wicked plan. Do not do what you think is right in your own eyes. Obey Jehovah God. Trust Him. And follow His commands and His path. Do not rebel against Him.'"

I saw the anger and bitterness disappear from On's face. God had indeed granted me favor and spoken through me to On's heart. As we sat there in my tent, he repented of his sin and sought forgiveness from God.

Afterward, he went to find Korah to tell him he was not going to be a part of the rebellion – and to counsel Korah and the others to turn from their wicked ways. Gratefully, On had ears to hear the truth of God that day ... but Korah and the others did not.

As Korah and his allies declared their rebellion, Moses threw himself face down on the ground. He immediately humbled himself before God and before the people, and agreed to let God decide what should be done. The contrast between the attitudes of Korah and Moses was a clear reminder that selfish ambition will always attempt to exalt itself, whereas surrendered ambition will always humble itself and submit to the will of the Father.

Moses rose to his feet and said to Korah and his two hundred fifty followers, "*Tomorrow morning the Lord will show us who belongs to Him and who is holy. The Lord will allow only those whom He selects to enter His own presence. Korah, you and all your followers must prepare your incense burners. Light fires in them tomorrow, and burn incense before the Lord. Then we will see whom the Lord chooses as His holy one. You have gone too far! The Lord is the one you and your followers are really revolting against!*"[6]

Moses then summoned Dathan and Abiram, the sons of Eliab, but they replied, "*We refuse to come before you! Isn't it enough that you brought us out of Egypt, a land flowing with milk and honey, to kill us here in this wilderness, and that you now treat us like your subjects? What's more, you haven't brought us*

into another land flowing with milk and honey. You haven't given us a new home-
land with fields and vineyards. We will not come." (7)

The next morning Korah and each of his followers prepared an incense burner, lit the fire, and placed incense on it. Then they all stood at the entrance of the tabernacle with Moses and Aaron. By now Korah had stirred up the entire camp against Moses and Aaron, and all the people surrounded the tabernacle entrance.

Then the glorious presence of the Lord appeared to our entire community, and the Lord said to Moses and Aaron, *"Get away from all these people so that I may instantly destroy them!"* (8)

But again, Moses and Aaron fell face down on the ground. *"O God,"* they pleaded, *"You are the God who gives breath to all creatures. Must You be angry with all the people when only one man has sinned?"* (9)

The Lord mercifully relented and said to Moses, *"Then tell all the people to get away from the tents of Korah, Dathan, and Abiram."* (10)

So Moses got up and rushed over to the tents of Korah, Dathan, and Abiram, followed by the elders of Israel. *"Quick!"* he told the people. *"Get away from the tents of these wicked men, and don't touch anything that belongs to them. If you do, you will be destroyed for their sins."* (11) So all the people stood back from the tents of Korah, Dathan, and Abiram.

Moses then said, *"This is how you will know that the Lord has sent me to do all these things that I have done – for I have not done them on my own. If these men die a natural death, or if nothing unusual happens, then the Lord has not sent me. But if the Lord does something entirely new and the ground opens its mouth and swallows them and all their belongings, and they go down alive into the grave, then you will know that these men have shown contempt for the Lord."* (12)

· · ·

Moses had hardly finished speaking when the ground shook and suddenly split open beneath the men. The earth swallowed them, along with their families and those who were standing with them and everything they owned. They were taken alive into their grave. The earth closed over them, and they all vanished from among the people of Israel.

The people around them fled when they heard their screams. *"The earth will swallow us, too!"* (13) they cried. Then fire blazed forth from the Lord and burned up the two hundred fifty men who were offering incense.

After witnessing the Lord's judgment, I thought my people would know not to complain against the Lord's anointed. But the very next morning a crowd began muttering against Moses and Aaron, saying, *"You have killed the Lord's people!"* (14) Just then the cloud covered the tabernacle and the glorious presence of the Lord appeared.

Moses and Aaron came and stood in front of the tabernacle, and the Lord said to Moses, *"Get away from all these people so that I can instantly destroy them!"* (15) But just as they had done the two previous days, Moses and Aaron again fell prostrate on the ground before the Lord.

Moses turned to Aaron and said, *"Quick, take an incense burner and place burning coals on it from the altar. Lay incense on it, and carry it out among the people to purify them and cover their sin before the Lord. The Lord's anger is blazing against them – a plague has already begun."* (16)

Aaron did as Moses instructed and ran out among the people, but the plague had already begun. Aaron burned the incense to purify the people. He stood between the dead and the living, and the plague stopped. But fourteen thousand, seven hundred people died in that plague, in addition to those who had died in the affair involving Korah, Dathan, and Abiram.

. . .

When the plague stopped, Aaron returned to Moses's side at the entrance of the tabernacle.

26

"I will finally put an end to the people's murmuring and complaining against you."[1]

* * *

The days, weeks, and months that followed were characterized by continuing reminders of the sinful and rebellious nature of our people. We may have been chosen by God – but, all too often, we chose to rebel against Him, His commands, and His servants.

Despite the judgment our people had experienced and witnessed as a result of rebellion against Moses and Aaron, some continued to rebel. Once and for all God determined to put an end to the controversy over who was to serve as His chosen priest on behalf of His people.

He instructed Moses to take the staff of the leader of each of our twelve ancestral tribes, together with Aaron's staff, representing the tribe of Levi. At God's direction, he placed the thirteen staffs in the tabernacle overnight. God declared that buds would sprout from the staff belonging to the man whom He had chosen to serve as priest.

. . .

As my sons and I watched the staffs being presented, I said to them, "All of these staffs were at one time the branch of a tree. Each of them was cut from the tree and is now a dry, lifeless stick. A dried, separated branch doesn't blossom; it can't bear fruit. Only a living branch, a branch connected to the tree, can blossom and bear fruit.

"All of these staffs are the same. Oh yes, some are shorter or longer, and some are thinner or thicker. They all came from different trees – different woods – so they all have a slightly different color and appearance. But they have all been turned into staffs by their masters. They all have been made for the same purpose – their masters' purpose."

That night as the staffs lay in the presence of God at the feet of His covenant, the one He chose – Aaron's staff – began to sprout and blossom and bear fruit. We all knew the fruit had been produced by God.

But we were amazed to see sprouts, blossoms, and almonds all at the same time on Aaron's staff. Even a living branch can only produce one thing at a time. But God was enabling those things to grow simultaneously as a reminder that He accomplishes His work in His way through the one He chooses. It would be His choice, not ours. And it would be His work, not ours.

This seemed to put the issue to rest. But some of our people overreacted and instead of displaying a reverent fear of God, they began to demonstrate an unhealthy fear of Him. They thought that anyone who came close to the tabernacle would be destroyed. His presence should have been a source of confidence; but for those who had yet to understand what it meant to be the people of God, it became a cause for alarm.

God instructed Moses to place the budding staff inside the Ark as a warning to any future rebels. The fruit remained on it as a lasting reminder of the work of God. And the barren staffs of the other tribal leaders served as a further reminder of each one's own inadequacy apart from Jehovah God.

* * *

We had now been following the pillar of cloud in the wilderness for many years. It was again early spring. The Lord led us to camp at Kadesh in the wilderness of Zin.

We longed to be in the Promised Land, but we knew we were only a little more than halfway through our forty-year exile. Our children were becoming adults. Babies were being born. And many who had begun the journey were being buried along the way.

Rebecca and I had seen our children grow in stature and maturity. My sons were becoming men of faith with hearts to follow and honor God. Their lives had become more shaped by their time wandering in the wilderness than by the slavery of Egypt. Memories of Egypt were fading – particularly for our younger children.

Our sons Iru, Elah, and Naam were now married with children of their own. Our daughters-in-law had become daughters to us – particularly to Rebecca. Our growing family now included twelve grandchildren. A generation was now being raised that never knew Egypt – a generation that had only ever known manna.

Our journey was full of joys and sorrows. Earlier in the week, Moses's and Aaron's sister Miriam died. Except for the incident in Hazeroth when jealousy had clouded her judgment, Miriam had been a constant source of encouragement to Moses. She had often spoken truth to him and Aaron when they needed it. Moses and Aaron were now in mourning and it didn't appear the pillar of cloud would lead us to leave anytime soon.

. . .

Since we were camped near a river, I took my two oldest grandsons to catch fish for that evening's dinner. Iru had chosen to name his firstborn son – my oldest grandson – Jephunneh, after my father. My father would have been proud of his namesake for his maturity, his abilities, and his walk with God.

Jephunneh was becoming a skilled fisherman despite not being able to fish that often. When we fished together, I knew we would return with a successful catch. Today was no exception. We had been at the riverbank for several hours when I saw Iru running toward me.

"Father," he gasped, "you need to come back to camp. Mother has fallen ill. One of the priests is attending to her. But we must get back quickly!"

When we arrived at the tent, my daughter, Achsah, met me with tears in her eyes. Before she spoke a word, I already knew the news. Rebecca was dead.

That morning when I left for the river, she had been fine. It was like any other day here in the wilderness. I never imagined what this day would bring. If I had known, I never would have left her side. I wasn't there to help her, to comfort her … or to say goodbye.

For thirty-six years we had stood side by side. For thirty-six years she had been my companion, my strength, my friend, and my helpmate. I thought back to my trips to the palace bakery just to get a glimpse of her. I thought about her knowing smile that seldom left her lips. I thought of her unwavering strength through every moment of our marriage. And I wept.

We buried Rebecca's body outside of camp later that afternoon before sunset. The fish that my grandsons and I had caught, together with food brought by our friends, became the condolence meal. For the next seven days mourners remained outside of our tent. Prayers were offered continually.

Moses and Aaron came to see me to express their condolences – just as Rebecca and I had done to them just a few days earlier. Life was surreal. I felt like I was outside of my body watching what was going on around me. I thought that at any moment I would awaken, and Rebecca would be right there beside me. But alas, that would not occur.

After seven days passed, the pillar of cloud ascended from the tabernacle as a sign that we were to continue our journey. Only part of me made the journey with my family and my people that day. Part of me remained by Rebecca's side. I now better understood why my father died just seven days after my mother.

But for the sake of my sons, my daughter, their families, and our tribe, I turned toward the cloud and followed. God had told me I would see the land of His promise. I always thought Rebecca would be by my side – but if she couldn't be by my side, she would be in my heart.

After several days of travel without encountering any water, our people began to complain and rebel. Many had not yet been born or were very young when our people had experienced the miracle at Meribah-Massah in the valley of Rephidim. They did not remember how God had provided water from a rock.

And yet, some of them sounded just like their parents. They murmured, they complained, they rebelled, and they blamed Moses. And just like their parents, they complained against God with bitterness instead of calling upon God for His provision. Now another place in the wilderness would be called Meribah (the place of arguing) – this one Meribah-Kadesh.

· · ·

The people came to Moses and said, "*If only we had died in the Lord's presence with our brothers! Why have you brought the congregation of the Lord's people into this wilderness to die, along with all our livestock? Why did you bring us here to this terrible place? This land has no grain, no figs, no grapes, no pomegranates, and no water to drink!*"[2]

Moses and Aaron turned away from the people and went to the entrance of the tabernacle, where they fell face down on the ground. Then the Lord appeared to them saying, "*Moses, you and Aaron must take the staff and assemble the entire community. As the people watch, speak to the rock over there, and it will pour out its water. You will provide enough water from the rock to satisfy the whole community and their livestock.*" [3]

Moses did as God directed. He took the budding staff from the Ark where it was kept before the Lord. He and Aaron summoned the people to come and gather at the rock God had shown them. "*Listen, you rebels!*" Moses shouted. "*Must we bring you water from this rock?*" [4]

But Moses did not follow the rest of God's instructions. Whether it was his grief over Miriam or his anger about the continuing complaints of our people – or both – Moses raised his hand and struck the rock twice with the staff. Though Moses had disobeyed God, the Lord still permitted water to gush out of the rock for hours, just as it had at Meribah-Massah. The entire community and all our livestock drank until they were satisfied.

But the Lord called Moses aside and said to him, "*Because you did not trust Me enough to demonstrate My holiness to the people of Israel, and did not do as I told you, you will not lead them into the land I am giving them!*" [5]

I was close enough to hear this exchange. I couldn't help but wonder what Moses had done that warranted such a severe punishment. It wasn't until several days later I was able to ask Moses about it.

. . .

Moses told me, "When I asked the people, 'Must we bring you water from this rock?' I kept the attention of the people on Aaron and me, as if we were the ones providing the people with water. I did not turn their attention to God. God intended to show His people that even the rocks obeyed Him, even when His people did not.

"God told me to speak to the rock, but instead I chose to speak to the people and strike the rock. My actions demonstrated I thought the word of God by itself would be insufficient to meet the need and I took matters into my own hands."

Moses went on to explain that God had called him to a place of leadership so He could teach the people to walk by faith, hope, and humility. Moses and Aaron both violated that commission that day through their actions. They had pointed people to the same agitation, anxiety, and anger that they themselves had demonstrated.

"Caleb," Moses said, "God's call to leadership brings with it a calling to greater accountability."

I couldn't help but feel sad for Moses. I had seen him endure more abuse than any leader – or any person – should have to endure. And now God had told him he would not be entering into the land of promise. I began to think of other faithful ones who would not see God's promise fulfilled.

I thought of my dear Rebecca, my father, my mother – and now Moses. But perhaps they had run their races and already finished well. My sadness diminished ever so slightly. I was beginning to see these events through eyes of hope – be it ever so dimly. I would trust God for He always knows best. Wherever He chose to lead me, I would follow.

* * *

27

Moses sent ambassadors to the king of Edom.[1]

* * *

My father taught me as a lad that Jacob, son of Isaac, was renamed "Israel" by God at the Jabbok River when he wrestled with Him and the Lord blessed him. Jacob's twin brother, Esau, was renamed "Edom" when he traded his birthright to Jacob for a meal of red meat stew. Israel had subsequently usurped Edom's blessing from their father through deception. The people of Edom and our people of Israel are the descendants of those twin brothers.

It had been over three hundred years since our two families had last seen one another in the land of Edom. That reunion had taken place immediately following Jacob's renaming at the Jabbok River. On that occasion, Edom had received his brother, Israel, with affection and with grace. Since that time the people of Edom had dwelt in this land and established their dominion over it.

. . .

We, on the other hand, had lived as strangers and slaves in a foreign land, and now we were wanderers through the wilderness. The only land to which we could lay claim, based on the promise God had given us, was still before us inhabited by others. So far, the people who had been deceived were faring much better than those of us who had received the blessing. The question was, would Edom again be gracious to Israel?

When we arrived at the borders of Edom, Moses sent Joshua and me as ambassadors to carry a word of greeting to our brothers. Though God Himself was leading us on our journey, Moses still thought it proper and wise to seek permission from the king of Edom to travel through their land. The Edomites knew the God of their fathers, Abraham and Isaac, had delivered us, had defeated our enemies, and was leading us through the wilderness. God's deliverance of us had become notorious!

But they also knew of the routing our people received at the hands of the Canaanites and the Amalekites when we had attempted to enter the Promised Land in defiance of God's command. The sin of our people had caused us to be viewed with contempt by our enemies – and perhaps, even our brothers, the Edomites.

This was the message that we carried to the king of Edom:

"This is what your relatives, the people of Israel, say: You know all the hardships we have been through. Our ancestors went down to Egypt, and we lived there a long time, and we and our ancestors were brutally mistreated by the Egyptians. But when we cried out to the Lord, He heard us and sent an angel who brought us out of Egypt. Now we are camped on the border of your land. Please let us travel through your land. We will be careful not to go through your fields and vineyards. We won't even drink water from your wells. We will stay on the king's road and never leave it until we have passed through your territory." [(2)]

We were seeking permission to continue our travel on the king's road. This road was the caravan route from Egypt through the Sinai Peninsula into the eastern lands of the Edomites, the Moabites and the Ammonites, and the eastern borders of the Mediterranean Sea. It was the most direct route from here into the land to which God was leading us.

But the king of Edom denied us entry saying, *"Stay out of my land! Or I will meet you with an army!"* [(3)] With that, he sent Joshua and me back to Moses under the watchful eye of his imposing warriors to demonstrate his resolve.

As we journeyed back, we wondered how the Lord would respond to this affront. Would God choose to destroy them? If so, what means would He use? But when we reported the king's response to Moses, God made it clear that He was choosing not to destroy the Edomites that day. He would lead us in a different direction.

We knew He must have a sovereign purpose for doing so. We did not doubt our God was able to lead us through the land of the Edomites, but He was choosing not to do so. And it had nothing to do with the size or might of the Edomite army.

God led us from there to the base of Mount Hor. It was there the Lord said to Moses and Aaron, *"The time has come for Aaron to join his ancestors in death. He will not enter the land I am giving the people of Israel, because the two of you rebelled against My instructions concerning the water at Meribah. Now take Aaron and his son Eleazar up Mount Hor. There you will remove Aaron's priestly garments and put them on Eleazar, his son. Aaron will die there and join his ancestors."* [(4)]

Aaron had long been preparing Eleazar for this day. He had taught him through the words of God as conveyed through Moses. He had taught him through his actions – both the good and the bad. And he had taught him by allowing Eleazar to assume greater responsibility along the way.

. . .

So, Moses removed the priestly garments from Aaron and put them on Eleazar. The transition was now complete. Aaron died peacefully and was buried on the summit of the mount.

Across the centuries from the time of Abraham and Sarah, God had shown us He would raise up growing numbers of men, women, and children to be a part of the story of His glory. The cast of characters would continuously change, but God's plan would be constant. It is God who chooses the cast of characters. It is God who makes the assignments. And it is He who determines the length of our performance.

It was God's time in the season of His story and in the life of Aaron. Aaron was far from perfect in his obedience to God. In fact, it was because of his disobedience that God prevented him from entering the Promised Land with the people. But Aaron had carried the mantle of leadership of God's people with his brother Moses.

Though we could all quickly enumerate his failures, we could not disregard his faithfulness. He had been our high priest interceding for us before God. On many occasions he had interceded for God's grace and mercy on our behalf. He was now over one hundred twenty years old. Physically and emotionally, he was tired.

He had been faithful to train the leadership that would take his place. And now it was time for him to step from this earthly assignment into eternal peace. Our people would grieve his passing, but he had entered into a place far greater than the Promised Land. He had entered into the kingdom of heaven.

As I reflected on Aaron's passing, I took my sons aside and told them, "In the days ahead, there will continue to be many more transitions in leadership. Already the mantle of leadership is being transferred to you and your generation. Be mindful of three important truths as you walk through those transitions.

- "We are not called to make our own assignments; we are called to follow Jehovah God. Do not go anywhere He is not leading you; and do not stay anywhere once He has led you to leave.

- "Be faithful to carry out all He has set before you, including the preparation of those He places in your path to continue the work.

- "Hold onto the garment of service He has clothed you in lightly. The garments do not belong to you, they are His. He has placed them on you for this season, but in His time, you must be prepared to relinquish them to His next servant."

We departed from Mount Hor and journeyed to the Negev. The Negev is the southern desert wilderness that divided the land of Canaan from the Sinai Peninsula. This was where the eleven other spies and I had journeyed when we explored the Promised Land over thirty years earlier.

There was a city by the name of Arad just north of the Negev. It marked the southern boundary of Canaan. The men of Arad had been part of the force that defeated our people decades earlier in the errant attempt to enter the Promised Land in disobedience to God. They had sent our people running in retreat that day. That defeat had actually taken place outside the city of what is now known as Hormah.

The Canaanite king of Arad heard we were approaching on the road to Atharim and had assembled his men in the Negev to attack us. They still remembered and celebrated the sweet victory they had enjoyed over our people. At the time, they had heard of our people and how our God had delivered us from Egypt. They had heard of the defeat of the Egyptian army at the hand of our God. They knew that their Amalekite brothers had experienced defeat at our hands on the day when Aaron and Hur had upheld Moses's raised arms.

. . .

So imagine their relief and their elation when they routed our people that day at Hormah. They had determined that the gods of the Canaanites must be greater than the God of Israel. It had been an easy victory. It had taken little effort on the part of the Canaanites.

The king of Arad had been a boy when that battle took place. He, like most of the men now under his command, had heard the story retold time and again about how their armies had crushed these upstarts wandering in the wilderness along with their God. A few of the men who had been present that day were a part of this group now gathered in the Negev. And as the Aradites heard we were again headed in their direction, I'm sure they were probably looking forward to another victory.

Also, defeating us would provide a great opportunity for the king of Arad to make a name for himself. No longer would people speak of his father's victory. Now they would speak of his! His arrogance and that of his fighting men was a lot like the arrogance our people had demonstrated when they thought they could defeat an army in disobedience to God.

As a matter of fact, the Aradites surprised us in their initial attack and took some of our people as prisoners. But this time, we were not going to attempt to fight them on our own. We called out to God saying, *"If You will help us conquer these people, we will completely destroy all their towns."* (5)

The Lord heard our cry, and He went before us. The Aradites had no idea that God hadn't gone before our people the first time; but they were about to experience the mighty hand of the Lord God Jehovah. God gave us an overwhelming victory that day. It was victory so complete that the Aradite army and their cities were utterly destroyed. That's why the area came to be known as Hormah, which means "complete destruction."

Our people called this victory the lesson of Hormah. The first time, without God going before us, our people had been defeated. The second time, with God leading us, our enemy had been destroyed. The lesson we learned was that apart from our God, we are at the mercy of our enemies. We will experience defeat, ridicule, and destruction.

But, we had learned there is no enemy God is not able to destroy. He will give us victory over any and every enemy we encounter if we will walk with Him – in obedience to Him, by His side, following His steps. And that which God defeats, He utterly destroys!

I prayed we would always remember the lesson of Hormah!

* * *

28

But the people grew impatient with the long journey, and they began to speak against God and Moses.[1]

* * *

The pillar of cloud led us away from Hormah along the road south to the Red Sea, which would take us around the Rift Valley. We should have been heading north, but we were taking a significant detour in order to avoid the land of Edom.

But when my people realized how much extra travel this detour required, they began to grow impatient and grumble. It started with comments about those "inconsiderate" Edomites. "Who do those Edomites think they are by not allowing us to travel through their land? Don't they realize we are the favored children of Isaac? How dare they treat us this way!"

I also heard some in the crowd say, "Why didn't God just destroy them like He did the Aradites? Why did He bow to their demands? Is God not greater than the Edomite king?"

· · ·

Then they began to complain more loudly against God and Moses saying, *"Why have you brought us out of Egypt to die here in the wilderness? There is nothing to eat here and nothing to drink. And we hate this horrible manna!"* [(2)]

By the time we stopped that night, the people were literally shouting their complaints and shaking their fists against Jehovah God. Even some within my tribe were doing so. I attempted, without success, to calm them down.

Suddenly, I heard a scream. It was quickly followed by another scream, and then another. As I went to investigate, I found our camps were being overrun with poisonous snakes. People were being bitten and dying. Shouts were coming from throughout the camp … but they soon turned to wails of grief.

We all began to realize the snakes were God's punishment for the sin of our people. The issue that day didn't have anything to do with manna, or the wilderness, or even the Edomites; it had to do with the heart condition of our people.

When would we learn that other people or our circumstances could not "make" us angry or agitated or bitter? They could not "make" us sin. The anger, the bitterness, and the agitation were there long before we encountered these people or circumstances.

The wilderness was and always had been infested with snakes. To this point, for almost forty years God had protected our people from them, but on this day, He allowed the snakes to invade our camp. It wasn't so much that He "sent" the snakes; rather, He withdrew His protective hand from around us.

I also noticed the snakes did not appear everywhere. There were no snakes in or immediately surrounding my family's campsite, for example – nor in the campsites of other families who had not joined in the complaints. The appearance of the snakes was selective, just as the plagues had been in Egypt. The snakes attacked only those who had spoken against God, just as the plagues had only blighted the Egyptians.

God's plan here was for cleansing and redemption. Yes, God would not tolerate our people's sin, and the price of their sin was death; but God made a way in the wilderness for them to be cleansed – He made a way for the redemption of their sin.

The people begged Moses to call out to God saying, *"We have sinned by speaking against the Lord and against you. Pray that the Lord will take away the snakes."*[3]

In response, God instructed Moses to make a bronze snake and lift it up on a pole above the people. He told the people that those who turned toward it and looked upon it would recover.

I have to admit, I didn't think that plan made much sense. It was too simple! All the people had to do was look at the bronze snake. They didn't have to go through protracted acts of contrition or a healing ritual; all they had to do was turn their gaze toward the bronze snake on the pole, believing God would forgive them. But many died because they wouldn't turn to look. It just seemed too good to be true!

But those who did look at the bronze snake received forgiveness. I hoped they had also repented of what was in their hearts. But that remained to be seen.

I couldn't help but wonder if God had permitted the detour in our journey to surface the dross in our hearts. He was preparing us to enter His Promised Land. Perhaps the detour was so we might experience the cleansing, the healing, and the forgiveness we needed beforehand.

· · ·

We remained camped in that place so our families could bury their dead and grieve their loss. But we never saw any more snakes in the camp.

Eventually the Lord led us to continue our journey around the land of Edom. We were soon approaching the edge of the Promised Land. Despite the Edomites' refusal to permit us passage, God was leading us where we needed to go. Another lesson God taught us through the detour was the enemy may sometimes cause us to change course, but he can never prevent us from arriving where God intends. Our God is sovereign even in the midst of detours.

Along the way, we stopped to refill our water supplies at a place called Oboth. God knew we would need those supplies for the long journey ahead through a dry and parched land.

But six days later when we arrived at a place called Beer, all our water supply was exhausted. Miraculously, for the first time in almost forty years when our water supply ran out, not one person in the camp complained!

Our people looked to the Lord God Jehovah to see how He would provide. As a matter of fact, we broke out in song! We trusted Jehovah God would supply ... and He didn't disappoint!

God instructed me and the remainder of our seventy elders to place our staffs in the ground. We were all surprised He did not have Moses strike the rock or even speak to it. As a matter of fact, He didn't even work through Moses for this miracle. He worked through our group of elders. As we placed our staffs in the ground, water sprang forth. And there was more than enough for everyone, including our animals.

This was another lesson from our detour. Though God rarely meets similar needs in the same way, He always meets the need – and in ways that bring Him glory. When we pray according to God's will, He hears us and He answers. And as He answered that day in Beer, our people responded with joy and thankfulness!

The detour around the land of Edom finally ended with our crossing from the eastern wilderness into the valley of Moab.

From the beginning of our journey, God had given us a promise: *"For My angel will go before you and bring you into the land of the Amorites, Hittites, Perizzites, Canaanites, Hivites, and Jebusites, so you may live there. And I will destroy them."* [(4)] We had now arrived at the land of the Amorites!

Again, Moses sent Joshua and me out as ambassadors. We approached the Amorites as gentlemen. We did not swagger or address them with arrogance. Though we had the assurance of victory from God, we brought a peaceable message to King Sihon of the Amorites:

"Let us travel through your land. We will be careful not to go through your fields and vineyards. We won't even drink water from your wells. We will stay on the king's road until we have passed through your territory." [(5)]

But King Sihon refused to let us cross into his territory. He was well aware of how the Canaanites had defeated us almost forty years before, and he knew that more recently the king of Edom had refused us passage through his land. He had no inclination to grant us passage through his land, either.

He mobilized his entire army and dispatched them in an unprovoked attack against us near the city of Jahaz. But King Sihon made the same miscalculation the king of Arad had made. He failed to factor in that Jehovah God was going before us, and this time, He had no intention of taking a detour.

· · ·

Joshua led us into battle and God went before us. He gave us steps that were sure. He provided us with strength that was unmatched. And He granted us victory that was complete. We slaughtered the Amorites and occupied their land from the Arnon River to the Jabbok River.

Moses reminded us that the first land God was giving us included the place where our patriarch Jacob wrestled with God – the Jabbok River – where God changed his name to Israel and blessed him. That same blessing was now continuing to us, his descendants, over three hundred years later. The victory God had given us this day had put us in possession of the land; but it was the promise that God gave Jacob those many years before that assured us of this victory.

God did not lead us to cross the border into the land of the Ammonites that day. Their land was not a part of His promise to us. And therein was another important lesson for us: we were assured we would possess *all* of the land within the boundaries of His promise, but we must never step beyond the boundaries of His promise.

Later, I realized all the land God promised us was currently in the hands of the Amorites, Hittites, Perizzites, Canaanites, Hivites, and Jebusites – the nations that were to be driven out.

The land God was now giving us had at one time been possessed by the Moabites. But God had told us we could never possess any land belonging to Moab, the descendants of our patriarch Abraham's nephew, Lot. God was honoring the promise Abraham had made to Lot. Since He wanted us to have this particular portion of land, though, God allowed the Amorites to take it from Moab.

In essence they had become temporary caretakers of the land for us – until it was God's time for us to possess it. It was a reminder that God accomplishes His purpose according to His promise in His time, and it will never violate His Word.

. . .

Though our journey was far from over, we began to inhabit the land of God's promise that day. There were still many miles to go and many battles yet to be fought. There was still much land to be possessed and obstacles to overcome. But through that victory over the Amorites, God had reaffirmed His promise to us.

The next day, God led us to march up the road to Bashan. Og was the name of the Amorite king who ruled the city of Bashan. Og had heard about the defeat of Sihon, king of Heshbon, but he was not deterred. Og was one of the last of the race of giants that had inhabited this land since before the days of Abraham.

This whole region of Bashan, Gilead, and Argob was called the land of giants. These were the people we saw when we spied out the land. Og was somewhere between twelve and thirteen feet tall! It was because of this king and people like him that our people had been afraid to enter the Promised Land. And now he was going to be one of the first enemies we would face!

Though Og was head and shoulders over the rest of his army, most of them were head and shoulders over the rest of us. When Og and his army attacked, there was a moment when Moses thought to himself, "There is no way we can defeat these men!"

But then he turned to God and the Lord said, "*Do not be afraid of him, for I have handed him over to you, along with all his people and his land. Do the same to him as you did to King Sihon of the Amorites, who ruled in Heshbon.*"[6] It was God's assurance we would not just defeat Og, we would utterly destroy him.

And not a single survivor remained! God gave us complete victory that day with few casualties on our part. He showed us there was no giant too tall or too strong for Him to overcome and that we would defeat if we followed Him!

As we were leaving the city of Bashan, my sons and I went to the place Og used to live. We found his iron bed, which was more than thirteen feet long and six feet wide. We took that bed and brought it back to our camp. We carried it with us everywhere we went.

The bed served as a reminder that there is no enemy too big for God to defeat! Many times, we had been so fearful looking up at the giants that we had forgotten how powerful our God is. But He faithfully reminded us He would help us defeat whatever giants we encountered for His glory!

29

"O Lord, You are the God who gives breath to all creatures. Please appoint a new man as leader for the community. Give them someone who will guide them wherever they go...."[1]

* * *

M oses had experienced personal loss in the wilderness just like the rest of us. Not only had his sister and brother died, so had his wife. He had continued on, like we all had, but there was a joy absent from his life these days.

His two sons – Gershom and Eliezer – had also died in the wilderness. Both were adults when God declared that all over twenty years of age, except Joshua and me, would perish in the wilderness. God had not made an exception for Moses's sons. Gershom was one of the men carrying the Ark of the Lord's Covenant when we went into battle with King Sihon near Jahaz. He was fatally wounded by an Amorite arrow and perished on the battlefield.

. . .

Similarly, Eliezer was one of the few men killed in the battle against King Og and his forces. Some of Og's warriors had attempted to seize the Ark early in the battle. The contingent of the Kohathite clan carrying and protecting the Ark immediately rose to its defense. God gave them swift victory and all of Og's warriors were slain, but not before an Amorite sword had cut down Eliezer as he bravely fought.

Moses also knew that his own body would remain in the wilderness. God had told him at the waters of Meribah that he would not lead the people into the Promised Land. Now as the time approached, God prompted him to make preparations for the remainder of us to enter into the land without him. One of those preparations was the selection of a new leader.

The responsibility of high priest had already passed from Aaron to his son Eleazar; and God had made it clear that Phinehas would follow his father Eleazar when that time arrived. Aaron's descendants had been chosen by God to serve Him permanently as priests, and the Lord had declared the balance of the tribe of Levi would continue to assist Aaron's descendants in that task.

That meant that Moses's descendants were to serve in a subordinate role to Aaron's descendants. Aaron, the one who had given in to the pressure from the people at Sinai and crafted the golden calf. Aaron, the one who had on more than one occasion taken the "safe" posture of going along with the crowd. His descendants would forever be in a position of authority over the descendants of Moses as a part of the Kohathite clan.

It was not uncommon for positions of leadership and privilege to pass within a family from one generation to the next. But Moses knew God was the leader of our people. We were His people and He would select His chosen leader to succeed Moses. And to Moses's credit, he made no effort to proffer a member of his family to succeed himself. Moses, as he often did, demonstrated a humility and a self-denial rarely seen among leaders. Moses was never about building a kingdom for himself or his family – he was about serving the Lord God Jehovah.

. . .

Moses was a man who sought the counsel of God and obeyed His command. It was ironic that he was not leading the people into the Promised Land because of a rare instance of disobedience. But I also believe it was because Moses had completed the assignment God had for him, and now God was allowing him to enter into his rest and reward.

God had long been at work leading Moses to prepare Joshua to be our next leader. For most, if not all, of our forty years in the wilderness, Joshua had served as Moses's understudy and assistant. Moses had kept him at his side so he could watch and observe and learn.

Moses did as God instructed and transferred leadership to Joshua. He set him apart before Eleazar and our whole community by laying hands on him and blessing him. Then he publicly acknowledged Joshua's elevation to this position of authority, making sure everyone was aware. Next, he charged him with the responsibility of leading the people. In essence, Moses stepped aside so we would clearly see Joshua as our leader.

The Lord directed that from this day forward: *"When direction from the LORD is needed, Joshua will stand before Eleazar the priest, who will determine My will by means of sacred lots. This is how Joshua and the rest of the community of Israel will discover what they should do."*[2]

I knew better than most how God had uniquely prepared and divinely appointed Joshua to govern our nation and lead us to conquer the land. Joshua had received great training under Moses and had successfully completed forty years of experience in leading our people in his subordinate position.

Joshua had been selected by God and was filled with His Spirit; and yet God made it clear that Joshua was to do nothing without first asking for and receiving the Lord's counsel. God knew it could be tempting for Joshua, either in his haste or in his own self-confidence, to make decisions without first seeking God.

Joshua knew God would decide the course of action to be taken and would show him the beginning point, the stepping off point, and the direction to go. And God would direct the execution of His plan. Nothing would be left to chance.

But though Moses had stood face to face before the Lord, Joshua was to stand before the high priest Eleazar. Though God would not hide His will from Joshua, He would reveal it through the high priest by means of sacred lots known as the Urim (meaning "light") and the Thummim (meaning "truth"). According to God's instruction, the Urim and Thummim were inserted into the pocket of the breastplate worn by the high priest. That way, they were carried over his heart as he went before the Lord in the Holy Place. God had said the high priest *"will always carry the objects used to determine the LORD's will for His people whenever he goes in before the LORD."*[3]

The Urim and Thummim were used to determine the will of God when His direction was not clearly understood. Each was marked to indicate "yes" and "no." Then, when thrown, if they both came up "yes" or both came up "no," that was an indication of God's will for that situation. God would determine the outcome.

Joshua was not chosen by God for his abilities; he was chosen for his availability and willingness to be led by God. He would not accomplish anything because of his greatness; anything accomplished would be due to the greatness and the goodness of God.

It was time for Joshua to lead us the rest of the way of our journey, walking boldly and confidently in God's truth. Here was a leader I could follow, without question, as we went forth to conquer the enemies before us and possess the land that was promised to us!

It was hard to believe the time we had been waiting for so long was almost here. Every adult who was living when our people refused to follow God into the Promised Land – with the exception of Moses, Joshua and myself – were now dead. Their bodies were buried in sites throughout the wilderness. We had borne the grief and the sorrow. The elders of our people were now those who had been children when we left Egypt – like my sons and daughter. But the greatest number of our people were those who had been born in the wilderness these past forty years – like my grandchildren and great-grandchildren.

A whole new generation was preparing to enter into the land. And a whole new generation of leaders was now being assembled to assist Joshua and Eleazar in determining how the land would be divided among our people. In many ways, this new group replaced our group of twelve who had been sent to spy out the land over thirty-eight years ago.

But unlike our original group that was chosen by Moses, this group was chosen and appointed by God. Moses had endeavored to choose wisely. He had chosen based on everything he could observe about the men on the outside. But God could see into each man's heart. And this time, there would be no rebellion. They – and we – were going to follow our God in obedience to His commands and trusting His promises.

By God's merciful grace, He chose me to represent our tribe of Judah on this group, as well. I was the only original member since Joshua was now the leader of our people. Our responsibility had also now been significantly narrowed. We would not be responsible to spy out the land. Rather, we would assist Joshua and Eleazar in assuring the land was being divided in accordance with the Lord's instructions.

·   ·   ·

There would be only ten members of the group this time. The tribes of Reuben and Gad had recently chosen to remain on the east side of the Jordan and inhabit land outside the borders of the Promised Land. Therefore, they would not have a say in the apportionment of the Promised Land and were not members of the group.

And though some of the clans of the tribe of Manasseh had chosen to do the same, the remainder had decided to inhabit God's Promised Land. A member was chosen to represent the half of that tribe that would be crossing into the land.

None of the men chosen had any direct family connection to those who had served as spies except me. Those original men had been men of prestige and position, and so were their families. But not only did those men die in the wilderness due to their faithlessness, their immediate descendants were also divested of their right to serve in any leadership capacity. It was another reminder of what God had said about the sins of the fathers having implications on future generations.

This group of men had been groomed in the wilderness for this place of service. The other members of the group and the tribes they represented were:

- Shemuel, son of Ammihud, of the tribe of Simeon,
- Elidad, son of Kislon, of the tribe of Benjamin,
- Bukki, son of Jogli, of the tribe of Dan,
- Hanniel, son of Ephod, of the tribe of Manasseh,
- Kemuel, son of Shiphtan, of the tribe of Ephraim,
- Elizaphan, son of Parnach, of the tribe of Zebulun,
- Paltiel, son of Azzan, of the tribe of Issachar,
- Ahihud, son of Shelomi, of the tribe of Asher, and
- Pedahel, son of Ammihud, of the tribe of Naphtali.

These men, like our previous group of twelve, had been chosen for a specific task in accordance with His purpose. Both groups were uniquely equipped and uniquely gifted. But the members of our first group had been known primarily for our personal and individual achievements – our strengths and successes.

This new group was known more for who we were in our relationship with God. Most in the original group became disoriented by their own wisdom and understanding. Prayerfully, this new group of leaders was prepared to seek and follow God's wisdom and His direction.

30

These are the words that Moses spoke to all the people of Israel while they were in the wilderness east of the Jordan River.[1]

*** * ***

We were camped in the Jordan Valley on the east side of the Jordan River. All that remained of our journey was to cross the river and enter the land of God's promise. For eighty years I had heard God's promise. For the last half of my life I had been on a journey to possess God's promise. And now I could look across the river and see the promise. We were almost there.

Soon after we arrived in the valley, Moses suffered one last personal loss – his brother-in-law Hobab died. Hobab had been true to his word. He had remained by Moses's side from the time we departed the peninsula of Sinai until now. When many of our people had been faithless, this Midianite had remained faithful.

When he committed to assist us on our journey into the land of Canaan, he had anticipated a journey of days or maybe weeks. He never thought it would take over thirty-eight years. When others had chosen to rebel, he had remained faithful – to his brother-in-law, to his commitment, and to his new-found Jehovah God.

When others had chosen to worship a golden calf, this Midianite had stood firm in his faith, not bowing a knee to anyone or anything other than the Lord God Jehovah. For years, he had helped us overcome the hardships of the wilderness as we followed God. There was no question he had been a part of the Lord's provision to us. But now as we stood on the edge of God's promise, Hobab's work was complete.

In some ways, Moses's grief was greater for Hobab than it had been for Aaron. Hobab had never turned away from him. Hobab had become a part of our people, as had his family. And though he would not be entering the Promised Land with us, his family would be.

And since Moses would not be crossing into the land with us, either, he had some words he needed to leave with us. He had led us throughout the journey for the past forty years. As a prince of Egypt, he had stood before pharaoh and demanded our release. As a shepherd of God, he had listened to our complaints and interceded for us before God.

Moses had served us tirelessly. He deserved our honor and respect. Whatever he had to say to us, he had more than earned the right to tell us. So, he stood on a hill as he had so many times before and called us to gather around him one last time.

As we stood there quietly, I wondered what he would say.

We had endured forty years in the wilderness with all of its hardships and challenges. We had experienced the grief of seeing an entire generation die in the wilderness. We had traveled for long periods without access to fresh water. Many of us had grown up in the wilderness with no place to call home. And through it all, our people had persevered. Would he speak words of affirmation to us?

Or maybe he would rally us to courageously advance to create and build a nation for our children and our children's children. It would be a place we could call home, a place where we would be master and not slave, and a place that would be safe and secure for our future generations. Maybe Moses would outline a military strategy for us to follow to ensure victory over the inhabitants of the land.

Instead, Moses reminded us of the faithlessness of our fathers. He reminded our people of the faithless report of the ten spies and the murmuring and complaining of the people. He reminded our people of the feeble attempt to disobey God and enter the land after God had commanded us to turn back to the wilderness. He reminded us of the thirty-eight years of wandering that resulted from such faithless disobedience.

And he reminded us that despite that faithlessness, God had been faithful through it all. He recounted God's provision, His protection, and His proficiency. He rehearsed His favor, His grace, and His mercy.

He then challenged us saying, *"Be careful never to forget what you yourselves have seen. Do not let these memories escape from your mind as long as you live! And be sure to pass them on to your children and grandchildren. Never forget the day when you stood before the Lord your God at Mount Sinai, where He told me, 'Summon the people before Me, and I will personally instruct them. Then they will learn to fear Me as long as they live, and they will teach their children to fear Me also.'"* [2]

It was a moment of history remembered so it would not be an era of history repeated. The Lord was again setting the land before us. Moses was admonishing us not to repeat the sins of our fathers and once more be turned away.

． ． ．

As we stood at the boundary of the Promised Land, Moses was reminding us this land would come at a cost – including battles against giants and fortified cities – but the Lord God Jehovah would enable us to pay the cost. He would go with us and fight for us. He would tear down walls. He would give us strategy. He would enable us to fight victoriously. Yes, He would grant us favor.

"Remember, O Israel," Moses said, *"Yahweh is Elohim, He is One."*[3] In that brief statement God had originally spoken through Moses to our people, God had given us a revelation of Himself and confirmed His triune nature. As Yahweh, He revealed His eternality, without beginning and without end. Though we did not understand it at the time, as Elohim He revealed His plurality as Father, Son, and Spirit. And in His statement that the Lord is one alone, He revealed His unity as the sovereign, almighty, all-sufficient God.

As our Heavenly Father, He had repeatedly demonstrated His wholehearted love for us, and now He commanded us to commit to Him wholeheartedly – now and for generations to come. Moses reminded us God had charged us with the responsibility of teaching, training, and nurturing His next generation of children through words and actions.

Moses told us to model God's Word in our homes, when we were away, while we were lying down, and when we were getting up. At all times, we were to reflect God's Word through our actions and lifestyles.

"God has prepared you to receive your inheritance," Moses said, "the fruit of His promise." We were about to receive and experience all the things we had lacked in the wilderness. We were about to inhabit cities and houses we did not build, enjoy goods and furnishings we did not produce, satisfy our thirst with water from wells we did not dig, and dine on fresh fruits and vegetables from gardens we did not plant. And God's provision was not going to be just enough to get by; He was going to provide abundantly.

But Moses went on to caution us, *"Be careful not to forget the Lord, who rescued you from slavery in the land of Egypt."*[4] Moses knew that the curse of blessings is, that all too often we forget or neglect the Giver of those blessings. And he admonished us to be careful never to forget from whom those blessings have come.

Then Moses asked us what we had done to deserve the Promised Land. Was it our size or our strength? Was it our intelligence or our might? Was it our hard work or our dedication? Was it our goodness or our greatness? Was it our faithfulness or our godliness? No, time and again we had demonstrated that we were a stubborn and ill-natured people. There was nothing to entitle us to the blessings of God. It was simply because the Lord loved us, and He was keeping His promise to us.

Moses reminded us we were a holy people. Holy, not because of our efforts or our attributes, but because God set us apart unto Himself. We belonged to God, and in His holiness anything that belonged to Him was holy. It was not a matter of who we were – but rather *whose* we were.

God was reminding us through Moses to stay separate. The nations that currently occupied the Promised Land had long ago turned from God. They had turned to immoral indulgences and idolatrous worship. We were to utterly destroy these people and make no treaty with them.

God had promised we would experience His blessing above all the nations of the earth if we were obedient to Him. He promised that we and our livestock would be fruitful and multiply, and be protected from illness and destruction.

. . .

The crowd began to stir with excitement as we listened to Moses's words. Our God had been faithful, and He would continue to be so. As Moses's time with us was concluding, he left us with these words of blessing:

> *"You will experience all these blessings if you obey the Lord your God:*
> *Your towns and your fields will be blessed.*
> *Your children and your crops will be blessed.*
> *The offspring of your herds and flocks will be blessed.*
> *Your fruit baskets and breadboards will be blessed.*
> *Wherever you go and whatever you do, you will be blessed."*[5]

But then we became more sober when he added these words of admonition:

> *"But if you refuse to listen to the Lord your God and do not obey all the commands and decrees I am giving you today, all these curses will come and overwhelm you:*
> *Your towns and your fields will be cursed.*
> *Your fruit baskets and breadboards will be cursed.*
> *Your children and your crops will be cursed.*
> *The offspring of your herds and flocks will be cursed.*
> *Wherever you go and whatever you do, you will be cursed."*[6]

He finished up by saying,

> *"Today I have given you the choice between life and death, between blessings and curses. Now I call on heaven and earth to witness the choice you make. Oh, that you would choose life, so that you and your descendants might live! You can make this choice by loving the Lord your God, obeying Him, and committing yourself firmly to Him. This is the key to your life. And if you love and obey the Lord, you will live long in the land the Lord swore to give your ancestors Abraham, Isaac, and Jacob."*[7]

The people had been silent as Moses spoke. It was as if His words were settling into our very souls.

Then Moses went up to Mount Nebo from the plains of Moab, climbing Pisgah Peak across from Jericho. And the Lord showed him the entirety of the Promised Land. Moses never returned to us. We believe the Lord buried him there, but no one knows the exact place.

Moses was one hundred twenty years old when he died, yet his eyesight was clear, and he was as strong as ever. There has never been another prophet in Israel like Moses, whom the Lord knew face to face. The Lord sent him to perform all the miraculous signs and wonders in the land of Egypt against pharaoh, and all his servants, and his entire land. And with mighty power, Moses performed amazing acts in the sight of all Israel.

We remained there on the plains of Moab for thirty days mourning the passing of God's servant who had so faithfully led us.

* * *

31

"In three days you will cross the Jordan River and take possession of the land the Lord your God is giving you."[1]

* * *

We had been camped in Moab for many months and some among us had even put down roots. We had planted crops for the first time in forty years and were augmenting our meals of manna with fresh produce from the land.

So when Joshua sent word we would leave in three days, it was very short notice for such a monumental move. Though we knew this day would eventually arrive, we had given up trying to anticipate when it would happen. At this point, no one dared to think we were only three days away from crossing into the land.

Once again, the Lord was teaching us – this time, that even when we are waiting, we must stand ready. Being prepared meant we needed to harvest and prepare the produce we would be taking. We needed to repack our belongings and break down our camp for travel.

. . .

Joshua told us we would be crossing the Jordan River. Ironically, in all the months we had been camped there, never once did we ask Joshua how we were going to get across the river! Instead of growing produce, our time may have been better spent building a flotilla of rafts, boats, and ferries to transport us to the other side. But no one ever suggested that possibility. Even now, with our departure only three days away, no one was making any preparations for a water crossing!

I don't know if it was because we were excited or just busy, but I never heard one critical word or question about how we were going to cross the river. Apparently, Joshua was trusting God to make a way. Could it be the rest of us were content to trust God without grumbling, complaining, or wringing our hands?

My grandsons asked me, "Grandpa, will Jehovah God part the river just like He parted the sea so long ago? Will Joshua use the staff of Aaron to make a dry pathway for us?"

"I do not know how our Lord God will make a way," I replied. "But I know He will make a way. If He has taught us anything over the past forty years, it has been that He will always accomplish what is needed to fulfill His promise!"

My son, Iru, spoke up. "The land is God's gift to us. We have done nothing to earn it, and we certainly don't deserve it. But when someone gives you a gift, your part is to graciously receive it. So, let's be ready and trust Him. Let's always be ready to adjust our lives to Him and gratefully receive His gifts!"

Although the tribes of Reuben, Gad, and half of the tribe of Manasseh would be staying on this side of the Jordan River, God still required those men to lead us across the water as fully armed warriors.

. . .

I was struck by the selfless commitment exhibited by the men of those tribes. Shammua would have been proud of his tribe of Reuben. They were displaying a bravery that he, in his younger days – before his faithless report – was best known for. It was a willingness to do whatever is required without reservation.

Similarly, Gaddi would have been proud of his tribe of Manasseh. They were willing to go wherever their leader directed them. But they weren't going on their own; their leader was going with them. Gaddi had always shown that same spirit when we were boys – that willingness to go wherever Joshua and I led him.

As I considered the tribe of Gad, I thought of the allegiance they were demonstrating to all of our tribes – their commitment to walk in community with the rest of us. Geuel had demonstrated that commitment – regrettably to a fault on the day he chose to stand with the majority that recommended we not enter the Promised Land.

Maybe his actions were a good reminder that sometimes our strength can become our greatest weakness. Regardless, today the tribe was committing their very lives to the rest of us to help us possess the land we had been promised.

All the leaders were a great example to the rest of us in other ways, too. They showed us how to follow Joshua as our new leader. We could have easily mourned Moses instead of respecting Joshua's authority. But those tribes showed us that those to whom God has granted favor deserve our honor and esteem.

They also did something my people had not demonstrated for over forty years – they encouraged our leader. We had become known for our grumbling, not our encouragement. But here were these three tribes encouraging Joshua and admonishing him to *"be strong and courageous."* [2] It was not a question of his character, but rather it was a vote of confidence in his leadership. They encouraged our leader, built him up, and spoke truth into his life.

Later that morning, Joshua came to me and my sons. "Iru and Elah," he said, "I have an assignment for you. I need you to *scout out the land on the other side of the Jordan River, especially around Jericho."* [3] Sending out spies was not a lack of faith on Joshua's part but rather an exercise of wisdom. He was not questioning if we should go, he was seeking out how God was making a way for us to go.

I had seen Jericho over thirty-eight years ago. It had been a fortified city with impenetrable walls and massive gates. I doubted much had changed, which meant it would be a difficult city to conquer. But, then again, that was from our perspective – not God's! And I was certain God already had a plan.

Like most parents, I was proud of my sons and the men they had become. But I couldn't have been any prouder when Joshua entrusted them with such an important assignment. There was a part of me that was a little jealous I would not be joining them, but I knew this was a job for younger men. So, with a full heart – and my full blessing – I watched as they walked out of camp to follow their leader's command.

I continued to keep watch for them over the next two days. When I spotted them returning on the third day, I walked out to meet them and joined them as they made their way to Joshua. My sons reported they were able to swim across the river without much difficulty.

"Once we were on the western shore," Iru said, "it was a short journey from there to the city of Jericho. It was mid-afternoon when we arrived. The city gates were still open, so we mingled with a crowd of merchants and travelers and easily made our way inside."

• • •

"Soon after," Elah began, "a man who looked as if he were an official approached us. 'You look like foreigners,' he said. 'Where are you from?' Iru told him we were weary travelers from Moab."

"I told him we were going to Hebron and had entered the city to rest for the night," Iru chimed in. "We would continue our journey in the morning. I asked the man if he had any recommendations where we might find food and lodging for the night. He pointed us in a direction and off we went. We noticed he continued to watch us as we walked away. We saw him call another man over and then point at us. It looked like he was dispatching the other man to follow us."

Elah picked up from there. "Right then the wheel fell off a merchant's cart carrying pomegranates. The cart's contents spilled and scattered in every direction. People nearby ran to help the merchant gather his fruit. In the midst of that commotion, the man who had first questioned us and the one he had sent to follow us became distracted.

"That gave us enough time to turn down another walkway without being seen. We then walked briskly – not wanting to call attention to ourselves by running – and headed in the opposite direction of where the man had pointed us."

"A woman stepped out of a doorway and stopped us," Iru broke in. "She said, 'You two look like you need help. Follow me.' I can't explain how we knew, but we knew Jehovah God had placed her in our path. We could tell by looking at her that she was a prostitute, but we knew we were supposed to follow her. So, we did not hesitate. We went with her and soon we arrived at her dwelling.

• • •

"She told us," Iru continued, "that as soon as she saw us, she knew she was supposed to help us. She said, 'I don't know why; I just know I'm supposed to help you. Who are you and why are you here?'"

Elah continued with the story from there. "We told her our names and that we were the oldest sons of our father Caleb, of the tribe of Judah of the people of Israel. She told us her name was Rahab and she had heard of our people. She said, 'More importantly I have heard of your God – the One who goes before you as a pillar of cloud by day and a pillar of fire by night. He is the God who defeated the Egyptian army and the armies of Sihon and of Og. Our people fear your God. Why have you come here?'

"We explained that our God was leading us to this place – to conquer this land – and we would be following Him. As night was falling, there was a pounding on her door, and a voice called out, 'Rahab, we have a message for you from our king!'

"She told us to quickly step out onto her roof and hide in the midst of bundles of flax. After giving us a moment to hide, she opened her door. We could hear everything clearly. We recognized the voice of the man who was speaking. It was the man who had first stopped us in the city."

Iru nodded and said, "The man told her, *'Some Israelites have come here tonight to spy out our land.* The king has sent us to arrest those men. Your neighbors said they saw you with them. *Bring out the men who have come into your house.'*(4)

"*'Yes, the men were here earlier,'* Rahab replied, *'but I didn't know where they were from. They left the town at dusk, as the gates were about to close. I don't know where they went. But if you hurry, you can probably catch up with them.'* "(5)

· · ·

"So, the man and the king's men who were with him hurriedly left and went looking for us.

"After some time had passed, Rahab came up on the roof. *'I know your God has given you this land,'* she told us. *'We are all afraid of you. Everyone in the land is living in terror. No one has the courage to fight after hearing what your God has done. For the Lord your God is the supreme God of the heavens above and the earth below.*[(6)]

"'*Now swear to me by the Lord that you will be kind to me and my family since I have helped you. Give me some guarantee that when Jericho is conquered, you will let me live, along with my father and mother, my brothers and sisters, and all their families.'*"[(7)]

"So we told her," Elah said, *'We offer our own lives as a guarantee for your safety. If you don't betray us, we will keep our promise and be kind to you when the Lord gives us the land.'*[(8)]

"Then, since her house was built into the town wall, she let us down by a rope through her window. *'Escape to the hill country,'* she told us. *'Hide there from the men searching for you. Then, when they have returned, you can go on your way.'*[(9)]

"Before we left, we told her, *'We will be bound by the oath we have taken only if you follow these instructions. When we come into the land, you must leave this scarlet rope hanging from the window through which you let us down. And all your family members – your father, mother, brothers, and all your relatives – must be here inside the house. If they go out into the street and are killed, it will not be our fault. But if anyone lays a hand on people inside this house, we will accept the responsibility for their death. If you betray us, however, we are not bound by this oath in any way.'*[(10)]

. . .

"'*I accept your terms,*'[(11)] she replied. And when we left, the scarlet rope was hanging from the window."

My sons went on to explain how they went up into the hill country and stayed there until the men who were chasing them had returned to the city.

"*The Lord has given us the whole land,*" Iru said, "*for all the people in the land are terrified of us.*" [(12)]

"What faith this Rahab has demonstrated!" Joshua said. "Flesh and blood did not reveal to her to help you. God by His grace has revealed Himself to Rahab and she has acknowledged Him as the one true God. She has acted by faith, despite personal peril. Surely God has confirmed His direction to us! And we will honor the commitment you have made to His servant Rahab."

* * *

32

"Early the next morning Joshua and all the Israelites left Acacia Grove and arrived at the banks of the Jordan River."[1]

* * *

The next day, Joshua told us to set up camp along the banks of the Jordan River to make the final preparations for crossing the water. Most of the year the Jordan was about one hundred feet wide and between three and ten feet deep. But it was now early spring. The melting snow in the mountains of Lebanon caused the river to rise to flood stage, overflowing its banks and rising in some areas to a depth of fifty feet.

This was not the most opportune time to cross the river. It would have been much easier a month or two earlier. But that had been neither Jehovah God's timing nor His plan.

Apparently, the Canaanites weren't worried about our coming across the water this time of year. Even though they knew my sons had been in Jericho within the past week, they had not bothered to assemble a show of force to discourage our crossing.

. . .

I was a little surprised that some of our youngest members had not voiced their fears about crossing a rushing river. Those under forty did not know how to swim since they had grown up in the desert. Some of them thought "final preparations" meant we were going to build a flotilla of some kind to ferry us across the water.

But we quickly learned that Joshua had something altogether different in mind when he announced, *"Purify yourselves, for tomorrow the Lord will do great wonders among you."* (2)

The last time we had been told to purify ourselves was at the base of Mount Sinai when we were preparing for God to make His presence known. We were told to cleanse and prepare our hearts and cleanse our garments. Most of our people could not remember that day thirty-eight years ago. They were either too young or had not been born. Joshua was telling us to prepare to enter into the presence of God – not to navigate a rushing river.

We did as he instructed. No one questioned or complained. We all busily and reverently went about purifying ourselves. I listened with a joyful heart as my children explained to their children what it meant to purify themselves using the very same words Rebecca and I had used with our children years earlier.

Next, Joshua called together the leaders of each tribe and sent us out with this message for the people: *"When you see the Levitical priests carrying the Ark of the Covenant of the Lord your God, move out from your positions and follow them. Since you have never traveled this way before, they will guide you. Stay about half a mile behind them, keeping a clear distance between you and the Ark. Make sure you don't come any closer."*(3)

. . .

The pillar of cloud that had guided us to these plains of Moab was no longer going to lead us. God had used the pillar to guide and protect us in the wilderness, but from here on we were to follow the Ark. The Ark was no longer to go with us, it was to go before us – representing the manifest presence of Jehovah God.

I reminded my grandchildren that inside the Ark were three important elements Jehovah had given us: the stone tablets He had written containing His law, the blossoming staff He had used in the hands of Moses and Aaron to perform His miracles, and a sample of the manna He had provided each day.

On the outside of the Ark was the mercy seat – representing His judgment and grace. Together, the Ark was the picture of God's divine law, power, and provision under His judgment and grace – a perfect example of not only His presence but also His favor.

"The Ark is a reminder to us and a communication to everyone else that sees it that we are God's chosen people," I explained, "and He goes before us!"

The separation between our people and the Ark enabled us to clearly see God's direction so we would not turn to the side or run ahead. Rather, we would stay on pace with Him – keeping Him clearly in our sights.

On the morning of the tenth day of the first month of what was now the forty-first year – almost forty years to the day since we had left Egypt – Joshua said to the priests, "*Lift up the Ark of the Covenant and lead the people across the river. When you reach the banks of the Jordan River, take a few steps into the river and stop there.*" [4]

To their credit, and to the credit of all of our people, no one questioned Joshua. No one sarcastically asked if he intended for us to walk through the water. The priests began the journey as they had been directed and the rest of us followed. No one had any idea what would happen next. Only God knew – and we were all walking in obedience and faith.

As soon as the priests' feet touched the river's edge, the water immediately began backing up. We later learned that it backed up a great distance away at a town near Zarethan, northward past Jericho. And the water below our point of entry flowed south to the Dead Sea. Within moments, the riverbed was completely dry.

Those of us who were older immediately thought back to the parting of the Red Sea. But unlike that day, when we walked a somewhat narrow path between walls of water, the winds were not blowing. The water simply dried up and we walked en masse across a dry riverbed as far as we could see. Except for the leading priests carrying the Ark, none of us even got our feet wet.

Joshua directed the priests to stop at the halfway point of the riverbed and remain there as the rest of our people passed by. They waited there for our entire nation of Israel to cross the Jordan onto dry ground.

While we were crossing, the Lord told Joshua to choose twelve men, one from each tribe. I was humbled he chose me to represent the tribe of Judah among the eleven other men.

"Take twelve stones," Joshua told us, *"from the very place where the priests are standing in the middle of the Jordan. Carry them out and pile them up at the place where you will camp tonight."*[5]

Joshua also instructed us to set up another pile of twelve stones in the middle of the Jordan, at the place where the priests who carried the Ark of the Covenant were standing. We set up the twelve stones in the middle of the riverbed, which remain there to this day. Then we took another twelve stones from the middle of the Jordan River and each of us carried one to the shore.

When everyone was safely across, the priests came ashore and the water returned and overflowed its banks as before.

The armed warriors from the tribes of Reuben, Gad, and the half tribe of Manasseh had followed the priests and gone before the rest of us as we crossed the Jordan. These armed men – about forty thousand in number – were ready for battle. But there were no opposing forces to meet us as we arrived on the western shore. We continued to Gilgal, just east of Jericho, where we made camp for the night.

It was there Joshua had us pile up the twelve stones we had taken to build the memorial. Without God's prompting, it would have been easy for Joshua not to memorialize God's supernatural work that day. There were many distractions as we watched for enemy forces and ensured the safety and welfare of our families, our livestock, and our possessions while crossing the riverbed.

But even in the midst of that busyness, God knew for the sake of our spiritual walk, our service to Him, and to glorify His Name, we needed to memorialize His miraculous work.

Even the date of our crossing was a significant spiritual marker. It was exactly five days shy of forty years. God had said we would wander in the wilderness for forty years, and now He brought us into the Promised Land five days before that forty-year mark. He did this so we could enter Canaan four days before the annual observance of Passover and on the exact day our preparations for the observance were to begin. It was another illustration of God's faithfulness as the Alpha – the One who led us out of Egypt – and the Omega – the One who led us into the Promised Land.

· · ·

Though Joshua had been our leader for several weeks, it was on this day the Lord made Joshua a great leader in the eyes of our people. We all respected him now as much as we had revered Moses.

As we gathered around him and around the memorial of stones we had built, he said, *"In the future your children will ask, 'What do these stones mean?' Then you can tell them, 'This is where our people crossed the Jordan on dry ground. For the Lord our God dried up the river right before our eyes, and He kept it dry until we were all across, just as He did at the Red Sea when He dried it up until we had all crossed over. He did this so all the nations of the earth might know that the Lord's hand is powerful, and so you might fear the Lord your God forever.'"* [6]

As Joshua led us in that time of remembrance, the faces of family members and friends who had died during our journey flashed before my eyes. Most notably, I thought of my dear Rebecca, as well as my father and mother. I thought of their faith and confidence in God that this day would arrive. It was as if they, too, were now rejoicing with us!

But I also thought about the spies who had explored the land with Joshua and me. They had died a tortured death, fully aware of the consequences of their faithlessness. I couldn't help but wonder if their souls knew we had finally made the journey and now stood in the Promised Land. Were they marveling at God's faithfulness despite their faithlessness? I prayed that no more of our people would have to die with the regret of faithlessness.

As Joshua said, *"God did this so all the nations of the earth might know that the Lord's hand is powerful,"* [7] and I prayed that knowledge and understanding might begin and remain with us!

* * *

33

When all the Amorite kings west of the Jordan and all the Canaanite kings who lived along the Mediterranean coast heard how the Lord had dried up the Jordan River so the people of Israel could cross, they lost heart and were paralyzed with fear because of them. [1]

* * *

Yesterday we awoke on the eastern shore of the Jordan. This morning we were camped on the western shore at Gilgal. Yesterday no one was inhabiting this parcel of land. Today there were almost two million of us, together with our livestock, camped in our sprawling city of tents. Yesterday we gathered our manna in the wilderness. Today we gathered it in the Promised Land.

I couldn't see any Canaanite spies keeping a careful watch on us, but I knew they were there. The river the Amorites and Canaanites were trusting to keep us at bay no longer stood between us and them. I can imagine how overwhelmed their spies felt looking down on us. But it wasn't us who intimidated them – it was our God.

. . .

The Canaanites had seen the miracle at the Jordan River with their own eyes! And if they were as fearful as Rahab said, imagine their fear now! We were no longer concerned they would attack us. We knew they were just watching to see what we would do. They were not going to be foolhardy like Og. They were keeping a safe distance.

The Lord told Joshua it was time for our covenant with Him to be renewed. Four hundred seventy years earlier, God had entered into a covenant with our patriarch, Abraham, and his descendants.

The covenant was: *"I will always be your God and the God of your descendants after you. And I will give the entire land of Canaan … to you and your descendants. It will be their possession forever, and I will be their God…. Your responsibility is to obey the terms of the covenant. You and all your descendants have this continual responsibility. This is the covenant that you and your descendants must keep: Each male among you must be circumcised."*[2]

God had given a promise to that first generation of Israelites and had entered into a covenant with them. Their part of the covenant was to obey the terms and seal it through the circumcision of every Israelite male.

But for thirty-eight years no Israelite male had been circumcised because our people had broken covenant with God and rebelled against Him. As a result, a generation of our people had died in the wilderness never receiving God's promise. And now an entire generation raised up in the wilderness did not bear the seal of that covenant.

Our wandering in the wilderness had been God's reproach for our faithlessness; but now our triumphal entry into this land was God's reminder of His faithfulness. And now He required the men and boys born during our time in the desert to be circumcised as a seal of His continuing covenant with our people and the generations to follow. With the first generation, it was a promise that had been given; now with this generation, it was a promise that had been granted.

. . .

Some of our men, though, questioned God's timing. "Is now a good time to renew the covenant? Is this a good time to incapacitate every Israelite male – age thirty-eight and younger – for a few days while their circumcision heals?" they asked. "Has God forgotten what happened when our patriarchs Simeon and Levi came against the Shechemites right after every male in their town was circumcised?[3] No one lived to tell about it! Why not delay until our enemies have been overcome and we are settled in the land?"

But God said now was the time! He told Joshua, *"Make flint knives and circumcise this generation of Israelites."*[4] God in His wisdom knew this was the very best time! I could think of four reasons why.

- God was reminding us we were not governed by conventional wisdom; we were under His direction. Our inability to defend ourselves during this time would only magnify His divine care. It was a clear signal and message to our enemies that our security was in God; not in our own strength.

- God knew the battles we would face. Confirming the covenant with us now would provide us with an assurance of His victory in the future. It would be a continuing reminder in the days ahead.

- It definitely was a teaching moment. It was a matter of our understanding we must always make Him first!

- I think it also was a picture of offering ourselves as a living sacrifice. Just like our patriarch, Isaac, we had to be willing to lay down our lives on the altar and walk in holiness and complete obedience to our Lord.[5]

When the younger males had been circumcised, the Lord told us through Joshua, *"Today I have rolled away the shame of your slavery in Egypt."*[6]

. . .

I can only imagine what the Canaanite spies thought when they witnessed a mass circumcision instead of our men practicing military maneuvers for an attack on Jericho!

And I am also certain the spies were not ready for what happened next. Because our fifth night in the Promised Land was the fourteenth day of the first month of Nissan – the night we observed the Passover!

God had given us very specific instructions on how to observe Passover and now He was attending to every detail for this special remembrance. On the tenth day of the first month, each family was to *"choose a lamb or a young goat for a sacrifice."*[7] On the tenth day of the first month of this year, God had made a way for all of our families and all of our livestock (from which the animal sacrifices would be chosen) to cross over into this land.

On the eleventh day of the first month of this year, God had led us to renew our covenant with Him through circumcision. On the two days following, while those men and boys were healing from the circumcision, the rest of us readied the other preparations for the Passover meal.

I marveled at how God left nothing to chance. When we crossed the Jordan, the Canaanites had withdrawn inside the walls of Jericho, leaving their barns and fields unattended. They had unwittingly provided the grain we needed to make bread and provide roasted grain for two million people – sufficient for all seven days of our observance.

Then at the twilight of our fourth full day in the land of Canaan (the fourteenth day of the month of Nissan), our whole assembly slaughtered the sacrificial animals. The meat was roasted over a fire and eaten along with bitter salad greens and bread made without yeast.[8]

. . .

Forty years ago, to this very night, the angel of death had passed over our homes. As we gathered as a family, my youngest son, Naam, recounted to his children, his nieces and nephews, and their children, how he and I had smeared the blood of a young goat on the doorframe of our home using a hyssop branch.

"Throughout the night we heard the cries from the homes of the Egyptians as the firstborn of each family died," Naam explained.

"Our journey to this Promised Land began with that solemn Passover, and now we celebrate the completion of our journey through another solemn Passover," I reminded them.

"We observed the second Passover thirty-nine years ago in the wilderness of Sinai," I explained to family members too young to remember. "But we have not had another celebration of Passover for thirty-eight years as a consequence of the faithless decision of our people to turn from God and turn away from His Promised Land.

"So, this observance is not only a remembrance of God's faithfulness in leading us out from our Egyptian captivity, it is also a time to thank Him for His steadfast love that has now permitted us to enter into His promise. Tonight is a time of joyful remembrance of the wondrous works of His goodness and power that has brought us to this very place."

Then our family bowed to the ground and worshipped our Lord God Jehovah in thanksgiving.

The next morning was the beginning of our fifth full day on the west side of the Jordan. Last night we had celebrated our Passover meal. This morning the first of our people walked out from the camp to gather their family's daily portion of manna. Few of our people were old enough to remember the days when we did not eat manna. For most of them, it had been a basic staple of our diet for their entire lives.

But this morning, when our people went out to gather it – it wasn't there! Gathering manna in the morning had become part of our daily routine. Gossip was exchanged as manna was being gathered. It was a time to catch up on news from within the camp!

But now the question on everyone's lips was, where is the manna? It used to be everywhere – and now it is nowhere. Some of the people began to panic and quickly returned to camp to seek out Joshua and our other leaders, including me.

Joshua quieted their fears. "Do you remember when Moses had us place a sample of manna in the Ark? When God instructed Aaron through Moses, He told us the day would come when we would no longer need manna. God directed the sample be set aside in the Ark as a continuing reminder of His faithfulness to us. Well, apparently that day has arrived!"

From that day forward, we began to eat from the crops of the land. Initially, we ate the grain left by the Canaanite farmers, but soon we planted and ate from our own harvests.

But first, Jericho awaited.

* * *

34

Now the gates of Jericho were tightly shut because the people were afraid of the Israelites. No one was allowed to go out or in. [1]

* * *

We already knew the people of Jericho were afraid of our Lord God Jehovah. We knew they were living in terror. The king of Jericho had apparently decided the God of Israel would not be their Master. But rather than seeking war or peace, he had simply chosen to shut his people and his city off from us.

He could have led his warriors on the offensive to attack us. Jericho had the high ground. Iru and Elah had reported that the Jerichoites were strong warriors, so they did not lack fighting strength.

Or the king could have led his people to surrender and seek peace – to petition us and our God for mercy. Having heard of Jehovah's might and majesty, he could have petitioned Him for saving grace. Instead, he chose to hide his people behind their walls.

. . .

And those walls were impressive. Iru and Elah had told us the wall around Jericho was in fact a design of three walls. First the mound, or "tell," was surrounded by a great earthen embankment with a stone retaining wall at its base. That wall was fifteen feet high. On top of the retaining wall was a mudbrick wall six feet thick and twenty-five feet high.

Then from the crest of the embankment was a similar mudbrick wall also six feet thick that started at forty-six feet above the ground level (outside the retaining wall) and rose an additional twenty-five feet in the air. From the ground level these walls projected seventy feet into the air. The builders of the city of Jericho had taken great care and pride to build a virtually impregnable fortress.

The morning after our Passover observance concluded, Joshua called the tribal leaders together. The Lord had given him the plan for conquering the city. We gathered enthusiastically to hear what God's direction would be. The Lord had given us great victory in our recent battles, and we were anxious to hear what military strategy He would have us employ. God had promised He would give us these lands, so there was no fear in our hearts. We were ready for battle!

Joshua stood before us and said, "Here is what the Lord has said, '*I have given you Jericho, its king, and all its strong warriors. You and your fighting men should march around the town once a day for six days. Seven priests will walk ahead of the Ark, each carrying a ram's horn. On the seventh day you are to march around the town seven times, with the priests blowing the horns. When you hear the priests give one long blast on the rams' horns, have all the people shout as loud as they can. Then the walls of the town will collapse, and the people can charge straight into the town.*'"[2]

After Joshua finished speaking, we all looked at one another. We had envisioned a military strategy that involved battering rams – not a ram's horn. We had expected to line up in a fighting formation – not a marching formation. We couldn't quite believe our ears ... but then we remembered Who was speaking.

. . .

It was the One who had released His death angel to pass through the home of every Egyptian family. It was the Lord God Jehovah who had destroyed the Egyptian army while we simply watched. It was the One who had parted the river for us to cross on a dry riverbed. It was the One who had promised us victory. He was the One we would follow around that city. We would trust Him!

So Joshua called together the priests and said, *"Take up the Ark of the Lord's Covenant, and assign seven priests to walk in front of it, each carrying a ram's horn."* [3] Then he gave orders to all our men of fighting age, *"March around the town, and the armed men will lead the way in front of the Ark of the Lord."* [4]

The seven priests with the rams' horns started marching as God had directed. They blew the horns as they marched. And the Ark of the Lord's Covenant followed behind them. Some of our armed men marched in front of the priests with the horns, and some of us walked behind the Ark. But it was God who went before us!

"Do not shout; do not even talk," Joshua commanded. *"Not a single word from any of you until I tell you to shout. Then shout!"* [5]

We marched around the town once that day as the Ark of the Lord went before us. Then we returned to spend the night in our camp.

On the second day, we all awoke early and again marched once around the town. Then we returned to the camp. We followed that same pattern for six days.

On the first day, the Jerichoites hid behind their walls in fear as they watched us march. But each subsequent day, they became slightly more visible. By the fifth day, they started to taunt us. On the sixth day, they openly ridiculed us. They believed their walls would protect them. They were convinced their walls were mightier than our God.

On the seventh day, we got up at dawn and began our march around the town. But this time we went around the town seven times. The Jerichoites looked over their walls and pointed at us, throwing stones and trash at us. By our seventh time around, they were openly mocking and deriding us. Some of us thought they were going to open their gates and attack us.

At the conclusion of our seventh time around the walls, the priests sounded the long blast on their horns as they had been instructed. Joshua commanded us, "*Shout! For the Lord has given you the town!*[6]

"Remember," he continued, "*Jericho and everything in it must be completely destroyed as an offering to the Lord. Only Rahab the prostitute and the others in her house will be spared, for she protected our spies.*

"*Do not take any of the things set apart for destruction, or you yourselves will be completely destroyed, and you will bring trouble on the camp of Israel. Everything made from silver, gold, bronze, or iron is sacred to the Lord and must be brought into His treasury.*"[7]

We shouted as loud as possible – and the walls of Jericho suddenly collapsed. Those who had been shouting at us fell to their deaths as the walls collapsed. The walls fell inward killing many of the Jerichoites under the crushing weight of the rock. We could hear screams coming from every part of the city.

We charged straight into the town and captured it, completely destroying everything in our path as the Lord had instructed. Every man and woman, young or old, as well as cattle, sheep, goats, and donkeys were destroyed by the collapsing walls.

· · ·

Joshua directed Iru and Elah to keep their promise to Rahab the prostitute. *"Go,"* he said, *"and bring her out, along with all her family."*[8] My sons did as they had promised and rescued Rahab, her father, mother, brothers, and all the other relatives who were with her.

When they brought her out, Iru told us, "Amazingly, the outer wall of her home, which formed a portion of the city's wall, did not collapse in the area immediately surrounding her home. It remained intact. If the wall had collapsed, Rahab and her family would have died. But the Lord God Jehovah protected her!"

They brought her whole family to a safe place within our camp among our tribe of Judah. And she and her family continue to live among us to this day.

We gathered and kept only those things made from silver, gold, bronze, or iron that could be purified by fire so they could be placed in the treasury of the Lord's house. We burned everything else that remained of the town and all that was in it … or so we thought.

After we had finished destroying everything, Joshua invoked this curse: *"May the curse of the Lord fall on anyone who tries to rebuild the town of Jericho. At the cost of his firstborn son, he will lay its foundation. At the cost of his youngest son, he will set up its gates."*[9] Jericho, the walled city, had been utterly destroyed by our God – and was never to be rebuilt!

That evening we gathered together in our camp and praised God for His victory – and thanked Him for our protection. Not one life had been lost among our people.

The next morning Joshua sent several men from the tribe of Ephraim to the north to spy out the nearby town of Ai. When the men returned later that day, they reported to Joshua. *"There's no need for all of us to go up there; it won't take more than two or three thousand men to attack Ai. Since there are so few of them, don't make all our people struggle to go up there."* (10)

Ai did not have the imposing walls of Jericho. It was a much smaller town with a much smaller population and a much smaller fighting force. Defeating Ai would take no effort. And though they never said these words, their confidence, on the heels of their victory at Jericho, communicated as much – "we don't even need God to do this; we can handle this town ourselves!"

The Ephraimite spies were not the only ones who allowed their overconfidence to cloud their judgment. The same was true of me as I listened to their report. And the same was true of Joshua and all of our leaders. Our arrogance was so great we failed to seek God for His plan and His direction.

Joshua directed three thousand of our fighting men to go to Ai the next day to conquer the town. But the men of Ai didn't have any walls to hide behind so they immediately attacked our men. Our warriors were stunned and became paralyzed with fear. The men of Ai knew they had the upper hand and began to chase our men – halfway back to Jericho. Thirty-six were killed as they retreated. The courage of our people melted away as we heard the report of our defeat.

Joshua, the other elders, and I tore our clothing in dismay, threw dust on our heads, and bowed face down to the ground before the Ark of the Lord until that evening.

Then Joshua cried out as he remained prostrate before the Lord, *"Oh, Sovereign LORD, why did You bring us across the Jordan River if You are going to let the Amorites kill us? If only we had been content to stay on the other side! LORD, what can I say now that Israel has fled from its enemies? For when the Canaanites and all the other people living in the land hear about it, they will surround us and wipe our name off the face of the earth. And then what will happen to the honor of Your great name?"*[11]

But the Lord said to Joshua, *"Get up! Why are you lying on your face like this? Israel has sinned and broken My covenant! They have stolen some of the things that I commanded must be set apart for Me. And they have not only stolen them but have lied about it and hidden the things among their own belongings. That is why you are running from your enemies in defeat. For now, Israel itself has been set apart for destruction. I will not remain with you any longer unless you destroy the things among you that were set apart for destruction.*

"Get up! Command the people to purify themselves in preparation for tomorrow. For this is what the LORD, the God of Israel, says: Hidden among you, O Israel, are things set apart for the LORD. You will never defeat your enemies until you remove these things from among you.

"In the morning you must present yourselves by tribes, and the LORD will point out the tribe to which the guilty man belongs. That tribe must come forward with its clans, and the Lord will point out the guilty clan. That clan will then come forward, and the Lord will point out the guilty family. Finally, each member of the guilty family must come forward one by one. The one who has stolen what was set apart for destruction will himself be burned with fire, along with everything he has, for he has broken the covenant of the Lord and has done a horrible thing in Israel."[12]

Early the next morning Joshua brought all the tribes of Israel before the Lord as He had commanded. To my great dismay, it was my tribe – the tribe of Judah – that was singled out. Joshua directed the clans of Judah to come forward. My clan passed by first, followed by the other clans until the clan of Zerah was singled out.

Then the families of Zerah came forward and the family of Zimri was singled out. Every member of Zimri's family was brought forward person by person, until Achan was singled out.

. . .

As Achan stood before all of the people, Joshua confronted him, "*My son, give glory to the Lord, the God of Israel, by telling the truth. Make your confession and tell me what you have done. Don't hide it from me.*"[13]

Achan replied, revealing his remorse, "*It is true! I have sinned against the LORD, the God of Israel. Among the plunder I saw a beautiful robe from Babylon, two hundred silver coins, and a bar of gold weighing more than a pound. I wanted them so much that I took them. They are hidden in the ground beneath my tent, with the silver buried deeper than the rest.*" [14]

Joshua sent my sons and me to make a search of Achan's camp. We searched his tent and found the stolen goods hidden there, just as Achan had said, with the silver buried beneath the rest. We brought everything before Joshua and the people, and laid it on the ground in the presence of the Lord.

Joshua directed that Achan, the silver, the robe, the bar of gold, his sons, daughters, cattle, donkeys, sheep, goats, tent, and everything he had, be taken to the valley outside of camp. It was there that Joshua said to him, "*Achan, you have brought trouble on us. The Lord will now bring trouble on you.*" [15]

In obedience to the Lord, we stoned Achan and his family that night and burned their bodies. We piled a great heap of stones over Achan, which remains to this day. The place where we stoned him has been called the Valley of Trouble ever since.

After we all returned to camp, the Lord said to Joshua, "*Tomorrow you will attack Ai, for I have given them into your hands.*" [16]

* * *

35

"You will destroy them as you destroyed Jericho."[1]

* * *

Ironically, the name Ai in Hebrew means "ruin." And our efforts to try and take Ai on our own, without first seeking God's direction, had led to just that – ruin. If we had sought the Lord first, we would have known about Achan's sin and dozens of our fighting men would still be alive. I prayed the memories of Ai would always remind us to seek God first!

Now that we were again seeking the Lord's direction, we could advance confidently and with His assurance: *"Do not be afraid or discouraged."*[2] Once again, He taught us a valuable lesson – confidence that rests solely in ourselves will most often lead to destruction, but confidence that rests in our God will never disappoint as long as we stay true to His plan.

As I thought about God's plan for our defeat of Ai and His plan for the defeat of Jericho, I was struck by two glaring differences. God told us through Joshua, *"This time you may keep the plunder and the livestock for your-*

selves." [3] This was ironic since we had been defeated at Ai *because* Achan had kept plunder from Jericho.

If Achan had not taken matters into his own hands and disobeyed God, he would probably have been able to acquire those silver coins, a bar of gold and a robe – and possibly even more – at Ai. What's more, he wouldn't have needed to hide them; he and his family could have enjoyed them to their fullest. It reminded me of something I learned as a young boy: Though the temptation of sin's reward will often look sweet, the outcome of obedience will always be sweeter – and always without the sting and bitterness of sin.

The other difference was God's strategy for conquering the two cities. God directed us in a very detailed military strategy for our attack against Ai as opposed to having us march around the walls of Jericho.

"Set an ambush behind the town. Send out five thousand of your best warriors after nightfall to hide in ambush close behind the town and to stand ready for action. Then in the morning send out your main army of twenty-five thousand men to attack from the front. The men of Ai, emboldened by their recent victory over you, will come out of the city to fight as they did before.

"When they do, your men will turn and run away from them. That force will allow the Ai warriors to chase them until they have been drawn away from the town. For they will say, 'The Israelites are running away from us as they did before.' While that is taking place, the men waiting in ambush will jump up and take possession of the town. Because I will give it to you. When you have captured the town, set it on fire." [4]

Joshua and our fighting men set out to attack Ai according to the Lord's plan. And each of us obediently performed the vital role he had been assigned. We were not going to have a repeat of our previous defeat because of one man's disobedience.

• • •

The entire population of Ai was destroyed. Although the king of Ai and the people had heard about the fate of the Jerichoites, they refused to surrender their lives to Jehovah God, instead thinking they could wage war against Him and win. The town burned until it became a permanent mound of ruins, just as its name implied.

Word spread throughout the land about what our God had done to the people of Jericho and Ai – and the surrounding towns and villages became even more fearful of Him.

The town of Gibeon, which means "hill place" at an elevation of about two thousand four hundred feet, towered over most of the other cities of Canaan. Gibeon was a fortress city dating back to the early days of the patriarchs, soon after the great flood. It had now existed for about eight hundred years because it was easily defensible.

But, as it turned out, the leaders of Gibeon had a different strategy in mind for defeating us. They were not going to rely on their fighting skills or their elevated fortress; they opted to use the weapon of deception against us. And they were very good at it – down to the last detail.

They loaded their donkeys with patched wineskins and weathered saddlebags. They loaded their packs with dry and moldy bread. And they dressed themselves in ragged clothes and worn, patched sandals. God had provided us with fresh manna every day as we traveled through the wilderness, and our clothes and sandals had never worn out for forty years. Since we had never experienced mold, patches, or ragged clothes during our long travels, the Gibeonites looked very strange to us.

When they arrived at our camp at Gilgal, they told us, *"We have come from a distant land to ask you to make a peace treaty with us."*[5]

. . .

I spoke up first. *"How do we know you don't live nearby? For if you do, we cannot make a treaty with you."*[(6)]

"We are your servants,"[(7)] they replied.

"But who are you?" Joshua demanded. *"Where do you come from?"*[(8)]

"We have come from a very distant country," they answered. *"We have heard of the might of the Lord your God and of all He did in Egypt. We have also heard what He did to the two Amorite kings east of the Jordan River – King Sihon of Heshbon and King Og of Bashan. Our elders and all our people instructed us, 'Take supplies for a long journey. Go meet with the people of Israel and tell them, "We are your servants; please make a treaty with us."'*

"This bread was hot from the ovens when we left our homes. But now, as you can see, it is dry and moldy. These wineskins were new when we filled them, but now they are old and split open. And our clothing and sandals are worn out from our very long journey." [(9)]

We examined their food, but we had failed to learn our lesson at Ai because we did not consult the Lord! Joshua entered into a peace treaty with them and guaranteed their safety. All our leaders, including me, ratified our agreement with a binding oath.

Three days after making the treaty, we discovered these people actually lived nearby! We set out at once to investigate and reached their towns within three days. The names of the towns were Gibeon, Kephirah, Beeroth, and Kiriath-jearim. But we did not attack the towns because we had made a vow to them in the name of our Lord God Jehovah.

Our people rightly confronted us, as leaders, for having entered into the treaty. They knew God had told us not to enter into a treaty with any of the inhabitants of this land. We had no excuse. We had disobeyed God and made the decision in our own wisdom.

I replied on behalf of all of our leaders. "We were wrong. We did not seek God before entering into the treaty. Therefore, we have sinned against God, and we have sinned against you. *But since we have sworn an oath to the Gibeonites in the presence of the Lord, the God of Israel, we cannot touch them.*"[10]

Joshua then spoke up. "*This is what we must do. We must let them live, for divine anger would come upon us if we broke our oath. Let them live.*"[11]

Joshua summoned the Gibeonite leaders who deceived us and said, "*Why did you lie to us? Why did you say that you live in a distant land when you live right here among us? May you be cursed! From now on you will always be servants who cut wood and carry water for the house of my God.*"[12]

They replied, "*We did it because we – your servants – were clearly told that the Lord your God commanded His servant Moses to give you this entire land and to destroy all the people living in it. So, we feared greatly for our lives because of you. That is why we have done this. Now we are at your mercy – do to us whatever you think is right.*"[13]

Joshua did not allow our people to kill them. Rather from that day on, he made the Gibeonites the woodcutters and water carriers for our community and for the altar of the Lord – wherever the Lord would choose to have it built.

Having heard how the Gibeonites had deceived us and become our allies, King Adoni-zedek of Jerusalem and his people became fearful. Gibeon was a large town – as large as the other royal cities and much larger than Ai. The Gibeonite men were considered to be strong warriors, so their alliance with us created quite a stir among the other kings of the region.

. . .

News reached our camp that King Adoni-zedek had formed an alliance with the other Amorite kings of the hill country – King Hoham of Hebron, King Piram of Jarmuth, King Japhia of Lachish, and King Debir of Eglon. His plan was not to attack us; he feared us – and more importantly, our God – too much.

Rather, his plan was for this newly formed alliance to combine forces and attack the traitorous Gibeonites. He would deal us a setback by defeating our new ally, Gibeon, and at the same time communicate to all the Canaanite peoples that an alliance with the Israelites and their God would not be tolerated.

The five Amorite kings combined their armies for a united attack and surrounded the town of Gibeon. The men of Gibeon quickly sent messengers to Joshua in our camp at Gilgal. *"Don't abandon your servants now!"* they pleaded. *"Come at once! Save us! Help us!"*[(14)] The warriors of all the Amorite kings are poised to attack us!"

But this time, Joshua and the rest of us knew before we did anything, we must seek the Lord's direction. Though we knew helping the Gibeonites was the right thing to do – in light of the oath we had made – we knew we were powerless apart from the leadership of our God.

"Do not be afraid of them," the Lord said to Joshua, *"for I have given you victory over them. Not a single one of them will be able to stand up to you."*[(15)]

Our camp in Gilgal was a full three days' journey from Gibeon. Joshua led us to travel with haste, even throughout the night. This was not only a strategic and tactical decision to take the Amorites by surprise, it also was because of our commitment to come to the aid of our ally. Our quick arrival took the Amorites completely by surprise.

36

All these kings – of the northern hill country – came out to fight.[1]

* * *

But it wasn't so much our early arrival at Gibeon as it was the presence and work of Jehovah. He granted us favor and protection resulting in the slaughter of great numbers of the Amorites. As a result, the Amorites panicked and began to retreat. We chased them along the road to Beth-horon all the way to Azekah and Makkedah. As they fled, a terrible hailstorm began to pelt them. We had not seen anything like it since the plagues of Egypt – and like in Egypt, we were spared. The hail killed only the Amorites.

But these were not the only extraordinary works of God that day. As the day was ending, Joshua cried out to the Lord asking Him to cause the sun to stand still until the Amorites had been destroyed. And the God who created all things – including the sun, moon, and earth – did just that! He caused the sun to stand still over Gibeon and the moon to remain stationary over the valley of Aijalon to the east until the Amorites had been completely defeated.

. . .

During the confusion of the Amorite retreat, their five kings abandoned their people and escaped to a cave at Makkedah. When Joshua heard they had been found, he issued this command: *"Cover the opening of the cave with large rocks, and place guards at the entrance to keep the kings inside. The rest of you continue chasing the enemy and cut them down from the rear. Don't give them a chance to get back to their towns, for the Lord your God has given you victory over them."* [(2)]

More Amorite warriors were killed by the hail than by our swords. As we had seen time and again, it was not our strength or resolve, but the might and power of our God that had defeated our enemy. He had proven His faithfulness once again!

When the defeat was complete, Joshua directed the commanders of our fighting men, saying, *"Go remove the rocks covering the opening of the cave, and bring the five kings to me."* [(3)]

When they did, Joshua told them, *"Come and put your feet on the kings' necks."* [(4)] Then he said to us all, *"Don't ever be afraid or discouraged. Be strong and courageous, for the Lord is going to do this to all of your enemies."* [(5)] Then Joshua killed all five kings himself and had their bodies impaled on five sharpened poles, where they hung until evening.

As the sun set, Joshua gave instructions for the bodies of the kings to be taken down from the poles and thrown into the cave where they had been hiding. Then he ordered the opening of the cave covered with a pile of large rocks.

In the days immediately following, God granted us victory over the kings of Makkedah, Libnah, Lachish, Gezer, Eglon, Hebron, Debir, and all of their surrounding villages. The kings and their people were defeated and destroyed, leaving no survivors.

. . .

God led us through Joshua to conquer the entire southern region – the kings and people of the hill country, the Negev, the western foothills, and the mountain slopes. Everyone in the land was completely destroyed as God had commanded – from Kadesh-barnea to Gaza and from the region around the town of Goshen up to Gibeon. All of these kings and their lands were conquered in a single campaign, and we sustained minimal losses – thanks to the Lord.

Before we turned our sights to the north, Joshua told us to return to our families in Gilgal for a time of rest.

Meanwhile King Jabin of Hazor heard what our God had done in the southern region of Canaan. With the exception of the five kings who had formed an alliance, all of the other kings and kingdoms had been destroyed one at a time. King Jabin decided all of the kings and kingdoms of the north should band together. He believed that united they would be undefeatable.

I was told later that the kings of the northern region had never before united in such a fashion. As a matter of fact, many of the tribes of the region were avowed enemies of one another. They had fought among themselves for as long as anyone could remember. But in this instance, they perceived our nation and our God to be their enemy – and their enemy's enemy for this purpose would become their friend!

So, the king sent out messages to all the other kings in the land – in Madon, Acshaph, the northern hill country, the Jordan Valley above and below the sea, and both eastern and western Canaan. They represented the undefeated kings of the Amorites, Hittites, Perizzites, Jebusites, and Hivites. King Jabin persuaded them to set aside their differences for the singular purpose of defeating the God of Israel and His people.

The idea of seeking peace, surrendering to us, and submitting to our God never crossed King Jabin's mind – nor the minds of any of the kings. Their hearts were hardened, filled with selfish ambition and pride, and they were determined to fight to the death.

The kings joined together and established their camp at the waters of Merom – northwest of the Sea of Chinnereth. Their location on the high ground would give them the advantage. Their combined armies formed a vast horde – the likes of which had never before been seen. Our spies estimated their force to be three hundred thousand foot soldiers, with an additional ten thousand on horseback and twenty thousand on chariots.

With all of their horses and chariots, they covered the region like sand on the seashore. Militarily they had a great advantage over us, positionally and strength-wise. We had no warriors on horseback or on chariots; ours was simply a force of foot soldiers. From a human perspective we were greatly outmatched.

Tensions between their warriors ran high, but their kings continued to keep their armies focused on their common enemy and on the assured victory their overwhelming numbers would bring if they remained united.

It took us seven days to travel to Merom from our camp in Gilgal. All along the way, we continued to hear reports from our spies about the fighting force that awaited us. With each report, the situation looked bleaker for us. Yes, we knew that God was for us – but we had never encountered a fighting force like this. Even the Egyptian army was dwarfed by this assembly.

We continued to press onward knowing God was going before us. But fear was growing in all of our hearts – including mine! We had seen God do miraculous acts, and He had promised to give us victory – but we needed some more assurance.

. . .

The night before we arrived at Merom that assurance came. The Lord said to Joshua, *"Do not be afraid of them. By this time tomorrow I will hand all of them over to you as dead men. Then you must cripple their horses and burn their chariots."* [6]

As I thought about His promise that night, I realized that He was growing our trust and faith in Him one step at a time. The first step had been at Jericho, where there was no attack from an enemy, just those towering and intimidating walls. Then Ai, a much smaller city, whose forces had attacked us aggressively but were greatly outmatched by us. Next came the five kings of the south – a larger force but handily defeated again by the Lord. And now, this vast horde. I am grateful our Lord allowed us to grow in our trust and faith in Him and He did not start us out facing an enemy of this magnitude.

The next morning, we immediately began our attack when we arrived at the waters near Merom. We did not stop to form ranks or rest. Our sudden attack caught our enemy by surprise. We were already on them before they could mobilize their cavalry or their chariots to attack. Their kings and commanders became confused and soon their warriors began to flee in retreat.

God gave us the stamina to chase them for two days as far as Greater Sidon and Misrephoth-maim, and Joshua led us to follow the Lord's instruction completely, sparing no detail. It pained us to cripple their horses, but we did so in obedience to the command of our Lord, knowing that He was erasing all instruments of warfare that could be raised against us in the future. And we burned all the chariots.

From there, we marched to Hazor, capturing the city and killing King Jabin – who had remained in the city instead of fighting with his army. We destroyed every living thing in the city. Not a single person was spared. And then we burned the city.

. . .

We continued on to each city throughout the region, leaving no survivors just as Joshua – and Moses before him – had commanded. And we took all the plunder and livestock of the ravaged towns for ourselves, as the Lord had directed.

Even the descendants of Anak we encountered were destroyed. These were the giants that Joshua, the other spies, and I had reported about forty years earlier. The giants who had caused such terror in the hearts of a faithless generation of our people had now been destroyed. Their bulk and strength that ten of our number had thought to be unconquerable had been reduced to dust. The Lord made it clear that anything we view as an unconquerable giant is but a dwarf to our Almighty God!

In all, thirty-one kings were defeated. It did not matter their number, their size, their strength, or their fighting ability. It did not matter if they were giants or if they had advantage on the field. It didn't matter if they were better equipped than us with horses and chariots, or even weaponry. It did not matter that from our perspective they appeared undefeatable.

All that mattered was the Lord God Jehovah went before us, and we followed Him. All that mattered was the Lord God Jehovah faithfully fulfilled His promises. All that mattered was the Lord God Jehovah overcame anything or anybody who attempted to thwart His plan and His purpose.

Our conquered territory now extended all the way from Mount Halak, which leads up to Seir in the south, as far north as Baal-gad at the foot of Mount Hermon in the valley of Lebanon. Not one of the people in this region had attempted to make peace with us, except the Hivites of Gibeon.

Because of the pride and unwillingness of the other kings and their people to turn to the God of Israel, the Lord had hardened their hearts. Not unlike pharaoh, their unrepentant sin had led to God's judgment. They had chosen to make enemies of those who might have become friends. As a

result, the people and their cities were defeated and destroyed as
the Lord had commanded.

And now, the land finally had rest from war. Six years had passed since we
crossed into this land of promise. The victory was now complete. The land
was now ours to inhabit. No portion of the promise had been left out. But
the work of inhabiting the land was just beginning!

* * *

37

So Joshua took control of the entire land, just as the Lord had instructed Moses. He gave it to the people of Israel as their special possession, dividing the land among the tribes.[1]

* * *

We returned as victors to our families camped at Gilgal. Our focus was now on dwelling in the land. God reminded Joshua there were still pockets of people scattered throughout the land who would need to be conquered in the days ahead – but until then, He would drive them out ahead of us.

The first order of business was allotting the land to our tribes as God had directed. Now that we had traveled throughout the land, we were in a better position to do so.

The tribes of Reuben, Gad, and half of the tribe of Manasseh were already settled on the east side of the Jordan River so they were not included. Neither was the tribe of Levi since the Lord had dedicated them for service in the tabernacle. That service was not solely for our time in the wilderness; it continued in the Promised Land.

God had said, *"I will compensate them for their service in the Tabernacle. Instead of an allotment of land, I will give them the tithes from the entire land of Israel. The Levites will receive no allotment of land among the Israelites, because I have given them the Israelites' tithes, which have been presented as sacred offerings to the LORD. This will be the Levites' share. That is why I said they would receive no allotment of land among the Israelites."*[(2)]

So, the nine tribes, together with the remaining half of the tribe of Manasseh, received their grants of land by means of sacred lots.

My tribe – the tribe of Judah – was the first to receive its portion. This was a day for which we had all been waiting. But it also brought a unique reward for me. Today was the fulfillment of a promise the Lord God Jehovah had made to me personally forty-five years earlier.

I, together with my sons and grandsons, came before Joshua and said, *"Remember what the Lord said to Moses, the man of God, about you and me when we were at Kadesh-barnea. You and I were both forty years old when Moses, the servant of the Lord, sent us from Kadesh-barnea to explore the land of Canaan. You and I returned and gave an honest report, but our brothers who went with us frightened the people from entering the Promised Land. For my part, I wholeheartedly followed the Lord my God. So that day Moses solemnly promised me, 'The land of Canaan on which you were just walking will be your grant of land and that of your descendants forever, because you wholeheartedly followed the Lord our God.'*

"Now, as you can see, the Lord has kept me alive and well as He promised for all these forty-five years since Moses made this promise – even while Israel wandered in the wilderness. Today I am eighty-five years old. I am as strong now as I was when Moses sent me on that journey, and I can still travel and fight as well as I could then. So give me the hill country that the Lord promised me. You will

remember that as scouts we found the descendants of Anak living there in great, walled towns. But if the Lord is with me, I will drive them out of the land, just as the Lord said." [3]

Joshua blessed me as my Lord had promised and gave the fields and villages surrounding Hebron to me as the portion of land for me and my family.

Later, when I returned to my family's tent, I was overwhelmed with thanksgiving to God for His graciousness. He had given me the grace and strength to see this day. Joshua and I were the ancients among our people. We were twenty years older than the next oldest person. God had granted me long life to see His promise become reality. And today He had given me the hill country of Hebron.

"Father, why did you ask for the hill country?" my youngest son asked. "Why did you seek land that still needs to be tamed? You are eighty-five years old! If anyone deserves an easier allotment of land to tame and inhabit, it's you! You were faithful when so many others were not. You have earned your reward. Why Hebron? Why the land of the giants?"

But before I could answer, my daughter replied, "Because God has made our father to be a man of faith. He has given him courage and boldness. We have seen his character all of our lives – and he has shown us that age does not change that! He has chosen, just as he always has, to put his shoulder to the plow in the fields that are rocky."

"You are most gracious, daughter," I said. "But my reason for choosing the hill country of Hebron is simply because that is the land God has promised us. He has promised to go before us – and for eighty-five years He has never failed me! Yes, the hill country will require work. It will require faith. It will require courage and boldness. It will require strength. But if it didn't, we would not remain dependent on our Lord. And if He has taught me anything, it has been to remain in a posture of dependence on Him!"

. . .

The land allotment to the tribe of Judah – chosen first because we were the kingly tribe as well as the largest tribe of Israel – included the southern boundary of the Promised Land encompassing the royal cities of Jerusalem, Hebron, Gibeah, and Gibeon.

The tribes of Joseph's sons, Ephraim and Manasseh – specifically the portion of the tribe that had not received an allotment on the east side of Jordan – received their portions next. I was a little surprised when these tribes immediately protested that they had not been given enough land. Perhaps they had expected a larger portion since Joshua was a part of their tribe.

"Why have you given us only one portion of land as our homeland when the LORD has blessed us with so many people?"[4] they asked Joshua.

He wisely replied, *"If there are so many of you, and if the hill country of Ephraim is not large enough for you, clear out land for yourselves in the forest where the Perizzites and Rephaites live."* [5]

The descendants of Joseph responded, *"It's true that the hill country is not large enough for us. But all the Canaanites in the lowlands have iron chariots, both those in Beth-shan and its surrounding settlements and those in the valley of Jezreel. They are too strong for us."* [6]

I was disappointed by their response but grateful Joshua chided them to face the giants and turn back the "iron chariots." Somehow these favored sons had quickly lost sight that their God, who had been faithful throughout the wilderness journey and the battles, would be faithful as they now possessed the land.

. . .

From there the remaining tribes received their allotment. First was the tribe of Benjamin – the remaining son of Rachel. Next came the tribes of Simeon, Zebulun, and Issachar – the remaining sons of Leah. Simeon received its allocation from a portion of land that was surrounded on all sides by the territory of our tribe – Judah. Lastly came the tribes of Asher, Naphtali, and Dan – the remaining sons of Bilhah and Zilpah, the servant women of Jacob's two lawful wives.

All the tribes had now received their allotment, which included very specific boundaries and cities as directed by the Lord. There was no land not allotted to a tribe and no tribe left out. God's provision and plan allowed for all of His people. The size, shape, and location of the allotment looked different between the tribes. Some enjoyed a coastal boundary; some ran along the banks of the Jordan River. Some bordered the clear Sea of Chinnereth; some bordered the Dead Sea. Some were to possess the hill country; some were chosen to possess the lowlands.

The last to receive an allotment was my friend Joshua, whose name means "Jehovah is help." In his responsibility as one of the twelve spies, he represented his tribe with faithful integrity and faith-filled reason. His uncompromising character, unswerving faith in Jehovah, and selfless devotion to his Lord and to the people, was always evident in his leadership.

Joshua had led our people in victory after victory in the land of Canaan. He had led us to a place where we could now rest in the realization of God's promises. By every standard imaginable, he had been a great, effective, and successful leader. He was also at this point the elder statesman of our people. There was no one left among us who was older than he was – either in age, wisdom, or maturity. There was no one numbered among our people who deserved greater respect, admiration, and honor than Joshua.

In most cultures, to the victor goes the spoils – and to the leader goes the greatest spoils. We had seen in Egypt how a victorious leader was publicly honored and rewarded with lavish praise and recognition. But Joshua did not seek the attention or the praise or the reward. He always sought to simply serve.

When the Lord told him he could have any town he wanted, Joshua's choice, like every other aspect of his life, was a true reflection of his character. He chose a city that was part of the land allotted to his tribe of Ephraim. Success and leadership had never caused him to have an elevated view of himself – he was a servant of his Lord, of his family, and of his people.

His choice also was in close proximity to Shiloh – the city where the tabernacle would be erected. This reflected his priority to always remain close to the Lord, even in his physical proximity to that place of worship.

Like me, Joshua had chosen the hill country. Though he could have selected somewhere easier to settle, he did not shrink from the challenge. His choice was a town that needed to be rebuilt on a solid foundation.

One other important truth about Joshua's allotment was that we, as a people, "gave" the land to Joshua. Given his position, he could have chosen first. It would have been acceptable and reasonable to do so. But instead, he graciously received the gift that was extended. And in so doing, he honored the gift, the givers (our people), and his Lord.

Having received our allotments, our tribes now all began their separate journeys to establish their new homes in our new land. And on this journey, there would most assuredly be no grumbling or complaining!

* * *

38

"You have done as Moses, the servant of the LORD, commanded you, and you have obeyed every order I have given you."[1]

* * *

There were still two matters for Joshua, Eleazar, and our leadership council to finalize before we could depart for our new respective homesteads.

The first was to establish the cities of refuge. The Lord had given detailed instruction to Moses on the establishment of cities of refuge.[2] He had defined their purpose, detailed how they would function, and designated their locations – all before we had even entered the land, let alone possessed it. And now the Lord instructed Joshua to implement the plan.

The six cities designated were distributed throughout the region so one could be reached within a half day's journey from anywhere in the land. Three were on the west side of the Jordan River, and three were on the east side. Of the six, two were in the north, two were more central, and two were in the south. The cities would be under the control of the tribe of Levi.

God established the cities of refuge to protect those who had accidentally killed someone. Pending trial, a murderer could surrender to a city of refuge where he would be judged. If the slayer was found not guilty, he could live in the city of refuge without fear of retribution for the rest of his life. If he outlived the serving high priest, he would be free to leave the city of refuge as an innocent man.

Each of the cities was renamed to reflect the promises these cities represented. On the west side of the Jordan were:

- Kedesh in the hill country of the tribe of Naphtali, meaning *to sanctify, consecrate, and make holy.* Our God promised He would work in the lives of all who seek refuge to bring about His work of sanctification in them that they might be made complete.

- Shechem in the hill country of the tribe of Ephraim, meaning *the shoulder or the bearer of burden.* In the midst of any trial that led to the need for refuge, God desired for the afflicted to release their burden and cast it upon Him knowing that He would sustain them.

- Hebron in the hill country of the tribe of Judah, meaning *fellowship.* The time of trial that led to the need for refuge would be permitted by God so those who call upon Him could know Him more intimately and live in fellowship with Him. The land God had given me surrounded Hebron. It reminded me to walk in fellowship with Him knowing He would always be my refuge.

On the east side of the Jordan were:

- Bezer on a hill in the plain of the tribe of Reuben, meaning *fortification and stronghold.* It was a reminder for those walking through trials that He would uplift them. He would be a stronghold to all who trust Him.

- Ramoth on a hill in the territory of the tribe of Gad, meaning *high and exalted place.* Those of us who had climbed Mount Sinai with Moses had sat beneath the feet of Jehovah God. Ramoth was a reminder that our God was high and lifted up. No matter what trial was encountered, it would always be but a footstool under His feet.

- And finally, Golan on a hill in the land of the tribe of Manasseh, meaning *joy or exultation.* It was a reminder that God's presence would always bring about the fullness of His joy regardless of circumstances.

In addition to these cities, forty-two cities scattered throughout the land on the east and west sides of the Jordan were given as a tithe to the priests and the other members of the tribe of Levi. Every one of the towns and cities had pastureland surrounding them. The Levites would live among the rest of our tribes as they carried out their God-given assignment as the priestly order of our people.

We had now completed the allotment of the land and cities as God had instructed. All that remained for me and the others was to lead our families to the hill country God had given us – and to inhabit the land.

Not a single promise the Lord had given us was left unfulfilled. He had given us all the land He had sworn to give us almost four hundred eighty years earlier. And He provided a way for us to take possession of the land. The land had changed possession from tribe to tribe over the years, but God's promise had never changed. The seashores had changed with the tide; the mountaintops had changed with the wear and tear of the climate. But God's promise had never changed.

. . .

During our time in the wilderness, we had caused ourselves grief and heartache that God never intended. We were prone to miss the fullness of His promise because we kept trying to figure out our own way to achieve it. Our journey was a clear example. What should have taken less than a year took us forty years because we lost sight of God's promise. An entire generation perished without seeing its fulfillment.

After being a people without a home for four hundred eighty years, God had now enabled us to settle in a land we could call our own and experience rest on every side. Rest from slavery. Rest from our travels. Rest from the insults of our enemies. Rest from our battles. It wouldn't be rest from work. There was still much work to be done. But the work would be done without worry and weariness. We would accomplish the work as we rested in God and relied on His strength.

He kept all of our enemies from standing against us. Time and again we witnessed the reality that our enemies did not fear Joshua's leadership ability or our fighting ability; they feared the presence and power of our Lord God Jehovah.

He conquered all our enemies. Yes, there were still Canaanites that remained to be fought another day. He told us He would not drive out all our enemies at once; He would drive them out *"a little at a time."* [3] But those enemies would lack the strength or spirit to attack us.

Now that their work was complete, it was also time for the eastern tribes of Reuben, Gad, and half of the tribe of Manasseh to return to their homes and their families. Unlike the rest of our tribes, these tribes had received their allotment of land before they fought. They had chosen the land they knew (the land east of the Jordan) over the land they had not seen (the land west of the Jordan).

They had made a choice similar to the one of Abraham's nephew, Lot. [4] Instead of receiving God's gift to Abraham, [5] Lot had chosen what he could see versus what he could not. And, just like Lot, God permitted these tribes to take possession of that which they had chosen. In doing so, He had required them to join the rest of us as we crossed the Jordan to possess the land of Canaan. And to their credit, they committed without reservation to do as the Lord commanded. Now, almost seven years later, they had been faithful to fulfill their promise to the end.

They honored their promise to those whom God had placed in leadership over them. They did as Moses commanded them, and they obeyed every order that Joshua gave them. An important part of being faithful to their promise was honoring those whom God placed in authority over them.

They also honored and faithfully served us – their fellow Israelites. They faithfully took the lead. These men were the armed warriors out front whenever we marched, from the time we crossed the Jordan until now. And they were always ready for battle. They were prepared to lay down their lives for the rest of us. They faithfully filled their post. Throughout the seven years, separated from their families and away from their homes, they never deserted our other tribes.

As they were now preparing to return to their families, Joshua commended them, admonished them, and blessed them saying, "*You have done as Moses, the servant of the Lord, commanded you, and you have obeyed every order I have given you. The Lord your God has given the other tribes rest, as He promised them. So go back home to the land that Moses, the servant of the Lord, gave you as your possession on the east side of the Jordan River. And be very careful to obey all the commands and the instructions that Moses gave to you. Love the Lord your God, walk in all His ways, obey His commands, hold firmly to Him, and serve Him with all your heart and all your soul.*"[(6)]

Our massive camp in Gilgal was no more. Each of our tribes, clans, and families was now going in a separate direction. My family, together with Joshua and his family, traveled with members of the Kohathite clan of the tribe of Levi to Shiloh. There they would erect the tabernacle in its permanent home. God's presence would still remain in our midst.

. . .

From there Joshua and I parted ways, knowing we would see one another again in Shiloh. He and his family turned north to the hills outside of Shiloh, and my family and I began our five-day journey south to the hill country of Hebron.

* * *

39

So Caleb was given the town of Kiriath-arba (that is, Hebron), which had been named after Anak's ancestor.[1]

* * *

As I traveled with my family from Shiloh, I realized this was the first time in my life I was truly able to go anywhere I wanted to go. In Egypt, I had been under the mastery of my Egyptian taskmasters. In the wilderness, I had been under the authority of Moses. In this land of promise, I had been under the day-to-day leadership of Joshua. But for the first time in my life – at eighty-five years of age – as I led my family, I was not looking to any human leader for direction.

There was a sense of freedom my family had never known. As we sat around our campfire that first night – one day's travel south of Shiloh – I looked around at my family. First, there were my sons. The oldest two looked just like me. Iru was the huntsman. He had become the best hunter and fighter among our people (as we had seen too many times). His skill with the bow was unmatched, except maybe by me!

• • •

Elah was the wise one. I had learned to turn to Elah for sound wisdom whenever I needed to make a decision. My third son, Naam, favored my dear wife in appearance. He was the inquisitive one; he had never been reluctant to ask questions and learn. The strengths of my sons were a great compliment and comfort to me as we approached the land we would tame.

Each of my sons had married well, and my daughters-in-law had become like my own daughters. They honored me and watched out for me – particularly since my dear Rebecca had died. Between the three of them they had raised up twenty grandchildren – twelve grandsons and eight granddaughters – all of whom were now adults themselves.

My children had been born in Egypt, living in slavery in their younger days, but they had matured in the wilderness. My grandchildren had been born and raised in the wilderness. For all of their lives until now, they had been nomads without a permanent home who had never known a day without manna until the past seven years.

Most of my grandchildren were now married. My six married granddaughters were no longer with me. They now traveled with their husbands and their families. But the wives of my eight married grandsons had become a part of our family's camp, as had the twenty-four great grandchildren who now required much of their attention! My youngest great grandchildren had been born in the Promised Land! They had never known slavery and they had never known the wilderness!

My daughter, Achsah, was now fifty-three years old. She had her mother's beauty, strength, and cleverness. She had refused to marry after Rebecca died. Instead, she had chosen to watch after me, despite my protests. But my nephew Othniel always had his eye on Achsah, and she on him. Her stubborn nature – which she also got from her mother! – is what kept them from marrying years ago. But it was easy to see the love that bloomed between them. I was considering a plan to get them married once and for all!

. . .

Othniel was my younger brother, Kenaz's, son. Kenaz and his wife had died in the wilderness while we were camped in the valley of Moab. They were among the last of our generation to die and be buried in the wilderness. It pained me that they never saw the Promised Land – through no fault of their own. But I trusted our Lord had something even better in store for them. Since then Othniel had become like my own son.

There were twelve other young men and ten young women who had also become a part of our extended family. They were members of our clan whom we took in as family when their own parents died in the wilderness. A few of the young men seemed to be more than casually interested in my unmarried granddaughters, and a few of the young women seemed to be blushing around my unmarried grandsons. So, I imagined they would officially become family in the not-too-distant future!

That meant there were seventy-seven in our traveling number, thirty-one of whom were fighting men ranging from twenty years of age to eighty-five. Yes, I still considered myself one of those fighting men. By God's grace He continued to give me the strength and endurance. And in a few days that strength would again be tested.

My sons and I knew that though God had granted our army victory over the kings of Hebron and Debir a few years earlier, not all the people had been destroyed – particularly some of the Anakites. Some of the race of giants that Shammua and the other spies had feared over forty years ago still lived in the hill country God had given me.

It was now our land by the decree of our sovereign God, but we would need to fight to take possession. The giants were not merely going to turn it over to us. But the One who is greater than any giant would go before us!

. . .

Iru and I had trained our young men to be proficient with their bows and their swords. Most of them had experience fighting enemies here in the Promised Land. So none of us was a novice.

On the fourth night of our journey to Hebron, I gathered my family around me in the camp.

"Tomorrow," I said, "we will arrive in Hebron. Levites from the Kohathite clan and other members from our tribe of Judah will have already secured the city of Hebron. We will sleep there tomorrow night and secure a place of shelter for our family. Then we will make plans to scout out the surrounding villages.

"Much of the land we will travel tomorrow is the land Jehovah God gave us. It is ours by right. And Jehovah God will grant us the might to secure it. Do not forget the land is already ours. He has already secured our victory.

"In a matter of days, we will again encounter those who look like giants, but remember they appear as ants before our God. And they live in fear of Him. They know that if He is for us, they cannot defeat us. Trust Him and watch to see His presence and power again be made known among the Anakites!"

On the fifth and final day of travel, we arrived at Hebron and secured shelter. As soon as we arrived, the Judahites who had preceded us alerted us that Anakite warriors had attempted two sieges on the city within as many weeks. They had made it clear they rejected the God of the Israelites and would not bow their knee to Him.

"He may have given you this land," they had bellowed, "but we have not! There will not be peace in this land until you have been vanquished. The

Anakite does not bow to the God of Abraham! And we will fight you with our last breath if it comes to that."

We knew we had to act quickly to defend our people and secure our land. The following day I sent out Iru, Elah, and Othniel to spy out the surrounding Anakite villages. They returned three days later.

"The closest village to this city is Aphekah," Iru reported. "It is controlled by the Anakite clan of Sheshai. The next village as we journeyed west is Adoraim. It is occupied by the clan of Ahiman. From there we traveled south to Jezreel, which is controlled by the clan of Talmai. Once we have conquered those villages there will be no threat to Hebron from within one day's journey from here. We must begin with those three.

"The Anakites are on alert. They appear to be making plans for a concerted attack on Hebron. From what we could see, the attack is imminent. We must move swiftly."

"We cannot defeat them in hand-to-hand combat," Elah continued. "But they are very vulnerable to an archery attack. They do not appear to be fearful that we will attack them. They do not wear armor to protect themselves from our arrows, nor do they appear to be proficient with bows. If we attack in that way, God will grant us success."

Hearing their report, we sought our Lord for His direction. He gave us peace and assurance He would go before us. Another fifty Judahites who had come to settle in Hebron volunteered to join with us in our battle to thwart any further attacks on the city by the Anakites. That enlarged our fighting force to eighty-one men – plus God! Even though Iru, Elah, and Othniel had reported between two hundred and three hundred fighting men in each of the three villages, we knew that "plus God" tipped the balance heavily in our favor.

· · ·

I chose to lead the attack on the first village of Aphekah with my son Naam by my side. Aphekah was only one hour away from Hebron. I led our men out of Hebron before sunrise so we could take our positions surrounding the village in the cover of darkness. Our best archers were positioned at the most strategic vantage points on all sides with sight lines into the village. The remainder of our men were positioned at ground level around the village and were prepared to fend off any attempts of attack or retreat.

At first light, while the village was just beginning to awaken, we began our attack. Our arrows rained down on the village. Quickly we could see chaos in their camp. It was obvious we had caught them by surprise. As I watched, it reminded me of the turmoil within the ranks of the Egyptian army just before God had closed the waters of the Red Sea on top of them. They didn't seem to know what to do.

Just then, the Anakites began charging out of their village toward our men on the ground. Our men stood firm in their positions and bravely fought the advancing giants – at first by bow, but soon with spear and sword. Those of us at the higher vantage point were able to assist them by deploying our arrows.

Within minutes, the Anakites were defeated and the village was captured. By God's grace, all of our band had survived and only two of our men had been injured. We knew that could only be explained by the fact God had fought for us! The victory was not ours; it was His!

Over the next two days, we advanced on the other two villages of Adoraim and Jezreel. My son Iru led the attack of Adoraim and Elah led the attack at Jezreel. The results in both instances were the same. God granted us victory and He kept my family safe! The Anakite clans – the descendants of Sheshai, Ahiman, and Talmai – had now been defeated, destroyed, and driven away.

.   .   .

From there we went to fight the people living in the town of Debir, formerly called Kiriath-sepher. We were even more outnumbered there. Though the King of Debir and his warriors had been defeated, a new king had taken his place and gathered warriors around him. Though these were not Anakite giants, they were fierce fighting men, nonetheless.

I stood before my men and said, *"I will give my daughter Achsah in marriage to the one who attacks and captures Kiriath-sepher."* [2] I was confident only one man would speak up. He would see this as his opportunity to once and for all marry my daughter. And I was proud of him when he did!

Othniel led the attack and conquered Debir. Like the others who had stood against us, this new king of Debir and his army were utterly destroyed. The city was captured, and we could now return to our family in Hebron. There were still other cities and villages to be conquered. And we would continue to do so throughout the days ahead, knowing it was God who would continue to give us victory.

I gave the village of Adoraim to Iru in honor of his bravery. He had led in their defeat and he would reap the rewards. The village of Jezreel I gave to Elah as a reward for leading us to victory. The village of Aphekah I gave to Naam for leading bravely by my side. And to Othniel I gave Debir, with a grateful heart. But I was even more grateful the day Achsah became his wife.

A few weeks after their marriage, I traveled to Debir to see Achsah and my new son-in-law. As I approached the city, Achsah came out to meet me riding on a donkey. I noticed she looked melancholy, so I asked her, *"What's the matter?"* [3]

She was never more like her mother than when she replied, *"Give me another gift. You have already given us land; now please give us springs of water, too."* [4] What father could deny his loving daughter and the brave son-in-law who had faithfully walked by his side? I gave them both the upper and lower springs!

And there they continue to live – as do the rest of my children and grandchildren and great grandchildren – on the land God promised us so long ago!

* * *

40

"Cling tightly to the LORD your God as you have done until now."[1]

* * *

My great-great-grandson was born today on my ninety-fifth birthday! His parents honored me by naming him Caleb. And, I might add, he is a beautiful little boy! He is just beginning the race God has set before him – whereas my race will soon draw to a close. There is so much I want him to know and to hold onto in the years to come.

The experiences of the past ninety-five years will just be stories to him – but they have been my life. He, and those of his generation, will have no recollection of Egypt or the wilderness. By God's grace, they will never know what it means to be a slave. They will never taste manna. They will hear about the great miracles of God, but they will not have witnessed them firsthand.

A short while back, I saw my friend Joshua for what was probably the last time on this side of heaven. He had assembled all the tribes of Israel at

Shechem – near his home in the hill country of Ephraim. He, too, wanted us to remember the faithfulness of our Lord God Jehovah.

He reminded us of the victories in battle God had given us that we did not earn. It was not our swords, or our bows, or even our strength or fighting ability that won those conflicts. It was the sovereign and mighty hand of our Almighty God.

Joshua also reminded us we were living in towns we now call our homes that we did not build. A people who as slaves had nothing, now had been given homes that were prepared for us. God had freely given them to us – His people.

And we are eating from vineyards and groves we did not plant. God sustained us through our Egyptian taskmasters, cared for us throughout the wilderness, and now provided for us through plantings we called our own. It is all a testament to God's grace.

So, little Caleb, I have decided to write this account for you, your children, and your children's children, so you will know the faithfulness of your God.

Fear Him, little one, and serve Him wholeheartedly! Cling to Him; His strong right hand holds you securely. All you have is from Him. May He find you faithful with all He has entrusted to you ... and may you serve Him faithfully with all your heart, soul, and mind!

* * *

EPILOGUE

"Serve only the LORD your God and fear Him alone. Obey His commands, listen to His voice, and cling to Him" [1]

* * *

Caleb lived almost forty years as a slave in Egypt, forty years as a faithful follower in the wilderness, and twenty years as a warrior in the Promised Land. He saw the oppression of Egypt, the dependence of the wilderness, and the challenges and blessings of Canaan.

He observed more often than not that people turn to the Lord and His promises during dangerous and desperate times. But he also observed that during times of peace and prosperity the people would turn *from* Him. Because it is during those times that God's people, then and now, are most easily tempted to pull away from Him.

Caleb's life is a testimony of faithfulness to God and to the promises of God. When others saw giants, Caleb saw His God. When others saw the prospects of defeat, he held on to the promises of victory. He stood faithfully as a spy when the majority of his fellow explorers gave a faithless report. He remained courageous when most of his fellow Israelites turned against him with stones in their hands. He stepped forward bravely at the age of eighty-five to tame and inhabit the hill country God had promised to him.

Caleb's story reminds us there will be times in our lives we will need to stand firm on the faithful truth of God in the midst of a rising tide of faithless opposition. Caleb is a picture of a man who continued to cling to God no matter the circumstances. And God will grant us that same courage, faith, and strength to cling to Him and stand tall if we will look to Him and trust Him.

Let us also cling to the promises of God! The Israelites repeatedly forgot His promises. All too often, we do the same. Sometimes we only remember His promise until the next crisis occurs. And then we remember His promise through the crisis and forget it – or ignore it – in the midst of peace and prosperity. Our minds and hearts become dulled to the memories of God's grace and goodness, and we begin to drift in the current of popular opinion – be it ever so subtle.

i grew up in south Florida and spent a lot of time at the beach. i loved to lie on my back, close my eyes, and float in the ocean. There is nothing more relaxing than floating in calm water! But when i would return to shore, most often i had drifted downstream.

i had not done anything to cause the drifting – the current was responsible for that. Occasionally, as I floated, i would look to see if i could still see my towel on the shore. As long as i could see it, i wasn't concerned.

The beach patrol uses flags to warn swimmers of swimming conditions. The red flag means "don't go in." The yellow flag indicates "swim with caution." The green flag signals the waters are calm.

. . .

When the flag was red, i wouldn't go into the water to float. i knew to avoid those strong currents. When the flag was yellow, i would be cautious, making regular "course corrections" to offset the current and stay closer to where my towel was located on shore. But when the flag was green, i didn't pay much attention.

That's often how it is for us in life. The days the warning flags are red or yellow, we are more attentive to where we came from. But on those other days when the green flag is flying – those days of warmth and sunshine – we tend to drift and not be concerned.

Caleb lived a life of faithfulness whether, to use my analogy, the flag was red, yellow, or green. We would do well to learn from him. Don't be lulled by the peaceful current of the green flag in the Promised Land. Don't become discouraged by the challenges of the yellow flag in the wilderness. And don't become frightened by the red flag waving over the giants. Keep your eyes on the One who will always be faithful ... and cling to Him!

Let us hold fast the confession of our hope without wavering, for He who promised is faithful.[2]

* * *

PLEASE HELP ME BY LEAVING A REVIEW!

i would be very grateful if you would leave a review of this book. Your feedback will be helpful to me in my future writing endeavors and will also assist others as they consider picking up a copy of the book.

To leave a review, go to:
  amazon.com/dp/B07ZDGBGLD

Thanks for your help!

* * *

AND THE SERIES CONTINUES ...

... with the other books in the *"THROUGH THE EYES"* SERIES

Experience the truths of Scripture as these stories unfold through the lives and eyes of a shepherd, a spy and a prisoner. Rooted in biblical truth, these fictional novels will enable you to draw beside the storytellers as they worship the Baby in the manger, the Son who took up the cross, the Savior who conquered the grave, the Deliverer who parted the sea and the Eternal God who has always had a mission.

BOOK #2

Though the Eyes of a Spy

A Novel — **Caleb was one of God's chosen people –** a people to whom He had given a promise. Caleb never forgot that promise — as a slave in Egypt, a spy in the Promised Land, a wanderer in the wilderness, or a conqueror in the hill country. We'll see the promise of Jehovah God unfold through his eyes, and **experience a story of God's faithfulness – to a spy who trusted Him – and to each one of us who will do the same.**

Available through Amazon.

BOOK #3

Though the Eyes of a Prisoner

A Novel — **Paul was an unlikely candidate to become the apostle to the Gentiles** ... until the day he unexpectedly encountered Jesus. You are probably familiar with that part of his story, and perhaps much of what transpired in his life after that. **But two-thirds of his life story is not recorded in detail, though Paul gives us some hints in his letters.**

God is always at work in our lives; often before we realize it. The same can be said of Paul. **Through this fictional novel**, we'll explore how God may have used even those unrecorded portions of his life to prepare him for the mission that was being set before him. We'll follow him from his early years in Tarsus through his final days in Rome.

Throughout those years, Paul spent more time in a prison cell than we are ever told. It was a place where God continued to work in and through him. The mission never stopped because he was in prison; it simply took on a different form. Allow yourself to be challenged as you experience **a story of God's mission – through the eyes of a prisoner who ran the race that was put before him – and the faithfulness of God through it all.**

Available through Amazon.

* * *

IF YOU ENJOYED THIS BOOK ...

... you will also want to read "The Eyewitnesses" Collection

The first four books in these collections of short stories chronicle the first person eyewitness accounts of eighty-five men, women and children and their unique relationships with Jesus. You'll hear from some of the characters you met in *"Through the Eyes of a Shepherd"* and learn more about their stories.

Little Did We Know – the advent of Jesus (Book 1)

Not Too Little To Know – the advent – ages 8 thru adult (Book 2)

The One Who Stood Before Us – the ministry and passion of Jesus (Book 3)

The Little Ones Who Came – the ministry and passion – ages 8 thru adult (Book 4)

The Patriarchs — eyewitnesses from the beginning — Adam through Moses tell their stories (Book 5) — releasing in 2023

Now available through Amazon.

Scan this QR code using your camera on your smartphone to see the entire collection on Amazon:

* * *

THE CALLED SERIES

... you will want to read all of the books in "The Called" series

Experience the stories of these ordinary men and women who were called by God to be used in extraordinary ways through this series of first-person biblical fiction novellas.

A Carpenter Called Joseph (Book 1)

A Prophet Called Isaiah (Book 2)

A Teacher Called Nicodemus (Book 3)

A Judge Called Deborah (Book 4) - releasing May 20

A Merchant Called Lydia (Book 5) - releasing July 22

A Friend Called Enoch (Book 6) - releasing Fall 2022

Available in LARGE PRINT through Amazon.

Scan this QR code using your camera on your smartphone to see the entire series on Amazon:

* * *

LESSONS LEARNED IN THE WILDERNESS SERIES

The Lessons Learned In The Wilderness series

A non-fiction series of devotional studies

There are lessons that can only be learned in the wilderness experiences of our lives. As we see throughout the Bible, God is right there leading us each and every step of the way, if we will follow Him. Wherever we are, whatever we are experiencing, He will use it to enable us to experience His Person, witness His power and join Him in His mission.

The Journey Begins (Exodus) – Book 1

The Wandering Years (Numbers and Deuteronomy) – Book 2

Possessing The Promise (Joshua and Judges) – Book 3

Walking With The Master (The Gospels leading up to Palm Sunday) – Book 4

Taking Up The Cross (The Gospels – the passion through ascension) – Book 5

Until He Returns (The Book of Acts) – Book 6

The complete series is also available in two e-book boxsets or two single soft-cover print volumes.

Now available through Amazon.

Scan this QR code using your camera on your smartphone to see the entire series on Amazon:

For more information, go to:

wildernesslessons.com or kenwinter.org

ALSO AVAILABLE AS AN AUDIOBOOK

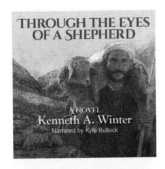

TIMELINE

The dates used in this timeline are approximations after review of the Egyptian and Israelite timelines. They are not intended to provide historical accuracy, rather to provide a relative timeline for this novel. Also italicized names, events, or timing of events listed in this timeline are either fictional or assumptions made for the purpose of telling the story.

* * *

Chapter 1 *(1909-1519 BC)*
    God's promise to the patriarchs
    History of the Egyptian pharaohs
    The reign of Ahmose I
    Moses becomes the adopted son of pharaoh's daughter
    The reign of Amenhotep I

Chapter 2 *(1518-1506 BC)*
    The reign of Thutmose I
    Marriage of Jephunneh (the Kenizzite) and *Miriam*
    Birth of Caleb
    Caleb growing up as a slave in Egypt
    An uncommon friendship

Chapter 3 (*1506-1492 BC*)
> *Friendship with Hoshea and Gaddi*
> *Caleb marries Rebecca*
> Caleb's son Iru is born

Chapter 4 (*1492-1480 BC*)
> The reign of Thutmose II
> *Caleb becomes master of the hunt*
> Caleb's other children are born – Elah, Naam, Achsah
> Egyptian taskmasters become harsher

Chapter 5 (*1480-1479 BC*)
> *Caleb becomes a leader of the tribe of Judah and begins to relate to leaders of the other tribes*

Chapter 6 (*1479 BC*)
> *Caleb approaches pharaoh*
> Moses returns

Chapter 7 (*1479 BC*)
> The plagues begin – the Nile River turned to blood

Chapter 8 (*1479 BC*)
> The plagues continue: frogs, lice, flies, animal plague
> *Caleb's refusal of pharaoh*

Chapter 9 (*1479 BC*)
> The plagues continue: boils, hail, locusts, darkness
> *Sapair's rejection*

Chapter 10 (*1479 BC* – Tuesday and Wednesday, 14th and 15th of Nissan)
> The Passover
> Thutmose II's son *Ramses* dies
> The exodus

Chapter 11 (*1479 BC* – Thursday thru Saturday, 16th thru 18th of Nissan)
> The place of the reeds

Chapter 12 (*1479 BC* – Saturday night thru Sunday, 18th and 19th of Nissan)

The crossing of the Red Sea

Thutmose I and Egyptian army die in the sea

A cry in Egypt – Queen Hatshepsut reigns

Chapter 13 (*1479 BC* – Monday thru Wednesday, 20th thru 22nd of Nissan)

Bitter waters

Chapter 14 (*1479 BC* – one month after leaving Egypt)

God provides manna and quail

Chapter 15 (*1479 BC*)

Water gushes from the rock

The Amalekites are defeated

Chapter 16 (*1479 – 1478 BC*)

Jethro's counsel to Moses

Jephunneh & Miriam die in the wilderness

Chapter 17 (*1479 – 1478 BC*)

The ten commandments are given

Chapter 18 (*1478 BC*)

A covenant meal

The golden calf

Chapter 19 (*1478 BC*)

A tent of meeting

A second trip to the mount

A tabernacle to build

Chapter 20 (*1478 BC* – one year after leaving Egypt)

The tabernacle is completed

The census

The tribal assignments

The Passover observed

Chapter 21 (*1478 BC*)

A new group of "spies"

Chapter 30 (*1439 BC*)
    Hobab dies
    Moses' final instructions

Chapter 31 (*1439 BC*)
    Preparing to cross the Jordan River
    The spies' report from Jericho

Chapter 32 (*1439 BC*)
    Crossing into the Promised Land

Chapter 33 (*1439 BC*)
    Renewing the covenant
    Observing the Passover
    No more manna

Chapter 34 (*1439 BC*)
    Capturing Jericho
    The defeat at Ai

Chapter 35 (*1439 - 1436 BC*)
    Ai defeated
    The deception of the Gibeonites
    The kings of the southern region unite

Chapter 36 (*1435 - 1433 BC*)
    The remainder of the Promised Land is conquered

Chapter 37 (*1433 BC*)
    Give me the hill country
    The land is allotted

Chapter 38 (*1433 BC*)
    Cities of refuge / cities given to Levites
    Eastern tribes return home

Chapter 39 (*1433 – 1418 BC*)

* * *

SCRIPTURE BIBLIOGRAPHY

Much of the story line of this book is taken from the Books of Exodus, Numbers, Deuteronomy and Joshua. Certain fictional events or depictions of those events have been added.

Specific references and quotations:

Preface
  (1) Exodus 1:6-7

Chapter 1
  (1) Exodus 1:8
  (2) Genesis 22:11-12
  (3) Genesis 22:2
  (4) Exodus 1:16 (ESV)
  (5) Exodus 1:22 (ESV)
  (6) Exodus 2:13
  (7) Exodus 2:14

Chapter 2
  (1) Exodus 1:11

Chapter 3

[1] Exodus 2:23a
[2] Genesis 28:13, 15

Chapter 4
[1] Exodus 2:23b

Chapter 5
[1] Exodus 2:25
[2] Genesis 12:14-20

Chapter 6
[1] Exodus 2:25
[2] Exodus 5:1
[3] Exodus 5:2
[4] Exodus 5:3
[5] Exodus 5:4-5
[6] Exodus 3:7-8, 15, 10

Chapter 7
[1] Exodus 3:19-20
[2] Exodus 5:15
[3] Exodus 5:17-18
[4] Exodus 5:21
[5] Exodus 6:6-8
[6] Exodus 7:1-5
[7] Exodus 7:9a
[8] Exodus 7:9b
[9] Exodus 7:17-18
[10] Exodus 7:19

Chapter 8
[1] Exodus 6:29
[2] Exodus 8:1-4
[3] Exodus 8:8
[4] Exodus 8:9
[5] Exodus 8:10
[6] Exodus 8:10-11
[7] Exodus 8:16 (NKJ)
[8] Exodus 8:19

[9] Exodus 8:20-21
[10] Exodus 8:25
[11] Exodus 8:26-27
[12] Exodus 8:28
[13] Exodus 8:29
[14] Exodus 9:1-5

Chapter 9

[1] Exodus 9:7
[2] Exodus 9:9
[3] Exodus 9:13-19
[4] Exodus 9:22
[5] Exodus 9:27-28
[6] Exodus 9:29-30
[7] Exodus 10:3-6
[8] Exodus 10:7
[9] Exodus 10:9
[10] Exodus 10:11
[11] Exodus 10:16-17
[12] Exodus 10:21
[13] Exodus 10:24
[14] Exodus 10:25-26
[15] Exodus 10:27-28
[16] Exodus 10:29

Chapter 10

[1] Exodus 11:1
[2] Exodus 11:4-8
[3] Exodus 12:21-23
[4] Genesis 15:14
[5] Exodus 12:31-32
[6] Exodus 12:32
[7] Exodus 13:19

Chapter 11

[1] Exodus 11:1
[2] Exodus 13:3-5, 11-12, 14-16
[3] Exodus 13:17
[4] Exodus 14:5

(5) Exodus 14:11-12

Chapter 12
(1) Exodus 14:10
(2) Exodus 14:13-14
(3) Exodus 14:25
(4) Exodus 15:1-3, 11-13, 17-18

Chapter 13
(1) Exodus 15:22
(2) Exodus 15:11
(3) Exodus 15:24
(4) Exodus 15:26 (paraphrase)

Chapter 14
(1) Exodus 16:1
(2) Exodus 16:3
(3) Exodus 16:7-8, 12
(4) Exodus 16:15
(5) Exodus 16:15-16
(6) Exodus 16:19
(7) Exodus 16:23
(8) Exodus 16:25-26
(9) Exodus 16:28-29

Chapter 15
(1) Exodus 17:1
(2) Exodus 17:2
(3) Exodus 17:2
(4) Exodus 17:3
(5) Exodus 17:4
(6) Exodus 17:5-6
(7) Exodus 17:7
(8) Genesis 25:29-34
(9) Exodus 17:16

Chapter 16
(1) Exodus 18:1
(2) Exodus 3:12

(3) Exodus 18:10-11
(4) Exodus 18:15-16
(5) Exodus 18:17-23

Chapter 17

(1) Exodus 19:3
(2) Exodus 19:3-6
(3) Exodus 19:8
(4) Exodus 19:10-13
(5) Exodus 20:19
(6) Exodus 20:20
(7) Exodus 20:1-17
(8) Exodus 24:3
(9) Exodus 24:8

Chapter 18

(1) Exodus 24:10
(2) Exodus 24:12
(3) Exodus 24:14
(4) Exodus 32:1
(5) Exodus 32:2
(6) Exodus 32:4
(7) Exodus 32:5
(8) Exodus 32:21
(9) Exodus 32:22-24
(10) Exodus 32:26
(11) Exodus 32:27
(12) Exodus 32:29
(13) Exodus 32:30
(14) Exodus 32:31-32
(15) Exodus 32:33-34

Chapter 19

(1) Exodus 33:1
(2) Exodus 33:1-3
(3) Exodus 33:12-16 (ESV)
(4) Exodus 33:17 (ESV)
(5) Exodus 34:1-3
(6) Exodus 34:6-7

(7) Exodus 34:9
(8) Exodus 25:8
(9) Exodus 35:5

Chapter 20
(1) Exodus 36:5
(2) Exodus 36:6
(3) Numbers 1:2-3 (ESV)

Chapter 21
(1) Numbers 10:12
(2) Numbers 10:30
(3) Numbers 10:31-32
(4) Numbers 11:11-15
(5) Numbers 11:12
(6) Numbers 11:15
(7) Numbers 11:16-17

Chapter 22
(1) Numbers 11:18
(2) Numbers 11:28
(3) Numbers 11:29
(4) Numbers 11:18-20
(5) Numbers 12:6-8
(6) Numbers 12:11

Chapter 23
(1) Numbers 13:2 (ESV)
(2) Numbers 13:17-20 (ESV)

Chapter 24
(1) Numbers 13:25 (ESV)
(2) Numbers 13:28
(3) Numbers 13:28
(4) Numbers 13:29, 32
(5) Numbers 13:31-32
(6) Numbers 13:30
(7) Numbers 14:2-3
(8) Numbers 14:4

(9) Numbers 14:7-9
(10)Numbers 14:11-12
(11)Numbers 14:13-19
(12)Numbers 14:20-25
(13)Exodus 3:8
(14)Exodus 15:5
(15)Exodus 23:23,28
(16)Exodus 33:2; 34:11
(17)Exodus 19:5-6

Chapter 25
(1) Numbers 14:26-27
(2) Numbers 14:26-35
(3) Numbers 14:40
(4) Numbers 14:41-43
(5) Numbers 16:3
(6) Numbers 16:5-7, 11
(7) Numbers 16:12-14
(8) Numbers 16:21
(9) Numbers 16:22
(10)Numbers 16:24
(11)Numbers 16:26
(12)Numbers 16:28-30
(13)Numbers 16:34
(14)Numbers 16:41
(15)Numbers 16:45
(16)Numbers 16:46

Chapter 26
(1) Numbers 17:5
(2) Numbers 20:3-5
(3) Numbers 20:8
(4) Numbers 20:10
(5) Numbers 20:12

Chapter 27
(1) Numbers 20:14
(2) Numbers 20:14-17
(3) Numbers 20:18

(4) Numbers 20:24-26
(5) Numbers 21:2

Chapter 28
(1) Numbers 21:4-5
(2) Numbers 21:5
(3) Numbers 21:7
(4) Exodus 23:23
(5) Numbers 21:22
(6) Numbers 21:34

Chapter 29
(1) Numbers 27:16-17
(2) Numbers 27:21
(3) Exodus 28:30

Chapter 30
(1) Deuteronomy 1:1
(2) Deuteronomy 4:9-10
(3) Deuteronomy 6:4
(4) Deuteronomy 6:12
(5) Deuteronomy 28:2-6
(6) Deuteronomy 28:15-19
(7) Deuteronomy 30:19-20

Chapter 31
(1) Joshua 1:11
(2) Joshua 1:18
(3) Joshua 2:1
(4) Joshua 2:2-3
(5) Joshua 2:4-5
(6) Joshua 2:9,11
(7) Joshua 2:12-13
(8) Joshua 2:14
(9) Joshua 2:16
(10) Joshua 2:17-20
(11) Joshua 2:21
(12) Joshua 2:24

Chapter 32
(1) Joshua 3:1
(2) Joshua 3:5
(3) Joshua 3:3-4
(4) Joshua 3:6,8
(5) Joshua 4:3
(6) Joshua 4:21-24
(7) Joshua 4:24

Chapter 33
(1) Joshua 5:1
(2) Genesis 17:7-10
(3) Genesis 34:24-26
(4) Joshua 5:2
(5) Genesis 22
(6) Joshua 5:9
(7) Exodus 12:3
(8) Exodus 12:8

Chapter 34
(1) Joshua 6:1
(2) Joshua 6:2-5
(3) Joshua 6:6
(4) Joshua 6:7
(5) Joshua 6:10
(6) Joshua 6:16
(7) Joshua 6:17-19
(8) Joshua 6:22
(9) Joshua 6:26
(10) Joshua 7:3
(11) Joshua 7:7-9
(12) Joshua 7:10-15
(13) Joshua 7:19
(14) Joshua 7:20-21
(15) Joshua 7:25
(16) Joshua 8:1

Chapter 35
(1) Joshua 8:2

(2) Joshua 8:1
(3) Joshua 8:2
(4) Joshua 8:2-8
(5) Joshua 9:6
(6) Joshua 9:7
(7) Joshua 9:8
(8) Joshua 9:8
(9) Joshua 9:9-12
(10) Joshua 9:19
(11) Joshua 9:20-21
(12) Joshua 9:22-23
(13) Joshua 9:24-25
(14) Joshua 10:6
(15) Joshua 10:8

Chapter 36

(1) Joshua 11:4
(2) Joshua 10:18-19
(3) Joshua 10:22
(4) Joshua 10:24
(5) Joshua 10:25
(6) Joshua 11:6

Chapter 37

(1) Joshua 11:23
(2) Numbers 18:21, 23-24
(3) Joshua 14:6-12
(4) Joshua 17:14
(5) Joshua 17:15
(6) Joshua 17:16

Chapter 38

(1) Joshua 22:2
(2) Numbers 35:9-34
(3) Exodus 23:29-31
(4) Genesis 13:10-11
(5) Genesis 13:14-17
(6) Joshua 22:2, 4-5

Chapter 39
(1) Joshua 15:13
(2) Joshua 15:16
(3) Joshua 15:18
(4) Joshua 15:18

Chapter 40
(1) Joshua 23:8

Epilogue
(1) Deuteronomy 13:4
(2) Hebrews 10:23 (ESV)

* * *

LISTING OF CHARACTERS

*Dates are all B.C. and are approximations to reflect a timeline within the story.
Italicized names are fictional characters within the story.*

* * *

The Patriarchs:

Abraham b.1984 d.1809

Isaac b.1884 d.1704

Jacob b.1824 d.1677

Joseph b.1714 d.1623

The Egyptians:

Pharaoh Merneferre Ay I b.NA d.1691

- elevated Joseph and welcomed Jacob

Pharaoh Ahmose I b.NA d.1544

- enslaved Israelites/ killed male children

- first pharaoh of 18th dynasty

Queen Ahmose-Nefertari b.NA d.NA

- wife of Ahmose I

Princess (Queen) Meritamun b.1579 d.1548

- daughter of Ahmose I

- adopted Moses

- became brother Amenhotep's queen

- mother of Thutmose I

Pharaoh Amenhotep I b.1570 d.1520

- son of Ahmose I

Pharaoh Thutmose I b.1550 d.1492

- son of Amenhotep I

- childhood "step-brother" of Moses

Queen Ahmose b.1548 d.1519

- sister and first wife Thutmose I

Queen Mutnofret b.1545 d.1481

- aunt and second wife of Thutmose I

- mother of Amenemhat

Prince Amenmose b.1530 d.1510

- first son of Thutmose I and Queen Ahmose

- died in battle

Prince Amenemhat (Pharaoh Thutmose II) b.1518 d.1479

- second son of Thutmose I and Mutnofret

- Caleb was his childhood playing companion

- died leading army in Red Sea

Queen Hatshepsut b.1520 d.1458

– sister and wife of Thutmose II

- mother of Princes Ramses and Wadjmose

- became ruler of Egypt after exodus

Prince Ramses b.1497 d.1479

- first-born son of Thutmose II and Hatshepsut

- died on the night of Passover

Prince Wadjmose (Pharaoh Thutmose III) b.1484 d.1425

- second son of Thutmose II and Hatshepsut

Rahotep b.NA d.NA

- Egyptian taskmaster

Sapair b.1518 d.1479

- Egyptian taskmaster's son

- childhood friend of Caleb

The Israelites:

Jephunneh b.1543 d.1478

- father of Caleb/ a Kenizzite (a hunter)

Miriam b.1540 d.1478

- wife of Jephunneh/ mother of Caleb

Caleb b.1518 d.1418
- *principal character/ Israelite spy*
- *son of Jephunneh and Miriam*
- *a leader of the tribe of Judah*
Rebecca b.1514 d.1458
– *wife of Caleb*
Iru b.1493 d.NA
– *son of Caleb*
Elah b.1492 d.NA
– *son of Caleb*
Naam b.1490 d.NA
– *son of Caleb*
Achsah b.1486 d.NA
– *daughter of Caleb*
Kenaz b.1503 d.1439
- *younger brother of Caleb*
Othniel b.1481 d.NA
- *son of Kenaz/ nephew of Caleb*
- *husband of Achsah*
Hoshea/ Joshua b.1518 d.1408
- *childhood friend of Caleb*
- *tribe of Ephraim/ Israelite spy*
- *God's anointed leader to lead His people to conquer the Promised Land*
Moses b.1559 d.1439
- *Prince of Egypt*
- *God's anointed leader to lead His people out of Egypt and through the Promised Land*
Tzipora b.1534 d.1455
- *wife of Moses/ daughter of Jethro*
Jethro/ Reuel b.1594 d.NA
- *father of Tzipora and Hobab*
- *Midianite priest*
Gershom b.1507 d.1440
- *first born son of Moses and Tzipora*
Eliezer b.1505 d.1440
- *second born son of Moses and Tzipora*
Miriam b.1569 d.1458
- *sister of Moses*
Hur b.1572 d.1478

- *husband of Miriam*
Aaron b.1562 d.1445
- *brother of Moses*
- *High Priest of Israel*
Elisheba b.1538 d.1456
- *wife of Aaron/ sister of Nahshon*
Eleazar b.1497 d.1406
- *son of Aaron/ second High Priest of Israel*
Hobab b.1509 d.1439
- *Midianite son of Jethro*
- *brother of Tzipora*
Nahshon b.1552 d.1440
- *brother of Elisheba/ tribal leader of Judah*

The other ten Israelite spies:

Shammua – *tribe of Reuben* b.1532 d.1478
Shaphat – *tribe of Simeon* b.1528 d.1478
Igal – *tribe of Issachar* b.1527 d.1478
Palti – *tribe of Benjamin* b.1524 d.1478
Gaddiel – *tribe of Zebulun* b.1517 d.1478
Gaddi – *tribe of Manasseh* b.1518 d.1478
- *childhood friend of Caleb*
Ammiel – *tribe of Dan* b.1526 d.1478
Sethur – *tribe of Asher* b.1524 d.1478
Nahbi – *tribe of Naphtali* b.1523 d.1478
Geuel – *tribe of Gad* b.1522 d.1478

The Canaanites:

Rahab – *Jerichoite prostitute* b.NA d.NA

* * *

ACKNOWLEDGMENTS

I do not cease to give thanks for you ....
Ephesians 1:16 (ESV)

* * *

With a grateful heart:
to my wife, life partner and best friend, LaVonne,
for walking faithfully by my side throughout this faith adventure;

to my family
for your faithful support all along the way;

to Sheryl,
for all you have done to help me better tell the story of God's faithfulness;

to Dennis,
for your God-given creativity and artistic touch;

to Aaron, Connie, Cyndie, Debby, Joanne, Larry, Leslie, Lorél, Lorena,
Robert and Theresa,
for your challenging insights and encouragement;

and most importantly,
to the One who this story is truly all about –
our Lord God Jehovah,
who is faithful through it all!

* * *

ABOUT THE AUTHOR

 Ken Winter is a follower of Jesus, an extremely blessed husband, and a proud father and grandfather – all by the grace of God. His journey with Jesus has led him to serve on the pastoral staffs of two local churches – one in West Palm Beach, Florida and the other in Richmond, Virginia – and as the vice president of mobilization of the IMB, an international missions organization.

Today, Ken continues in that journey as a full-time author, teacher and speaker. You can read his weekly blog posts at kenwinter.blog and listen to his weekly podcast at kenwinter.org/podcast.

* * *

And we proclaim Him, admonishing every man and teaching every man with all wisdom, that we may present every man complete in Christ. And for this purpose also I labor, striving according to His power, which mightily works within me.
(Colossians 1:28-29 NASB)

PLEASE JOIN MY READERS' GROUP

Please join my Readers' Group in order to receive updates and information about future releases, etc.

Also, i will send you a free copy of *The Journey Begins* e-book — the first book in the *Lessons Learned In The Wilderness* series. It is yours to keep or share with a friend or family member that you think might benefit from it.

It's completely free to sign up. i value your privacy and will not spam you. Also, you can unsubscribe at any time.

Go to kenwinter.org to subscribe.

* * *

Made in the USA
Columbia, SC
01 February 2023

11345346R00202